50 More Mysteries

50 More Mysteries

Selected By
Isaac Asimov,
Martin H. Greenberg.
And Joseph D. Olander

GOODWILL PUBLISHING HOUSE™
B-3, RATTAN JYOTI, 18, RAJENDRA PLACE, NEW DELHI-110008 (INDIA)
TEL.: 25750801, 25755519, 25820556 FAX : 91-11-25763428

This special low priced Indian reprint is published by arrangement with Sterling Publishing Company, Inc. New York, U.S.A.

Published in India by
GOODWILL PUBLISHING HOUSE™
B-3 Rattan Jyoti, 18 Rajendra Place
New Delhi-110008 (INDIA)
Tel. : 25750801, 25755519, 25820556
Fax : 91-11-25763428
E-mail : goodwillpub@vsnl.net
website : www.goodwillpublishinghouse.com

Printed at :-
Kumar offset
New Delhi

CONTENTS

INTRODUCTION

Snacks

by Isaac Asimov

As a man who constantly battles the upward-edging scale, I am perfectly ready (even delighted) to admit that nothing beats a nice roast duck dinner—or filet mignon—or brook trout—with, of course, all the fixings.

Yet even the best trenchermen among us will admit that there are times during the light-hearted conviviality of a successful cocktail party when nothing beats a carrot stick dipped into something garlicky, the cracker on which a bit of chopped liver or smoked salmon rests, the shrimp dipped in a tangy sauce.

There are, in other words, times for the full dinner and times for the snacks.

And so it is in literature. What is better than a long and exciting mystery novel when we have a day of leisure in which to track down the clues and follow the intricate play of action?

But suppose we need something for just those few minutes before dropping off, or for some minutes of comfort over a sandwich or while waiting for a train? In that case, how about all the excitement, thrills, and surprise of a mystery novel compressed into two thousand words or less? A snack, in other words.

If there's nothing like a snack at the right time, then here in this book are an even fifty of them, every one of them guaranteed by your humble anthologists. (And pray notice that even the introduction is snack-sized)

P.S. This anthology was inspired by the fact that I had done three previously on short-short science fiction, and I felt the same could be done for mysteries. It is hard, however, to do anything in the realm of the mystery anthology that the master, Ellery Queen, has not already done. In 1969 he published *Mini-Mysteries*, a collection of seventy stories, and this anthology follows in the tradition.

Sweet Fever

by Bill Pronzini

Quarter before midnight, like on every evening except the Sabbath or when it's storming or when my rheumatism gets to paining too bad, me and Billy Bob went down to the Chigger Mountain railroad tunnel to wait for the night freight from St. Louis. This here was a fine summer evening, with a big old fat yellow moon hung above the pines on Hankers Ridge and mockingbirds and cicadas and toads making a soft ruckus. Nights like this, I have me a good feeling, and I know Billy Bob does too.

They's a bog hollow on the near side of the tunnel opening, and beside it a woody slope, not too steep. Halfway down the slope is a big catalpa tree and that was where we always set, side by side with our backs up against the trunk.

So we come on down to there, me hobbling some with my cane and Billy Bob holding onto my arm. That moon was so bright you could see the melons lying in Ferdie Johnson's patch over on the left, and the rail tracks had a sleek oiled look coming out of the tunnel mouth and leading off towards the Sabreville yards a mile up the line. On the far side of the tracks, the woods and the run-down shacks that used to be a hobo jungle before the county sheriff closed it off thirty years back had them a silvery cast, like they was all coated in winter frost.

We set down under the catalpa tree and I leaned my head back to catch my wind. Billy Bob said, "Granpa, you feeling right?"

"Fine, boy."

"Rheumatism ain't started paining you?"

"Not a bit."

He give me a grin. "Got a little surprise for you."

"The hell you do."

"Fresh plug of blackstrap," he said. He come out of his pocket with it. "Mr. Cotter got him in a shipment just today down at his store."

I was some pleased. But I said, "Now you hadn't ought to go spending your money on me, Billy Bob."

"Got nobody else I'd rather spend it on."

I took the plug and unwrapped it and had me a chew. Old man like me ain't got many pleasures left, but fresh blackstrap's one; good corn's another. Billy Bob gets us all the corn we need from Ben Logan's boys. They got a pretty good-sized still up on Hankers Ridge, and their corn is the best in this part of the hills. Not that either of us is a drinking man, now. A little touch after supper and on special days is all. I never did hold with drinking too much, or doing anything too much, and I taught Billy Bob the same.

He's a good boy. Man couldn't ask for a better grandson. But I raised him that way—in my own image, you might say—after both my own son Rufus and Billy Bob's ma got taken from us in 1947. I reckon I done a right job of it, and I couldn't be less proud of him than I was of his pa, or love him no less either.

Well, we set there and I worked on the chew of blackstrap and had a spit every now and then, and neither of us said much. Pretty soon the first whistle come, way off on the other side of Chigger Mountain. Billy Bob cocked his head and said, "She's right on schedule."

"Mostly is," I said, "this time of year."

That sad lonesome hungry ache started up in me again—what my daddy used to call the "sweet fever." He was a railroad man, and I grew up around trains and spent a goodly part of my early years at the roundhouse in the Sabreville yards. Once, when I was ten, he let me take the throttle of the big 2-8-0 Mogul steam locomotive on his highballing run to Eulalia, and I can't recollect no more finer experience in my whole life.

Later on I worked as a callboy, and then as a fireman on a 2-10-4, and put in some time as a yard-tender engineer, and I expect I'd have gone on in railroading if it hadn't been for the Depression and getting myself married and having Rufus. My daddy's short-line company folded up in 1931, and half a dozen others too, and wasn't no work for either of us in Sabreville or Eulalia or anywheres else on the iron.

That squeezed the will right out of my daddy, and he took to ailing, and I had to accept a job on Mr. John Barnett's truck farm to support him and the rest of my family. Was my intention to go back into railroading, but the Depression dragged on, and my daddy died, and a year later my wife Amanda took sick and passed on, and by the time the war come it was just too late.

But my son Rufus got him the sweet fever too, and took a switchman's job in the Sabreville yards, and worked there right up until the night he died. Billy Bob was only three then; his own sweet fever comes most purely from me and what I taught him. Ain't no doubt trains been a major part of all our lives, good and bad, and ain't no doubt neither they get into a man's blood and maybe change him, too, in one way and another. I reckon they do.

The whistle come again, closer now, and I judged the St. Louis freight was just about to enter the tunnel on the other side of the mountain. You could hear the big wheels singing on the track, and if you listened close you could just about hear the banging of couplings and the hiss of air brakes as the engineer throttled down for the curve. The tunnel don't run straight through Chigger Mountain; she comes in from the north and angles to the east, so that a big freight like the St. Louis got to cut back to quarter speed coming through.

When she entered the tunnel, the tracks down below seemed to shimmy and you could feel the vibration clear up where we was sitting under the catalpa tree. Billy Bob stood himself up and peered down towards the black tunnel mouth like a bird dog on a point. The whistle come again, and once more, from inside the tunnel, sounding hollow and miseried now. Every time I heard it like that, I thought of a body trapped and hurting and crying out for help that wouldn't come in the empty hours of the night. I shifted the cud of blackstrap and worked up a spit to keep my mouth from drying. The sweet fever feeling was strong in my stomach.

The blackness around the tunnel opening commenced to

lighten, and got brighter and brighter until the long white glow from the locomotive's headlamp spilled out onto the tracks beyond. Then she come through into my sight, her light shining like a giant's eye, and the engineer give another tug on the whistle, and the sound of her was a clattering rumble as loud to my ears as a mountain rockslide. But she wasn't moving fast, just kind of easing along, pulling herself out of that tunnel like a night crawler out of a mound of earth.

The locomotive clacked on past, and me and Billy Bob watched her string slide along in front of us. Flats, boxcars, three tankers in a row, more flats loaded down with pine logs big around as a privy, a refrigerator car, five coal gondolas, another link of boxcars. Fifty in the string already, I thought. She won't be dragging more than sixty, sixty-five.

Billy Bob said suddenly, "Granpa, look yonder!"

He had his arm up, pointing. My eyes ain't so good no more and it took me a couple of seconds to follow his point, over on our left and down at the door of the third boxcar in the last link. It was sliding open, and clear in the moonlight I saw a man's head come out, then his shoulders.

"It's a floater, Granpa," Billy Bob said, excited. "He's gonna jump. Look at him holding there, he's gonna jump."

I spit into the grass. "Help me up, boy."

He got a hand under my arm and lifted me up and held me until I was steady on my cane. Down there at the door of the boxcar, the floater was looking both ways along the string of cars and down at the ground beside the tracks. That ground was soft loam and the train was going slow enough and there wasn't much chance he would hurt himself jumping off.

He come to that same idea, and as soon as he did he flung himself off the car with his arms spread out and his hair and coattails flying in the slipstream. I saw him land solid and go down and roll over once. Then he knelt there, shaking his head a little, looking around.

Well, he was the first floater we'd seen in seven months. The yard crews seal up the cars nowadays and they ain't many ride the rails anyhow, even down in our part of the country. But every now and then a floater wants to ride bad enough to break a seal, or hides himself in a gondola or on a loaded flat. Kids, oldtime hoboes, wanted men. They's still a few.

And some of 'em get off right down where this one had, because they know the St. Louis freight stops in Sabreville and they's yardmen there that check the string, or because they see the run-down shacks of the old hobo jungle or Ferdie Johnson's melon patch. Man rides a freight long enough, no provisions, he gets mighty hungry. The sight of a melon patch like Ferdie's is plenty enough to make him jump off.

"Billy Bob," I said.

"Yes, Granpa. You wait easy now."

He went off along the slope, running. I watched the floater, and he come up on his feet and got himself into a clump of bushes alongside the tracks to wait for the caboose to pass so's he wouldn't be seen. Pretty soon the last of the cars left the tunnel, and then the caboose with a signalman holding a red-eye lantern out on the platform. When she was down the tracks and just about beyond my sight, the floater showed himself again and had him another look around. Then, sure enough, he made straight for the melon patch.

Once he got into it I couldn't see him because he was in close to the woods at the edge of the slope. I couldn't see Billy Bob neither. The whistle sounded one final time, mournful, as the lights of the caboose disappeared, and a chill come to my neck and set there like a cold dead hand. I closed my eyes and listened to the last singing of the wheels fade away.

It weren't long before I heard footfalls on the slope coming near, then the angry sound of a stranger's voice, but I kept my eyes shut until they walked up close and Billy Bob said, "Granpa." When I opened 'em the floater was standing three feet in front of me, white face shining—scared face, angry face, evil face.

"What the hell is this?" he said. "What you want with me?"

"Give me your gun, Billy Bob," I said.

He did it, and I held her tight and lifted the barrel. The ache in my stomach was so strong my knees felt weak and I could scarcely breathe. But my hand was steady.

The floater's eyes come wide-open and he backed off a step. "Hey," he said, "hey, you can't—"

I shot him twice.

He fell over and rolled some and come up on his back. They wasn't no doubt he was dead, so I give the gun back to Billy Bob and he put it away in his belt. "All right, boy," I said.

Billy Bob nodded and went over and hoisted the dead floater onto his shoulder. I watched him trudge off towards the bog hollow, and in my mind I could hear the train whistle as she'd sounded from inside the tunnel. I thought again, as I had so many times, that it was the way my boy Rufus and Billy Bob's ma must have sounded that night in 1947, when the two floaters from the hobo jungle broke into their home and raped her and shot Rufus to death. She lived just long enough to tell us about the floaters, but they was never caught. So it was up to me, and then up to me and Billy Bob when he come of age.

Well, it ain't like it once was and that saddens me. But they's still a few that ride the rails, still a few take it into their heads to jump off down there when the St. Louis freight slows coming through the Chigger Mountain tunnel.

Oh my yes, they'll *always* be a few for me and Billy Bob and the sweet fever inside us both.

The Magnum

by Jack Ritchie

Amos Weatherlee clutched a magnum of champagne in one hand and a hammer in the other.

He paused in the wide doorway of the hotel bar.

At this hour of the afternoon, the barroom was nearly empty except for the three women in one booth with Pink Ladies and a middle-aged man alone in another.

Weatherlee approached him and extended the hammer. "Pardon me, but I would regard it as an extreme favor if you would smash my bottle."

Harry Sloan studied him warily. "Don't you think that would make quite a mess?"

Weatherlee's silver-gray hair was somewhat disheveled and he spoke with a slight slur. "I never thought of that. You don't suppose that the bartender has a basin or something like that we could use?"

Sloan sipped his whiskey and soda. "If you're really set on smashing that bottle, why don't you do it yourself?"

Weatherlee sighed. "I tried. I really tried. Captain O'Reilly did too. So did Carruthers and Larson and Cooper and I don't know how many more. It was quite a wild night."

"What was?"

"Our club meeting a year ago."

Sloan's attention was distracted by the procession of a dozen elderly men filing through the hotel entrance. At least half of them walked with canes. They moved slowly across the lobby toward the open doors of a private dining room.

Sloan showed some interest. "Who in the world are they?"

"Our club," Weatherlee said. "It's our annual reunion.

The members just finished a sight-seeing bus tour of the city and now we're going to have dinner." He watched as the group entered the dining room. "We were all members of the same National Guard Company. We formed the club right after the war."

"World War I?"

"No," Weatherlee said. "The Spanish-American War."

Sloan regarded him skeptically.

"That's Captain O'Reilly," Weatherlee said. "Wearing the broad-brimmed campaign hat." He sat down. "How old do you think I am?"

"I haven't the faintest idea."

"Ninety," Weatherlee said proudly. "I was eighteen when I enlisted."

"Sure," Sloan said. "And I suppose you were a member of Teddy Roosevelt's Rough Riders and charged up San Juan Hill?"

"No. Actually our outfit never got beyond Tampa before the war ended. Our only casualties were to yellow fever."

"You look pretty spry for ninety."

"I am," Weatherlee said firmly. "I take a brisk half-hour walk every day and I'm still in full possession of all my faculties. In full possession."

"Sure," Sloan said. "Sure."

"Of course we weren't all the same age when we formed the club. Captain O'Reilly, for instance, our oldest man, was thirty-six. Twice as old as I at the time. He joined the club more in the spirit of good-fellowship, rather than really expecting to drink the bottle."

Sloan eyed the magnum of champagne. "What kind of a club was this?"

"A Last Man club. Perhaps you've heard of them? We founded ours in 1898. Right after the war ended and we were waiting to get shipped home. We wanted one hundred members, but actually we could get only ninety-eight to sign up."

"And those are the survivors? What's left?"

"Oh, no. Those are only the members who could make it. The others are in hospitals, old age homes, and the like."

Sloan did some mental arithmetic. "You said that Captain O'Reilly was thirty-six when the club formed in 1898?"

"Yes."

"Are you telling me that Captain O'Reilly is now one hundred and eight years old?"

"That's right. Our oldest man."

"And at ninety, you're the youngest?"

"Yes," Weatherlee said. "And I'm Custodian of the Bottle. According to our by-laws, the youngest surviving member is Custodian of the Bottle."

Sloan finished his drink. "Just how many club members are still alive?"

"Ninety-five."

Sloan stared at him for a few moments. "You mean to tell me that only three of you people have died since 1898?"

Weatherlee nodded. "There was Meyer. He died in a train accident back in 1909. Or was it 1910? And McMurty. He stayed in the Guard and worked himself up to full colonel before he was killed in the Argonne in 1918. And Iverson. He died of acute appendicitis in 1921."

Sloan considered his empty glass and then sighed. "Care for a drink?"

Weatherlee smiled affably. "I guess one more won't hurt. I'll take whatever you're having."

Sloan caught the bartender's eye and held up two fingers.

Weatherlee leaned forward and lowered his voice. "Actually this isn't the original champagne bottle. I broke that in 1924."

Sloan studied it again.

"It happened at our convention that year," Weatherlee said. "I was riding the elevator at the time. In those days they didn't operate as smoothly as they do now. There was this sudden jerk as the operator stopped at my floor. The suitcase I was carrying sprang open and the bottle dropped to the floor. Couldn't have fallen more than a foot, but there it lay, shattered on the floor."

Weatherlee shook his head at the memory. "I was absolutely panic-stricken. I mean here I was the custodian of the club's bottle—a great responsibility—and there it lay, shattered on the elevator floor. Luckily I was the only passenger on the elevator at the time. No one but the operator knew what had happened."

"So you went out and bought another bottle?"

"No. I didn't see how I could duplicate it anywhere. The bottle was quite distinctive. Purchased in Tampa, twenty-six years before."

Sloan indicated the bottle. "Then what is that?"

"It was the elevator operator who saved me," Weatherlee said. "He went out and got an *exact* duplicate."

"How did he manage to do that?"

"I haven't the faintest idea. He seemed a little evasive, now that I remember, but I was too overjoyed to press him. He was really most apologetic about the accident. Most solicitous. Took care of the mess in the elevator and brought the new bottle to my room fifteen minutes later. Wouldn't even let me pay for it. Claimed that the entire incident was really his doing and wouldn't accept a cent."

Sloan took his eyes from the magnum. "You said something about Captain O'Reilly trying to break the bottle?"

"Yes. Last year at our meeting. I still don't know exactly why he tried it. But I do remember that he kept staring at the bottle all evening. That year I was the Treasurer and I'd just finished reading my report. We had $4,990 in the treasury. Our dues are actually almost nominal, but still after all those years and compounded interest, it reached that sum."

The bartender brought the drinks. Sloan paid him and took a swallow of his whiskey and soda. "So what about O'Reilly?"

Weatherlee watched the bartender leave. "Oh, yes. Well, just as I finished, he rose suddenly to his feet and began slashing at the bottle with his cane and shouting, 'That damn bottle! That damn bottle!' And then it seemed as though nearly everyone else went mad, too. They shouted and cursed and smashed at the bottle, some even with chairs. I really don't know how it would all have ended if the waiters hadn't rushed in and restrained them."

"But they didn't break the bottle?"

"No. It was most remarkable. The blows were really resounding, and yet it didn't break. I thought about that all year. All this long year."

Weatherlee took a deep breath. "I arrived here early this morning. I am not a drinking man, but on impulse I bought a pint of whiskey and took it up to my room. I just sat there drinking and staring at the bottle. I even forgot all about the bus tour. And then I don't know what came over me, but I picked up an ashtray—one of those heavy glass things that are practically indestructible—and struck the bottle. Again and again, until finally the *ashtray* broke."

Weatherlee took the handkerchief from his waistcoat pocket. "I was in a perfect frenzy. I rushed out of my room with the bottle, and down the hallway I found one of those maintenance closets with its door open. There was a hammer on one of the shelves. I put the magnum of champagne into the stationary tub in the cubicle and struck it again and again with the hammer."

"But the bottle still didn't break?"

Weatherlee dabbed lightly at his forehead with the handkerchief. "But what was most ghastly of all was that all the time I was trying to smash that bottle, I had the feeling that someone, somewhere, was *laughing* at me."

He glared at the magnum. "And then suddenly, the *conviction,* the *certainty,* came to me that neither I, nor *anybody* in the club could destroy that bottle. If it were done, it had to be done by someone on the outside."

Sloan frowned at his drink. "Just *why* do you want to destroy that bottle in the first place?"

Weatherlee sighed. "I don't know. I just know that I *do.*"

They were both silent for almost a minute and then Sloan said, "This elevator operator. What did he look like?"

"The elevator operator? Rather a distinguished sort of person. I remember thinking at the time that he wasn't at all what one would expect of an elevator operator. Rather tall. Dark hair, dark eyes."

One of the doors of the dining room across the lobby opened and a waiter stepped out. He came into the bar. "Mr. Weatherlee, we're serving now."

Weatherlee nodded. "Yes. I'll be there in a moment."

Sloan waited until the waiter was out of hearing. "When did you say you broke the original bottle?"

"In 1924."

"And nobody's died since then?"

"Nobody's died since 1921. That was when Iverson got his acute appendicitis."

Sloan stared at the bottle again. "I'd like to join your club."

Weatherlee blinked. "But that's impossible."

"Why is it impossible?"

"Well . . . for one thing, you didn't belong to our National Guard company."

"Do your by-laws say anything about members having to belong to that particular company? Or any company at all?"

"Well, no. But it was *assumed*. . . ."

"And you did say that you never did fill your membership quota? Only ninety-eight people signed up? That leaves a vacancy of two, doesn't it?"

"Yes, but you are so much younger than any of the rest of us. It would be unfair for us to have to compete with you for the bottle."

"Look," Sloan said. "I'm not a rich man, but I'll match what's in the treasury, dollar for dollar."

"That's very kind of you," Weatherlee said a bit stiffly, "but if you should outlive all of us, and that seems likely, you'd get it all back anyhow."

Sloan smiled patiently. "I'll sign an affidavit renouncing all claim to what's in the treasury."

Weatherlee rubbed his neck. "I don't know. I'm not the final authority on anything like this. I'm not even an officer this year, unless you want to count being Custodian of the Bottle. I really don't know what the procedure would be in a case like this. I suppose we'll all have to take a vote or something."

He rose and put the magnum under his arm. "I suppose there's no harm in asking, but frankly I think they'll turn you down."

Sloan put his hand on the hammer. "Better leave this here with me."

Sloan came to Weatherlee's room at nine-thirty the next morning.

He took an envelope from his pocket and handed it to Weatherlee.

Weatherlee nodded acceptance. "To be quite honest, I was a bit surprised that the club decided to accept you. Not without exception, of course. Captain O'Reilly was quite against it."

Sloan moved to the bureau and picked up the magnum of champagne.

Weatherlee blinked. "What are you doing?"

"Taking the bottle with me. You told me yourself that according to the club's by-laws, the youngest member is Custodian of the Bottle."

"Yes, but. . . ."

Sloan opened the door to the corridor. He smiled broadly. "We wouldn't want you to go around asking strange people to break it, now would we?"

When Sloan was gone, Weatherlee locked the door.

He went to the bathroom and began removing the make-up from his face. As he worked, a half century disappeared.

Maybe he could have taken Sloan for more than five thousand, but you never know. Getting too greedy could have blown the whole deal.

He smiled.

Finding the sucker was the hardest part of it.

But once you did, and learned approximately how much he could part with without undue pain, you went about arranging the set-up. That included going to the nearest Old Soldiers' Home and offering to treat a dozen of their oldest veterans to a dinner.

And the old boys did so enjoy an afternoon out.

Two Postludes

by Isak Romun

Desmond Blinn carved a dripping slice of the rare beef, pushed it down on a piece of rye, put another piece of bread on top of the meat, and took great bites, his free hand feeling his stubbled face. A beer was nearby, warm now, poured out too long ago, just before he began wrestling with his thoughts. But he drank it lustily, driblets of pale amber upon his new beard turning into small reflective beads perched on the tips of stiff hairs.

It was a good meal, a good last meal, hearty and rough as his life had been; and simple, simple and direct, as he knew his death was soon to be. A strange man, Bohlmann, the leader; a man for little rituals, careful observances, precise ceremony. The traditional "last meal" of the doomed man's choice, a case in point. What would take place soon?—a quick walk into the courtyard, Blinn's hands tied behind him, two strong boys, each with a paw upon a shoulder, pushing him gently but with no nonsense to his knees; a long wooden slat upon which thick, brushed letters proclaiming the crimes of ingratitude, treachery, and betrayal of which Blinn had been accused and, in Bohlmann's direct, thick-robed judgment, found guilty. And then, one gunshot up through the neck into the brain and eternity would fold out in front of Blinn.

Bohlmann had seen the method in a newsreel: Chinese Reds, the strips of wood calligraphed with records of infamy, executed by Nationalists—or the other way around; and the simplicity, not devoid of a certain economical pomp and high moral tone, was appealing, irresistible to his nature.

"Let us try that with the very next one we shoot," he had said jollily, and Desmond Blinn remembered, with a tremor, for it was he who had accommodated Bohlmann, who bent down, aimed the gun upwards, and pulled the trigger, then stepped back quickly as the two burly boys, like *pas de deuxing* dancers, sprang off to the sides to escape, with Desmond, the squirting blood and the small flying pieces of brain.

And now, he, Desmond Blinn, would again be a participant in this final ceremony. For what? A woman. So foolish, for there were so many women. Bohlmann secured them and spent them like copper coins, and soon Blinn would suffer because he rubbed one while there was some sheen still upon it. The woman had been disposed of, thrown down a well and left to die there. Women did not get to participate in the Ceremony, only men—the ones against whom Bohlmann mounted huge accusations, driving himself up a spiraling curve of vengeful rage until, convinced of the utmost perfidy, he pronounced the awful sentence: the Ceremony.

"Tomorrow," he had shouted at Blinn, his wet red mouth

quivering with anger and expectation. "Tomorrow, at dawn." It was always dawn, another nicety, another line in the format: a chiaroscuro effect cherished by Bohlmann.

But in the meanwhile, thought Desmond Blinn, there's this splendid beef, cut from a cow stolen, slaughtered, and cooked over a great fire that day, and the rough, simple bread, and the beer, though warm, satisfying but almost gone. Might they give him another?

As Blinn went to the door of the cell in the monastery the band had taken over, he felt a keen exhilaration over how well he was taking this whole thing, enjoying the meat and bread, even rattling his agateware cup, chips of its coating flying about, against the short bars of the small opening in the door and shouting down the corridor, demanding more drink. And, by God, see that it's good and cold!

He was certain he could hold out this way, relish what life he had left without indulging in false hopes that somehow it would go on beyond the approaching light, that at the last moment he would receive a reprieve and be welcomed back into the band. No, that would not happen, but Blinn would rob Bohlmann of some of the glee gained through the Ceremony. Hah!—for what was the Ceremony designed? Not to make a man stand tall and stare back upon his persecutor at that last moment, as against a wall to be shot or, rope around his neck, upon a nervous horse. No, the victim was pushed down, his head bent forward, the wooden slat a comical element in a piece already without dignity; and then in this ignominious position, almost fetal (strange, that), the muzzle of the gun was pushed up against the short nape hairs but not fired until Bohlmann, off to the side, fat and squalid in his canvas chair, his torpid face moving rhythmically to the steady chewing of browned sesame seeds, masking his inner elation, gave the signal. (Caligula at the Circus Maximus.) By this time, the miscreant was reduced to a quaking, screaming figure, explaining to Bohlmann, pleading with Bohlmann, assuring Bohlmann that whatever in the world he had done (and perhaps he honestly didn't know), it would never occur again. Never.

If only you'll let me live. That's what they all said, thought Desmond Blinn as his cup ceased its insistent, cadenced ring upon the bars, and his knees felt a certain wateriness when he thought of those wretches, each now in his thoughts, remarkably, with his own face, the fear-stricken face of Desmond Blinn.

He wiped this vision of an uncongenial immediate future from the slate of his mind and struck up again the racket of cup against bars, calling out loudly (too loudly?) for more beer. Then he resurrected the images so recently discarded and ran them through a mental projector so that each, miraculously transformed now, showed Desmond Blinn as staunch, unbreakable, tight-lipped, and not without a trace of annoying wryness playing about his features, robbing Bohlmann of his pleasure.

For now, as one of his guards came padding down the corridor, Blinn knew, *knew,* that he would go through the Ceremony as these last pictures showed him, that he would deny Bohlmann the circus scene he coveted.

But the approaching guard ignored Blinn's demand for more beer and pushed a face against the bars of the small opening and blew his sweetish breath into the cell as he whispered quick and precise instructions to the confined man. The guard was Pardrilone, an old-time member of the band.

Tomorrow it would be over, he told the prisoner, but not for Blinn. For Bohlmann. If the men didn't turn from him now, he said, each would, in time, march screaming to the same fate that their leader planned for Blinn. Bohlmann was mad!

It was, after all, Pardrilone explained, not for a woman that Blinn was to die, but because he represented a threat to the leadership of Bohlmann, just as Bohlmann had been a threat to *his* predecessor. The woman had been emplaced to provide Bohlmann with an immediate cause for ordering Blinn's extinction; and perhaps the woman's as well, for Bohlmann was tiring of her.

This was why Blinn must be the center of the band's revolt against their leader. The others were afraid or, weighted down by the awe in which they held Bohlmann, could not conceive of his overthrow being successful, as if he had been touched by divinity.

Blinn reeled back from the door and fell to his cot,

weakened as much by the prospect of deliverance as others are of death. He had been ready for death. His was a readiness that was absolute, that was devoid of self-deception. He knew that never would he be as ready, that the conditioning of his mind and soul undergone in the hours spent in the dark cell could not be replicated at some future date, could not be turned on, turned off, by some psychic finger pressing a button.

"What's the matter with you?" Pardrilone hissed through the bars. "Are you with us?"

Desmond Blinn nodded as he rose and moved back to the door. "How? The plan. Does Quesada know?" Quesada was a faraway revolutionary figure to whom the band of irregulars owed a tenuous allegiance.

"He'll approve. Later. Here's a gun. Loaded." The guard shoved between the bars an ugly automatic pistol. "The clip is full. One round is chambered."

"I'll kill Bohlmann with this?"

"Yes. When I come to get you, I'll tie your hands loosely. Make sure to wear your woolskin so it will hide the gun. When you're out there, work your hands loose, get the gun out fast, and shoot him as he sits watching."

"Right in his fat, pig face."

"No," Pardrilone cautioned. "Too chancy—you could miss. Place your shots in his chest, around the heart. Can you do it?"

Blinn said he could.

"Good. You will be our new leader. That's the way these things go."

The next day, the plan worked perfectly. But despite what Pardrilone said, Blinn fired at and placed two bullets squarely in Bohlmann's face and watched with satisfaction as the force of the shots toppled the fat man over backwards, his wide buttocks still clamped in the arms of the canvas chair which went over with him as he skidded and rolled to a stop against a car some six feet distant. Some of Blinn's satisfaction was stolen, however, by Bohlmann, who saw, in the instant between the appearance of the gun and its discharge, what was happening and looked at Blinn calmly, a hint of wryness about his lips.

Pardrilone went over to the body, examined it, then growled at Blinn. "You should have fired at the chest. If you had missed, many of us would have been doomed. It was a stupid chance to take."

"I didn't miss—he's dead, isn't he?" Blinn replied matter-of-factly.

Pardrilone pondered this logic, accepted it, turned to the other members of the band, and yelled, "Hail Blinn, our new leader!"

The shouts were ear balm for Blinn, who stood the center of an admiring throng, any one of whose members would have shot him out of hand just moments before. He held his arms above his head, hands cupped in the manner of a champion boxer. Outside the circle—forgotten now even by Evelyn, his latest woman, who now turned her hot, fox eyes upon Blinn—lay Bohlmann, his shattered face a jagged O.

After that, Blinn led the band on many daring raids that garnered them much spoils and a number of casualties. They were richer than ever but disgruntled at the chances they had to take. So, one day, they grasped Blinn, tied his hands behind him, and dragged him to an open field. From the moment they had their hands on him to the moment they fired one sure shot into his head, Blinn, a bag of twitching, sagging flesh, cried and begged for his life. He had few thoughts at the end, but one of them was of how well Bohlmann had died. And how well he, Blinn, might have died that same day.

A Deal in Diamonds

by Edward D. Hoch

It was seeing a girl toss a penny into the plaza fountain that gave Pete Hopkins the idea. He was always on the lookout for money-making ideas, and they were getting tougher to find all the time. But as he looked up from the fountain to the open window of the Downtown Diamond Exchange, he thought he had found a good one at last.

He strolled over to the phone booth at the other side of the plaza and called Johnny Stoop. Johnny was the classiest dude Pete knew—a real fashion-plate who could walk into a store and have the clerks falling over themselves to wait on him. Better yet, he had no record here in the east. And it was doubtful if the cops could link him to the long list of felonies he had committed ten years ago in California.

"Johnny? This is Pete. Glad I caught you in."

"I'm always in during the daytime, Pete boy. In fact, I was just getting up."

"I got a job for us, Johnny, if you're interested."

"What sort?"

"Meet me at the Birchbark Bar and we'll talk about it."

"How soon?"

"An hour?"

Johnny Stoop groaned. "Make it two. I gotta shower and eat breakfast."

"Okay, two. See you."

The Birchbark Bar was a quiet place in the afternoons—perfect for the sort of meeting Pete wanted. He took a booth near the back and ordered a beer. Johnny was only ten minutes late and he walked into the place as if he were casing it for a robbery or a girl he might pick up. Finally he settled, almost reluctantly, for Pete's booth.

"So what's the story?"

The bartender was on the phone yelling at somebody about a delivery, and the rest of the place was empty. Pete started talking. "The Downtown Diamond Exchange. I think we can rip it off for a quick handful of stones. Might be good for fifty grand."

Johnny Stoop grunted, obviously interested. "How do we do it?"

"*You* do it. I wait outside."

"Great! And I'm the one the cops grab!"

"The cops don't grab anyone. You stroll in, just like Dapper Dan, and ask to see a tray of diamonds. You know where the place is, on the fourth floor. Go at noon, when there's always a few customers around. I'll create a commotion in the hall, and you snatch up a handful of stones."

"What do I do—swallow them like the gypsy kids used to do?"

"Nothing so crude. The cops are wise to that, anyway. You throw them out the window."

"Like hell I do!"

"I'm serious, Johnny."

"They don't even keep their windows open. They got air conditioning, haven't they?"

"I saw the window open today. You know all this energy-conservation stuff—turn off the air conditioner and open the windows. Well, they're doing it. They probably figure four flights up nobody's goin' to get in that way. But something can get *out*—the diamonds."

"It sounds crazy, Pete."

"Listen, you toss the diamonds through the window from the counter. That's maybe ten feet away." He was making a quick pencil sketch of the office as he talked. "See, the window's behind the counter and you're in front of it. They never suspect that you threw 'em out the window because you're never near the window. They search you, they question you, but then they gotta let you go. There are other people in the store, other suspects. And nobody saw you take them."

"So the diamonds go out the window. But you're not

outside to catch them. You're in the hall creating a diversion. So what happens to the stones?"

"This is the clever part. Directly beneath the window, four stories down, is the fountain in the plaza. It's big enough so the diamonds can't miss it. They fall into the fountain and they're as safe as in a bank vault, till we decide to get them. Nobody noticed them hit the water because the fountain is splashing. And nobody sees them *in* the water because they're clear. They're like glass."

"Yeah," Johnny agreed. "Unless the sun—"

"The sun don't reach the bottom of the pool. You could look right at 'em and not notice 'em—unless you knew they were there. We'll know, and we'll come back for them tomorrow night, or the next."

Johnny was nodding. "I'm in. When do we pull it off?"

Pete smiled and raised his glass of beer. "Tomorrow."

On the following day, Johnny Stoop entered the fourth floor offices of the Downtown Diamond Exchange at exactly 12:15. The uniformed guard who was always at the door gave him no more than a passing glance. Pete watched it all from the busy hallway outside, getting a clear view through the thick glass doors that ran from floor to ceiling.

As soon as he saw the clerk produce a tray of diamonds for Johnny, he glanced across the office at the window. It was open about halfway, as it had been the previous day. Pete started walking toward the door, touched the thick glass handle, and fell over in an apparent faint. The guard inside the door heard him fall and came out to offer assistance.

"What's the matter, mister? You okay?"

"I—I can't—breathe . . ."

He raised his head and asked for a glass of water. Already one of the clerks had come around the counter to see what the trouble was.

Pete sat up and drank the water, putting on a good act. "I just fainted, I guess."

"Let me get you a chair," one clerk said.

"No, I think I'd better just go home." He brushed off his suit and thanked them. "I'll be back when I'm feeling better." He hadn't dared to look at Johnny, and he hoped the diamonds had gone out the window as planned.

He took the elevator downstairs and strolled across the plaza to the fountain. There was always a crowd around it at noon—secretaries eating their lunches out of brown-paper bags, young men casually chatting with them. He mingled unnoticed and worked his way to the edge of the pool. But it was a big area, and through the rippling water he couldn't be certain he saw anything except the scattering of pennies and nickels at the bottom. Well, he hadn't expected to see the diamonds anyway, so he wasn't disappointed.

He waited an hour, then decided the police must still be questioning Johnny. The best thing to do was to head for his apartment and wait for a call.

It came two hours later.

"That was a close one," Johnny said. "They finally let me go, but they still might be following me."

"Did you do it?"

"Sure I did it! What do you think they held me for? They were goin' crazy in there. But I can't talk now. Let's meet at the Birchbark in an hour. I'll make sure I'm not followed."

Pete took the same booth at the rear of the Birchbark and ordered his usual beer. When Johnny arrived the dapper man was smiling. "I think we pulled it off, Pete. Damn if we didn't pull it off!"

"What'd you tell them?"

"That I didn't see a thing. Sure, I'd asked for the tray of stones, but then when there was the commotion in the hall I went to see what it was along with everyone else. There were four customers in the place and they couldn't really pin it on any one of us. But they searched us all, and even took us downtown to be X-rayed, to be certain we hadn't swallowed the stones."

"I was wondering what took you so long."

"I was lucky to be out as soon as I was. A couple of the others acted more suspicious than me, and that was a break. One of them even had an arrest record for a stolen car." He said it in a superior manner. "The dumb cops figure anyone who stole a car would steal diamonds."

"I hope they didn't get too good a look at me. I'm the one who caused the commotion, and they just gotta figure I'm involved."

"Don't worry. We'll pick up the diamonds tonight and get out of town for a while."

"How many stones were there?" Pete asked expectantly.

"Five. And all beauties."

The evening papers confirmed it. They placed the value of the five missing diamonds at $65,000. And the police had no clue.

They went back to the plaza around midnight, but Pete didn't like the feel of it. "They might be wise," he told Johnny. "Let's wait a night, in case the cops are still snoopin' around up there. Hell, the stones are safe where they are."

The following night, when the story had already disappeared from the papers, replaced by a bank robbery, they returned to the plaza once more. This time they waited till three A.M., when even the late crowd from the bars had scattered for home. Johnny carried a flashlight and Pete wore wading boots. He'd already considered the possibility that one or two of the diamonds might not be found, but even so they'd be far ahead of the game.

The fountain was turned off at night, and the calmness of the water made the search easier. Wading in the shallow water, Pete found two of the gems almost at once. It took another ten minutes to find the third one, and he was ready to quit then. "Let's take what we got, Johnny."

The flashlight bobbed. "No, no. Keep looking. Find us at least one more."

Suddenly they were pinned in the glare of a spotlight, and a voice shouted, "Hold it right there! We're police officers!"

"Damn!" Johnny dropped the flashlight and started to run, but already the two cops were out of their squad car. One of them pulled his gun and Johnny stopped in his tracks. Pete climbed from the pool and stood with his hands up.

"You got us, officer," he said.

"Damn right we got you," the cop with the gun growled. "The coins in that fountain go to charity every month. Anybody that would steal them has to be pretty low. I hope the judge gives you both ninety days in the cooler. Now up against the car while we search you!"

The Last Day of Shooting

by Dion Henderson

By nine o'clock the sun was streaming warmly into the blind and Johnny Tennant's big retriever was asleep on the shooting platform, lying on a hunting coat with his head resting on the rucksack that held the lunch. Blackbirds worked noisily in the bog behind us, their red shoulder patches bright against the dead grass, and once three egrets lumbered whitely down the channel from the rice fields. "Snow geese," someone said quietly back in the marsh and laughed, and the words came distinctly across the water. The sky was very blue and of course the only birds moving out of the refuge a mile away were impossibly high; it would not have been so bad except that it was the last day. It was the last day of the duck season and the last time, for most of us, that we would hunt together, or even meet, except accidentally.

Down in the point blind, Tom Randall stood up suddenly, hooting and thrashing his arms over the sedge and willow that camouflaged the blind, and an alarmed mud hen that had blundered almost into his boat skittered across the channel, peeping wildly. There was subdued laughter from the other three blinds around the point at the familiar performance. It was all very much like other days in other years—with one difference that made it not like any of them at all.

"I wish he had not taken the big gun," Johnny Tennant said. He was sitting on the platform beside the sleeping dog, with his feet down in the boat. He had not smiled at the mud hen's alarm.

"Your 20-gauge will be big enough," I said. "The way the birds are flying."

"I wasn't thinking about the shooting. There won't be any shooting."

"If it really disturbs you for him to have the big gun, I'll row down and get it back."

"If he knew I was disturbed, he wouldn't give it to you."

"That's probably true. He always carried a joke too far."

"Even when it was not a joke," Johnny Tennant said, not smiling.

"It was only a joke, taking the gun."

"No. It wasn't a joke."

"Are things really as bad as all that between you and Tom?" I asked.

"Things have always been that bad," Johnny Tennant said. "But now they are beginning to show, because I do not have much left that he wants."

I did not say anything. I was sorry that he felt bad, and that this last trip was not turning out well for him. Most of us had come because he wanted us to, because he had planned it for us, and because we were sorry for Johnny Tennant—but there wasn't anything we could do, really. The Clam Point Chowder, Poker Playing and Duck Hunting Society was something left over from a long time ago, when we were all a lot younger. Things like that are always more important to some members than to others, and with us it was Johnny Tennant who had inspired it, kept it going, and to whom, now that the shooting didn't amount to much and the members were scattered and the lease had run out, it was important that we get together for one last day of shooting.

I guess that it all became more important to Johnny as it became less important to the rest of us. He took care of the boats, he kept the decoys in repair and spent a good deal of his time in the shack on the point. He was our gunsmith, and reloaded our shotgun shells to a powder-and-shot ratio he had figured out to be most effective for the kind of shooting we had along the channel. Johnny's troubles probably had some relation to all this. They kept quietly overtaking him, one by one: the business that he started with Tom Randall, which did not do well as long as Johnny was in it; the woman who could not make up her mind between them; and then Johnny giving up both the business and the woman. But he did it carelessly, with a shrug, and the only difference we noticed was that Johnny Tennant spent more time at the shack on the point and more time alone, carving minutely detailed miniature ducks for the rest of us to hang up in our dens at home, and working on the inlays and engraving of his own favorite shotgun.

He had started with very complicated checkering of the stock and forearm, and then he had gone gradually into steel engraving, high-relief chiseling, and gold and ivory inlays. He reproduced a scene of the point itself on one side of the receiver, and the channel blind on the other, with ducks flying and the dog retrieving—until the gun itself was a glittering encyclopedia of our times together on the point. Gun engraving is a highly specialized art in itself, and I do not know how Johnny's work compared with the real immortals like Rudolph Kornbrath or Arnold Griebel or Joseph Baver, but the gun was very beautiful.

Now the gun was out in the point blind with Tom Randall, and whether it was just because of thoughtlessness or a poor joke, the hunt was not the way Johnny had planned it; the whole thing was spoiled for him.

It began when Tom Randall dropped his own gun into the marsh. We had eaten breakfast in the shack by lantern light with the windows covered: fried bread, heavy with bacon grease, and eggs and potatoes in a mixture that would kill a man at home in the city, but out here in the marsh would burn just brightly enough in his belly to keep him from freezing to death. Then, bundled up in seaters under the shooting coats, walking clumsily in hip boots, we followed Johnny out into the frosty starlight and down the quarter-mile of trail through the oak scrub to the place where the boats were pulled up under the cypress.

Johnny pushed the skiff out and stepped into it himself. "I'll take the point blind alone," he said. "That way maybe I can turn some of the high fliers coming out of the refuge and bring them in so you all get some shooting."

He uncased his gun and the starlight sparkled on the inlays as he slipped three shells softly and invisibly into the magazine.

"You'd better keep that museum piece covered up," someone said, "or it'll scare the ducks in the next county with its reflections."

"I'll keep it in the shade," Johnny said, chuckling. He sounded very happy then. "It's a pretty thing, though."

That was when Tom dropped his own gun into the marsh, into a foot of water and another foot of ooze. He was trying to push a boat out, holding the piece under one arm, and his hands slipped on the frost-wet gunwale and he dropped the gun. It was not hard to find, but it would take an hour, and daylight, to clean it up so that it was safe to shoot. Randall stood darkly in the water and swore.

"Never mind," Johnny Tennant said patiently, pushing the skiff back ashore. "I've got another gun up at the shack you can use. It's only a 20-gauge that I use to keep the squirrels honest, but it'll do."

He left the skiff and ran lightly up the trail in the darkness while the rest of us stood around uncomfortably, not talking.

"The light is coming up fast," Tom Randall said suddenly. "If we're not in the blinds by first shooting light, we'll never see a bird within range."

"What do you suggest?" I said.

Tom Randall stepped into the skiff and sent it skimming out into the channel. "This," he said. "I'll take old Johnny's boat and shotgun and go on out to the point blind myself. He can shoot with one of you."

"Johnny won't like it."

"Johnny won't mind," Tom Randall said, laughing, although no one laughed with him. "Johnny doesn't mind anything."

He was gone when Johnny came back with the 20-gauge, but it appeared that he was right. Johnny just shrugged and got into the boat with me, and we matched with the others to see who would take the channel blind and who would take the others. Then we poled off into the darkness, feeling for the channels in the grass to the open water.

And of course there had been no shooting. The sun came up clear and full and burned the frost off the marsh. The warm air from the Gulf moved up the river, and the birds getting up off the refuge climbed their aerial staircase straight up into the wonderfully blue sky, and no one truly cared except Johnny.

A little later the mud hen came back across the channel, swimming in narrow suspicious circles, but pressed by curiosity to see what had frightened it the first time. It was forty yards from the point blind, craning its neck, when Tom Randall fired. The charge of No. 4 shot splattered against the water, catching the bird in the center of a lethal pattern four feet in diameter, and presently the bird floated feet up, dead in the water.

"It shoots as good as it looks," Tom Randall's voice said across the water. "I think I'll keep it."

Johnny Tennant sat on the platform in our blind, not smiling. The retriever, awakened by the gunshot, peered out at the distant mud hen, and then, in the absence of a command to fetch, went back to sleep.

"He's a very funny man," I said in disgust.

Johnny Tennant shrugged. "I suppose he had to try it," he said. "He couldn't just look at it."

"I'm really very sorry. We didn't have a chance to stop him."

"It doesn't matter. . . . Maybe he thought it was safer to take my gun than take the one I was getting just for him." He smiled a little this time.

"Sure," I said. "You might have fixed up the 20 just for him, with a nice plug rammed down the barrel, or something."

"That isn't a good idea. A ballistician could tell if a gun blew up because the barrel was plugged."

He smiled again, almost wistfully. "If I wanted to kill a man accidentally in a duck blind," he said, "there are better ways."

The sun was warm in the blind and there was no swell in the channel, but suddenly I felt the touch of a cold wind blowing.

"A worn sear," Johnny said. "Or a cracked bolt in the block, so that the receiver would come right on back into your face after a shot. And when you use hand-loaded shells, it would be easy."

I did not say anything.

"You could make all kinds of mistakes," he went on. "You

could pick up the wrong over-powder wads and block the blow-by just long enough to split a barrel. Or you could measure from a flask of rifle powder, instead of regular nitrocellulose."

He paused, and said, "You remember that just one grain of a nitrocellulose rifle powder can raise breech pressure by almost 10,000 pounds."

He was sitting on the platform, still smiling a little and rubbing the dog's ears, when the dog raised his head abruptly, looking at something in the sky beyond the point. We followed his gaze, from habit, and presently we could see a bird, coming in low, laboriously, head swinging.

"A young goose looking for the family," Johnny Tennant said. "It looks as though he might come right down the channel."

Hearing him talk about the goose made me feel better. The cold wind let up for a moment, and I said: "It looks as though Tom will get the shot. I'm glad he's already fired once."

Johnny Tennant looked at me with a strange expression. "Did I make you nervous, talking about mistakes?"

"I had an odd feeling, while you were talking. I'm really very glad he already fired that gun once."

"That doesn't prove anything," he said, gently. "If a man made a mistake loading a shell, he could only afford one mistake—and there's no way to tell where it would be in the magazine."

The hair rose on my neck and I stood up, but down in the point blind Tom Randall was already up on the shooting platform. The young goose was flaring over him, in easy range, and Randall swung the beautiful gun, the sun flashing on its scrollwork and its splendid inlays. As the goose hung in panic at the top if its flare, the whole top of the blind dissolved in a white flash that was quite distinct before the shattering sound of the explosion swept across the water.

I stood dumbly in the boat, hearing the emptiness after the blast, and then the patter of raindrop-falling shot and metal fragments in the water around us, and then, preposterously later, the heavy sound of the body falling in the point blind.

"Damn him," Johnny Tennant said, in a thick, sad voice.

I looked at him and the tears were running down his defeated face.

"Tom always took everything I wanted for myself," Johnny Tennant said. "Even this."

Blisters in May

by Jack Ritchie

Dr. Kaufmann wasn't sure he'd heard right. "You mean you want a transfer to the road gang?"

"Yes, sir," I said.

He shook his head. "Fred, you have one of the best jobs inside the walls. You're out of the sun and there's no sweat. Don't you like being a medical orderly?"

"Yes, sir," I said. "But . . ." I shrugged. "I guess you could say that I'd like a change of pace."

He thought about it for a few seconds. "How long are you in for, Fred?"

"Life," I said.

He smiled faintly. "All right, Fred. I'll arrange the transfer. But I'm making book that after a few days with a pick and shovel, you'll be begging to come back. Anyway, I'll keep your present job open. When would you like this change of pace?"

"As soon as possible, sir. If you could make it Monday? That's May 1st."

Before I left my job at the dispensary that day, I put a roll of adhesive tape in my pocket. On Monday, after breakfast, I fell in with the outside work crew and we marched to the waiting trucks. The gates opened for us and for the first time in nine years I was outside the walls.

The ride was short and I spent the time taping my hands.

The trucks pulled up in front of a large ramshackle shed which housed the tools and machinery. We got off and waited in formation while a guard unlocked the double doors. He went inside and a con named Mark Hanson followed him.

After a few moments, the rest of us single-filed into the building. Hanson was in charge of handing out the tools. He marked me down for an axe.

We lined up again outside and waited while Hanson went about the business of closing the doors. He was about to snap the padlock when he looked at the guard and grinned sheepishly, "I forgot my shovel."

Yes, I thought, you forget it twice a year.

Hanson disappeared back into the shed and came out twenty seconds later with a shovel. He padlocked the doors and fell into the rear of the formation.

We marched a quarter of a mile to the work site and started the day. It was make-work mostly, clearing the scrub pine and cutting pole wood.

At noon, I got my plate filled in the chow line and sat down in the shade of a tree next to Hanson. He contemplated the contents of his plate and I had the feeling he wasn't going to eat what was there. Not today, anyway. When he put down the plate untouched, I said, "How are the hands?"

He glanced at his palms automatically. Blisters were beginning to form. I got out my roll of adhesive. "Try this."

He shrugged a small thanks and accepted it.

"Kind of interesting about your hands," I said. "Every first of May or thereabouts you develop blisters bad enough to have to be treated at the dispensary. Been that way for every one of the four years you've been here."

He regarded me stonily. "So?"

"So the prison keeps a pretty thorough medical record of everything that happens to you—whether it's a sore throat, lumbago, or blisters. It's put down in your file."

"What's all that to you?"

I chewed a piece of my bread and swallowed. "But the thing that really interests me is your appendix. Two years ago, when Dr. Williams was still the medical officer, he took it out. And what do you know, four months ago Dr. Kaufmann had to do the same thing again."

He made sure that we were out of earshot of the other prisoners and the guards before he spoke again. "The records are wrong."

"No," I said. "They aren't. I'm the one who kept them." I tasted the cold tea in my tin cup. "When Mark Hanson went back into the shed alone for his shovel this morning, he had a small rip on the knee of his uniform. When he came out, the rip was gone."

I smiled and said, "The tool shed is outside the walls. It's locked, but not guarded at night. So you slipped inside last night and hid. Maybe under the floorboards or something like that. And when the Mark Hanson with the rip in his uniform got the chance to go back inside alone this morning, the two of you traded places real quick and you came out. How long are you staying with us this time?"

He studied me for a full minute before he made up his mind to admit anything. "May and June. Like always."

I nodded. "So I guess that makes you the real Mark Hanson. But if you can get the other one to do ten months for you, why not the whole year?"

"He's a family man. A wife and kids. He wouldn't touch this deal if it kept him away for the full seven years of my rap."

"Who is he? Your twin brother or something?"

"No. I used him for my double whenever I was worried about some of my friends and what they might have in mind. When this income tax thing hit me, I had a doctor work on him a little to make him even more like my mirror."

I put aside my empty tin plate. "So you get outside. Why don't you stay out? The world's a big place and they don't extradite from Brazil."

He shook his head. "Maybe so, but I got my business interests in the U.S. and they need my touch. I'm running things from behind a door right now, but in a few more years I want to be able to step out without having the Government tap my shoulder again."

He looked at me. "So now we talked. What do you want? Money? Or you'll toddle to the warden with a story?"

"No," I said. "I don't want money."

He frowned. "Hell, you don't expect me to arrange . . . ."

"Why not?" I said. "You got the connections and you ought to be able to find somebody with my face."

The guards blew their whistles and we got to our feet.

I rubbed at the pain in my back and then picked up my axe. This kind of work really wasn't for me, and I had the hunch that someone using my name would come to the same conclusion after about ten months and make noises about getting out.

I didn't think I'd hear him in Brazil.

The Collector

by Patricia A. Matthews

Allister Hugh loved olden times. He adored the quaint, revered the ancient, and often declared sadly with his hand held over his heart that, "Things today are not the way they used to be."

That is the reason he loved Lenadine Lou Le Clare. Not that Lenadine was old, far from it. She was young and very beautiful. And to Allister she was the embodiment of all the charms credited to the belles of long past years.

Her beauty was of the Dresden china type. Her hair pale gold and simply styled. She tóok tea at precisely three each afternoon and often fainted when upset.

Every Sunday afternoon Allister called upon her. They had tea upon the terrace and spoke of gentle things.

He presented her with flowers and once—much moved by her rendition of the Moonlight Sonata played upon an old-fashioned spinet—he composed a sonnet entitled "Lovely Hands of Palest Ivory," which he dedicated to her.

All went well. She received him with dignity and poise. Their courtship proceeded as gracefully as a minuet, and Allister was happy. He was certain that ultimately she would be his; a fitting culmination to years of collecting museum pieces.

One lovely afternoon as they sat late at their tea upon the

terrace, Allister decided that this was the moment to declare his intentions.

The breeze was soft, the air fragrant with the scent of flowers from the garden. He sank to his knees beside Lenadine's chair.

"Lenadine," he declared, looking passionately into her sea-green eyes. "Lenadine, I am mad about you. Will you do me the honor of becoming my wife?"

"Oh, Allister," she answered in emotion-choked tones. "Long have I awaited the day when you would offer me your heart."

"My heart," he declared movingly, "my soul, my life, are at your feet."

They were married. It was a lovely old-fashioned wedding and after a discreet honeymoon in Niagara Falls the couple took up residence in the old mansion Lenadine had inherited from her first husband.

Allister found Lenadine all he had ever desired in a woman, and the old mansion was filled with the relics of bygone days which he loved. There was only one flaw. He could not interest Lenadine in his hobby. It was perhaps unrealistic of him to wish to do so, for who expects the collector's item to be interested in the collection of which it is a part? But as many people will who have an absorbing interest, he wished to share it.

One day he said to her, "Lenadine, my love, since you do not share my interest in antiques, perhaps you should have a hobby of your own."

Lenadine smiled sweetly. She always smiled sweetly, it was one of the things he admired in her.

"Oh, I have a hobby of sorts," she replied roguishly; and not a word more would she say on the subject.

He thought it a feminine whim. Women were unpredictable creatures. He let it pass.

Then one day he discovered the locked door. It was a heavy door, well reinforced and bolted. Curious, he asked Lenadine about it.

She was vague.

His curiosity became stronger. He insisted.

She cried.

After that he insisted no more, but his curiosity grew. He decided to break the lock and see for himself what the room contained. He determined to do it that very night, when Lenadine and the servants were asleep.

That evening he was especially attentive to Lenadine, for he felt a trifle ashamed of what he planned to do. She, however, was much subdued that evening.

"Come, my love," he cajoled her. "Why is my little bird so quiet this evening?"

"I did not wish to tell you," she said, "but tonight is the very night that my former husband—" Here she burst into soft sobs which she muffled in her lace handkerchief.

"Ah, my dear," answered Allister sympathetically, knowing that her first husband had died in some vague but tragic manner. "Of course, love. It is natural that you should think of him. I am not offended. Perhaps it would be better if you retired now."

Lenadine smiled gratefully and, kissing him coolly upon the cheek, retired to her room.

Allister was now free to examine the locked room. He secured a candle—he much preferred a candle to a flashlight—and approached the concealing door.

It took him considerable time to force an entry. The lock was extremely difficult. But at last the door stood open and Allister was able to enter the room.

He lit the candle and went in. The door swung slowly shut behind him. The flame from the candle flickered, but its pale light was sufficient to illumine the strange altarlike block of stone with the odd, dark stains upon it and the queer, round jars sitting in precise rows upon a shelf; each of the jars contained an unidentifiable object suspended in liquid.

With a feeling of dreadful anticipation, Allister raised the candle and advanced toward the jars.

The candle flickered perilously, there was a draught as if someone had opened a door. But before the candle went out Allister was able to see quite clearly the contents of the jars.

And in the first frightful blackness after the extinguished flame, he recalled Lenadine's words that sunny afternoon upon the terrace.

"Oh, Allister, I have waited so long for you to give me your heart."

House Call

by Elsin Ann Graffam

She dialed the number and waited. Two rings, three— Maybe he wasn't in on a Saturday, maybe—

"Hello? Dr. Reed? This is Joe's mother, Mrs. Forte. Yes. Well, please, you've *got* to come over and see my Joe! He looks awful bad and I'm so worried. What? Oh, no, he can't come to your office. He's—he don't look good at all. You can come here, maybe? You will? In a half hour? Oh, thank you, thank you so much, Doctor!"

She hung up the telephone slowly and smoothed back stray strands of gray hair. Her fingers were gnarled, but strong and muscular from forty years of taking care of her boys. Her boys. There had been five of them once, but now all she had left with her was her Joe. A good boy, he was; nothing bad would ever happen to her Joe. That's why she had to make the doctor come to her home, had to get everything taken care of.

She tiptoed down the hall to Joe's bedroom and carefully opened the door. He was sitting on the edge of the bed, his body rigid and his face as vacant as it had been the last five times she'd looked in on him.

"Joe?" she whispered.

He didn't look at her.

"Joe, everything will be all right. You wait and see. I'll take care of you."

Closing the door as softly as she'd opened it, she looked at the hands of the old clock in the hall. Twenty-five minutes to wait. She'd go crazy just sitting, waiting—

Going into the living room, she picked up her knitting and began to work on the sweater she'd started the week before. A bright shade of blue, it was Joe's favorite color. He'd be real surprised when he saw it.

"Oh, Ma," he'd say, "you shouldn't have gone to all that trouble for me!"

But he'd slip it over his head and grin at her like a little boy. Yes, her Joe would be pleased with the sweater. It was worth the pain from the arthritis in her fingers to make her boy happy. After all, what's a mother *for,* if it isn't to take care of her boys?

She dropped the yarn when the bell rang and went to the door. Peeking around the side of the curtain, she was relieved to see the doctor standing there.

"Dr. Reed, oh, thank you so much for coming over so quick. I'm so grateful—

He brushed past her and strode into the hall.

"That's all right, Mrs. Forte. Where is he?"

"What?"

"Joe. Where is he?"

"Oh. Well, if you could—if we could just talk for a bit first, in the kitchen, maybe?"

He sighed. "I really haven't too much time, Mrs. Forte. It *is* Saturday afternoon, you know, and my office hours were supposed to be over an hour ago."

"Please, Doctor?"

She stood there, her eyes pleading, and when she turned and went ahead of him into the kitchen he shrugged and followed her.

"A cup of coffee for you, Doctor?"

"No, I—"

"Ah, coffee for the good doctor. No matter how rich and important he gets, he still comes to our house to take care of us. For the good doctor a nice cup of coffee. Here, let me—"

She poured the steaming liquid into one of her two best china cups and pushed it across the table to him.

Sighing again, he picked it up and sipped. "These old women. These *old women!*" he thought with exasperation. " 'A cup of tea? A cup of coffee?' And if you decline their hospitality they get so damned offended."

"Now," he said aloud, "what about Joe?"

"He's in his room, Doctor, just sitting on his bed, staring at nothing. Been like that since he got home last night. He wouldn't talk to me or nothing. Couple of hours ago he sort of came out of it for a few minutes and told me what the matter was, but then he turned his head away. He had tears in his eyes. Tears! My Joe!"

She shook her head with the memory of it.

"You're not drinking your coffee, Doctor," she said then.

"I am. I am. Please go *on*."

"Well, my Joe, he's an important man, really. In this group, you know."

"No, I don't know." He drank the last of his coffee and started to rise.

"Doctor!"

The tone of her voice startled him and he sat down.

"The group," she went on, "they call it 'Our Thing'."

Ignoring the intent look on the man's face, she said, "They—the bosses, they gave Joe a job to do. And he *has* to do it. When they say do something, you do it or else, right?"

"Uh-huh," replied the doctor.

"But my Joe, he's so *sensitive!* He was always the most delicate of my boys."

She smiled, remembering. "When he was only, oh, eight or nine, he fell off his bike and you had to sew up his knee. He fainted, remember? That's how he is, Doctor. A real man, you understand, but so *sensitive*."

Dr. Reed grunted.

"Well, it seems like there's this man around the neighborhood who's been—how did Joe put it?—'horning in on the drug traffic' or something like that. And, see, they told Joe to get rid of him—to kill him, you know. Because they don't like no competition, they don't like that at *all*.

"But my Joe, he just couldn't *do* it. 'Maybe a stranger, Ma,' he said, 'but not—'. And he started to cry. Cry! Think of how I felt, his mother, when I saw them tears running down his face!"

"Ah," said the doctor.

"This man Joe's supposed to kill, he's a real respected man around here. A doctor. . . . Doctor?"

She watched impassively as the doctor slid off the chair and landed on her kitchen floor with a thud.

He hadn't, she noted with relief, broken her china cup in his fall. She picked it up and carried it over to the sink, scoured it and the coffee pot with extra care; then, stepping over the doctor, she went to her son's room.

"Joe? Joe!"

He turned and looked at her dully. "What, Ma?"

"It's all taken care of, just like I said. Come into the kitchen and look!"

That's Ma for you. She always takes care of her boys.

The Adventure of the Blind Alley

by Edward Wellen

Feeling his way through the pea-soup fog, Police Constable Cooper paused at the noise of a struggle. He stared hard to hear. At the first outcry and the noise of scuffling his hand had whisked to his whistle. But before he could blow a blast to frighten off the attacker, he heard the sickening sound of a cosh on a skull, then the thump of a falling body.

He withheld the blast and with heavy caution, in order to catch the assailant red-handed, he lifted his boots towards the rough breathing and the tearing of cloth.

P.C. Cooper smiled tightly to himself. He knew this to be a narrow cul-de-sac and himself to be between the attacker and escape. He had the culprit all but in his arms.

He winged out his cape and moved slowly but steadily into the blindness of the alley. But a kerb leaped out of nowhere. P.C. Cooper's stumble and his muffled oath warned the attacker. The constable blew a savage blast. "In the name of the law, stand fast!"

P.C. Cooper heard fleeing footsteps, the ring of a hob-nailed boot striking an iron mudscraper, then the creak of a door and the snick of a latch. The culprit, then, was a denizen of this unsavoury alley.

The constable swore under his breath. He had his man—and yet he did not have him. He knew there were a half-dozen doors on either hand. Unless the constable located the right door straightway, the culprit would have time to change from his wet outer clothes and to hide what he had stolen from the victim.

The victim. A dozen paces deeper into the alley, and the constable saw the shape of the victim on the cobblestones.

Feeling sudden clamminess and chill, P.C. Cooper stood over the fallen man. He eyed a familiar hawklike profile, a bloodied deerstalker cap, a still-clutched violin case. Rents showed in the victim's clothes where hurried hands had torn away a watch chain and snatched a wallet. That the mighty manhunter should have fallen prey to a common robber!

The victim stirred. A word came forth. "Constable . . ."

P.C. Cooper knelt, careless that his knee touched the wet stones. The blood-blinded face had not turned towards him. How had the man known to call him constable?

The whistle, of course. The habits and skills of a lifetime would not have failed him even in the direst of moments. Though stunned, the great detective would have taken note of some clue, and most likely clung to consciousness now solely to impart that clue.

"Sir, did you see your assailant? Can you describe him?"

A painful shake of the hand.

"Do you know where he ran to?"

A painful nod.

P.C. Cooper's heart surged, but the man only consciousness enough to point vaguely and gasp, "A flat . . ."

The constable grimaced in disappointment. The great detective had told P.C. Cooper only what P.C. Cooper already knew.

A flat, indeed! This was an alley of roominghouses—nothing but flats.

P.C. Cooper removed his cape and wadded it under the great detective's head as a cushion. Then the constable rose and duty took over. His whistle guided answering whistles.

Each blast, each echo, ached. It hurt him to think that his colleagues would find him simply standing there, waiting, while the culprit was safe behind one of those unseen doors.

A flat . . .

P.C. Cooper shook his head. Why should those words keep ringing in his mind? They had originated in the poor stricken mind of the great detective.

A flat . . .

Pounding boots pulled up. P.C. Cooper recognised the figure of P.C. Lloyd.

Lloyd was a Welshman, and Welshmen are famous for having perfect pitch.

Swelling with authority, Cooper seized Lloyd's arm and pointed him.

"Man, hurry and kick the mudscrapers with your great hobnailed boots and find the one that sounds A flat."

The Unfriendly Neighbor

by Al Nussbaum

When I sat down at the breakfast table today, my wife had the morning newspaper folded beside my plate as she always did. I took a sip of coffee, then opened the paper to the first page and got the shock of my life. There, staring back at me, was a picture of Elmer Sesler. I read the accompanying article and couldn't keep from laughing.

"What's so funny?" my wife asked.

"It's a long story, honey. It began twenty years ago." Then I told her about Elmer Sesler . . .

I was a freshman in high school when the Seslers moved in next door. There was just Elmer, who was my age, and his parents. His father, who was a minor executive with an insurance company, had been transferred to our city to work in the local office.

Elmer had stood out immediately, and not because of his

jug-handle ears or freckled face. He had his own car. Few seniors had cars, but here was a lowly freshman who not only had a car, he had one that was almost new. A couple of guys tried to throw sour grapes on the situation by saying the car was probably his father's, but I put a stop to that.

"His father drives this year's model," I said. "That one's his, all right."

If anyone was unconvinced, Elmer's actions soon convinced them. He began to take the car apart. One day he'd arrive at school with the hood and trunk lid missing; the next day the doors might be gone. After the first few days, no one ever saw that car completely assembled again. The car *had* to be his. No one could get away with treating his father's car that way.

On evenings and weekends I'd look across the hedge that divided our back yards and see him tinkering with his car or working on something else in his garage. He had a workbench set up and far more tools than I could name. One time he had his car's engine completely disassembled and scattered across the ground with each separate part resting on a piece of clean newspaper. Other times he was hovering over an old TV and a vacuum cleaner he had spread out on his workbench. He seemed to have an insatiable curiosity and a genuine talent for taking things apart.

If it hadn't been for his car, however, he'd have been a social failure. He had all the tact of a kick in the teeth. He always ignored me when he saw me watching him, even though he must have recognized me from school where we had several classes together. Finally I spoke to him, and he walked over to the hedge.

"Yes?" he said in a flat tone.

"I'm Bill Ford," I said, reaching across the hedge to shake hands.

He ignored my hand and kept a level stare on me until I pulled my arm back in confusion.

"Just because we're neighbors doesn't mean you can ride to school in my car," he said.

"Who said anything about riding to school in your car?" I demanded. "*I* didn't say anything about your old car, or about riding in it."

"No, but you were thinking about it," he said.

He turned his back on me and returned to the garage where he had a washing machine torn apart on the cement floor.

I stood there for several minutes, shaking with anger. My fury was all the more intense because he'd been right. I *had* been thinking about how convenient it would be to have a ride to school, instead of having to walk the fifteen blocks every morning.

It turned out I wasn't the only one he accused of having designs on his car. He accused almost everyone, but apparently I was the only one who hated him for it. Perhaps because he was wrong about them, the other kids at school were able to laugh it off, while I resented having my mind read.

From then on I belittled everything Elmer Sesler did, and never passed up a chance to attack him verbally. Though everyone else seemed to consider him some kind of budding, eccentric genius, I made it clear I thought he was just a lunatic.

"He might even be dangerous, the way he thinks everyone is trying to use him," I said. "Just because he can take things apart doesn't mean he's a genius. I see him in his back yard every day, and half the stuff he tears into never does get back together. Take his car, for example—it doesn't look or run as well as it did before he started messing with it."

Nothing I said, though, had any effect. As far as the other students were concerned, Elmer Sesler was going to be famous someday. He was voted the most likely freshman to succeed, while I was given the wet blanket award.

Then, after that one year, Elmer's father was transferred to another city, and I never saw or heard of Elmer again . . .

"So what was so funny in the newspaper?" my wife asked. "Did he invent something?"

"No, he didn't invent anything," I said, "and I guess it's really not very funny. Elmer Sesler murdered his wife. The police found her body in Chicago, and Detroit, and Cleveland, and Buffalo."

A Feline Felony

by Lael J. Littke

Jerome Kotter looked like a cat. However, this did not bring him any undue attention from his schoolmates since almost all of them had an unusual quality or two. Beverly Baumgartner had a laugh like a horse. Bart Hansen was as rotund as an elephant. Carla Seaver's long neck resembled that of a giraffe. And Randy Ramsbottom always smelled remarkably like a dog on a rainy day.

The only person who worried about Jerome's unusual appearance was his father, who quietly set about arming his son to face a world in which he was a bit different. He taught Jerome gentle manners, assuring him that no matter how different he looked he would always get along fine if he acted right. He taught him to recite all the verses of *The Star-Spangled Banner* by heart. He encouraged him to read the Bible. And he taught him to sing the songs from the best-known Gilbert and Sullivan operettas. He felt Jerome was well equipped to face the world.

When Jerome got to high school he became the greatest track star that Quigley High had ever produced, although he had to be careful because the coaches from rival schools cried foul when Jerome resorted to running on all fours.

Altogether, Jerome's school years would have been quite happy—if it hadn't been for Benny Rhoades.

Whereas Jerome was tall, polite, studious, and well-groomed with silken fur and sparkling whiskers, Benny was wizened, unkempt, rude, and sly. His face was pinched and pointed and his hair stuck up in uneven wisps. He hated anyone who excelled him in anything. Almost everybody excelled him in everything, and since Jerome surpassed him in the one thing he did do fairly well—running—he hated Jerome most of all. When Jerome took away his title of champion runner of Quigley High, Benny vowed he would get even if it took him the rest of his life.

One of Benny's favorite harassments was to tread on Jerome's tail in study hall, causing him to yeowl and thereby incurring the wrath of the monitor. Benny tweaked Jerome's whiskers and poured honey in his fur. He did everything he could think of to make Jerome's life miserable.

When it came to Benny Rhoades, Jerome found it hard to follow the admonitions of his father—that he should love his enemies and do good even to those who used him spitefully. He looked forward to the day when he would finish school and get away, for he had to admit in his heart that he loathed the odious Benny. It rancored him to think that Benny was the only person who could make him lose his composure and caterwaul in public, thus making people notice that, despite his suave manner and intellectual conversation, he was a bit different. To keep his temper he took to declaiming *The Star-Spangled Banner* or passages from the Bible. Once he got all the way through the "begats" in Genesis before he took hold of himself and regained his composure.

Just before Jerome was graduated from college, Benny stole all the fish from Old Man Walker's little fish cart and deposited them in Jerome's car, after which he made an anonymous phone call to the police. The police, who had always regarded Jerome as the embodiment of what they would like all young men to be, preferred to believe his claim of innocence; but then again, looking as he did, it was natural for them to believe that he might have swiped a mess of fish.

People began to whisper about Jerome when he passed on the street. They pointed out that although his manners were perfect, he did have those long sword-like claws, and they certainly wouldn't want to be caught alone with him in an alley on a dark night. And wasn't there a rather feline craftiness in his slanted eyes?

Jerome left town after graduation enveloped in an aura of suspicion and an aroma of rotting fish which he never could dispel completely from his car.

Jerome decided to pursue a career as a writer of advertising copy in New York, reasoning that what with all the strange creatures roaming about in that city no one was apt to notice anything a bit different about him. He was hired at the first place he applied, Bobble, Babble, and Armbruster, Inc., on Madison Avenue. Mr. Armbruster had been out celebrating his fourteenth wedding anniversary the night before and had imbibed himself into near-oblivion trying to forget what devastation those fourteen years had wrought. When Jerome walked into his office, he naturally figured him to be related to the ten-foot polka-dot cobra that had pursued him the night before and thought he would fade with the hangover. After ducking behind his desk for a little hair-of-the-dog, he hired Jerome. By the time Mr. Armbruster had fully recovered from his celebration, Jerome had proved himself capable at his job and affable with the other employees, so he was allowed to stay. Mr. Armbruster naturally put him on the cat food account.

Before long, Jerome fell in love with his secretary, Marie, a shapely blonde who thought Jerome's sleek fur and golden eyes sexy. He wanted to ask her for a date, but first, in all fairness, he thought he should find out how she felt about him.

"Marie," he said one day as he finished the day's dictation, "do you like me as a boss?"

"Oh, yes," breathed Marie. "Gee, Mr. Kotter, you're the swellest boss I ever had. You're so different."

Jerome's heart sank. "Different? In what way, Marie?"

"Well," said Marie, "Mr. Leach, my old boss, used to pinch me sometimes. And he used to sneak up behind me and kiss me." She peered coyly at Jerome from under her lashes. "You're a perfect gentleman, Mr. Kotter. You're real different."

Jerome was enchanted and wasted no further time asking her out to dinner.

For several weeks everything was wonderful. Then, unexpectedly, Benny Rhoades turned up. Jerome looked up from his desk one day to see his nemesis standing in the doorway.

"Man," said Benny, "if it ain't Jerome Kotter." He grinned.

"Benny Rhoades," exclaimed Jerome. "What are you doing here?"

"Man, you're the most," said Benny softly. "I work in the mail room, man. You're gonna see a lot of me, Jerome."

Jerome's tail twitched.

"Why did you come here?" he asked. "Why don't you leave me alone?"

Offended innocence replaced the calculating look on Benny's pasty face.

"Why, man, I ain't done a thing. A man's got to work. And I work here." He lounged against the door jamb. "I hear you're a real swingin' cat around here. I wonder how long that's gonna last."

"Get out," said Jerome.

"Sure, Mr. Kotter, sir. Sure. Think I'll drop by your secretary's desk. Quite a dish, that Marie."

"You stay away from her." Jerome could feel the fur around his neck rising. His whiskers bristled.

Benny smiled and glided away like an insidious snake.

From that time on, Benny did what he could to torment Jerome. He held up his mail until important clients called the bosses to complain about lack of action on their accounts. He slammed Jerome's tail in doors, usually when some VIP was visiting the office. Worse of all, he vexed Marie by hanging around her desk asking for dates and sometimes sneaking up to nibble at her neck. Marie hated him almost as much as Jerome did.

Jerome didn't know quite what he could do about it without jeopardizing his job, of which he had become very fond. The other people at the agency liked him, although they regarded him as a trifle eccentric since he always insisted on sampling the cat food he wrote about. But then everyone to his own tastes, they said.

Things came to a head one evening when Jerome invited Marie to his apartment for a fish dinner before going out to a show. They were just sitting down to eat when the doorbell rang.

It was Benny.

"Cozy," he murmured, surveying the scene. He slammed the door shut behind him.

"A real swingin' cat," he said, sidling into the room. He produced a small pistol from his pocket.

"Are you out of your mind, Benny?" said Jerome. "What do you think you're doing?"

"I lost my job," smiled Benny.

"What's that got to do with me?"

"Marie complained that I bothered her. They fired me." Benny's small eyes glittered. "I'll repay her for the favor, then I'll take care of you, Jerome. I'll fix it so they'll think you shot her for resisting your charms, and then shot yourself. Everybody knows a big cat like you could go beserk anytime."

"You're a rat," said Marie. "You're a miserable, black-hearted little rat."

Jerome stepped protectively in front of her.

"Sticks and stones may break my bones but names will never hurt me," chanted Benny gleefully.

Jerome was looking at Benny thoughtfully. "A rat," he said. "That's what he is. A rat. Funny it never occurred to me before." His tail twitched nervously.

Benny didn't like the look on Jerome's face. "Stay away from me, man. I'll shoot."

Before Benny could aim, Jerome leaped across the room with the swift, fluid motion of a tiger. He knocked Benny to the floor and easily took the gun from him.

"A rat," repeated Jerome softly.

Benny looked at Jerome's face so close to his own. "What are you going to do?" he squeaked, his own face pinched and white and his beady eyes terror-stricken. "What are you going to do?"

Jerome ate him.

It took a long time to get the police sergeant to take the matter seriously. Marie had urged Jerome to forget the whole thing, but Jerome felt he must confess.

"You say you ate this guy Benny?" the sergeant asked for the twentieth time.

"I ate him," said Jerome.

"He was a rat," said Marie.

The sergeant shook his head. "We get all kinds," he muttered. "Go home. Sleep it off." He sighed. "Self-defense, you say?"

"Benny was going to shoot both of us," said Marie.

"Where's the body?" asked the sergeant.

Jerome shook his head. "There is no body. I ate him."

"He was a rat," said Marie.

"There's no body," said the sergeant. "We sent a coupla men up to your apartment and there's no body and no sign of anybody getting killed. We even called this Benny's family long distance to find out if they knew where he is, but his old man said as far as they are concerned he died at birth. So go home."

"I ate him," insisted Jerome.

"So you performed a public service. I got six kids to support, buddy. I don't want to spend the next two years on a head-shrinker's couch for trying to make the Chief believe I got a six-foot cat here who ate a guy. Now go home, you two, before I get mad."

Jerome remained standing in front of the desk.

"Look," said the sergeant. "You ate a guy."

"A rat," corrected Marie.

"A rat," said the sergeant. "So how do you feel?"

"Terrible," said Jerome. "I have a most remarkable case of indigestion."

"You ate a rat," said the sergeant. "Now you've got a bellyache. That's your punishment. Remember when you ate green apples as a kid?" He sighed. "Now go home."

As they turned to leave, Jerome heard the sergeant muttering to himself about not having had a vacation in four years.

Despite his indigestion, Jerome felt marvelous. "Let the punishment fit the crime," he said with satisfaction. He took Marie's arm in a courtly fashion and sang softly as they walked along. "My object all sublime, I shall achieve in time, to let the punishment fit the crime, the punishment fit the crime . . ."

"Gee, Mr. Kotter," said Marie, gazing up at him in admiration. "You're so different from anyone else I ever went with."

"Different?" asked Jerome. "How, Marie?"

"Gee," said Marie, "I never went out before with anybody who quoted poetry."

Don't I Know You?

by Henry Slesar

The man was well-groomed, in a sleek, furry way midway in style between Broadway and Bond Street. His hands were buried in the deep pockets of his camel's-hair coat, and he blew a frosty breath of winter past his mink mustache as he waited for the light to change.

The other man, smaller, not so well-groomed, his brown tweed overcoat threadbare in comparison, looked at him sharply, looked away, looked back, and was finally rewarded by an answering stare, equally puzzled and involved.

They crossed the street together, matching stride for stride, and then stopped at the opposite corner and looked at each other again. The mustached man cracked the silence first, with a smile and the words:

"Don't I know you?"

It took the smaller man a longer time to thaw. He said, "I sure as heck think I know *you.* Only I can't remember—"

"Carmody's the name," the mustached man said, in a manner suggesting the click of heels or the presentation of a card. Actually, he didn't move his well-shined shoes or remove his hands from his pockets.

"My name's Siegel," the smaller man said. "Frank Siegel. And if we *do* know each other"—here he finally managed the smile—"must have been a heck of a long time ago. You don't come from Michigan, by any chance?"

"Never been there," Carmody said. "But I've traveled a lot. South mostly, Florida, the Caribbean, southern Europe. I like the sunshine—hate this beastly cold." He said the adjective without a hint of English accent.

"No," Siegel said, "Never been to any of those places."

"School, maybe? No, I suppose not. I went to Washington and Lee."

"City College."

"Must have been some place," Carmody said. "The more I look at you, the surer I am."

"Same with me," Siegel said.

"Look," Carmody said, searching the east and west of the street, "I'm in no great hurry, are you? We could stop for a drink—nice warm bar—puzzle it all out."

"Well," Siegel said uncertainly. But he wasn't in a hurry. "All right," he finished. "One drink."

They chose a small uncrowded cocktail lounge on 50th Street and took a booth in the rear. Carmody had a martini, and Siegel, who didn't like liquor much, had a beer. He was content to let Carmody do the probing of the past.

"Mutual friends, maybe?" Carmody said. "Know anybody named Martin? My life is loaded with people named Martin. No? How about George LeRoy? Carl Kramer? Lillian Dietz?"

Siegel kept shaking his head. He began to feel tired, and even to lose interest, until Carmody said, "Well, I know one thing. We don't have the same occupation." He lifted his glass. The gin twinkled and so did his eyes. "I'm a thief," he said.

Siegel's eyebrows met. "How do you mean that?"

"Why, literally, my friend, literally," Carmody said. "I'm a member of a vanishing species. A good thief. Society thief. Used to be the darling of the fiction writers and Sunday supplements—but no more."

"You're kidding me," Siegel said, in an injured voice.

"No, I wouldn't do that," answered Carmody. "I steal for a living. Steal very nice, pretty things, with high price tags. Only from people who can afford it, of course—that's my one principle."

He took his left hand out of his pocket for the first time. There was a jeweled bracelet in the hand. Rows of neat diamonds made blue daggers of light in the darkened booth.

"Beautiful, isn't it? Belonged to a widow who hasn't worn it in fifteen years. I'm doing everybody a favor by restoring it to circulation."

"And you really stole this bracelet?"

"This morning," Carmody smiled. "It was very easy, really. And of course, now I'll sell it—to anybody who wants it. I'll even sell it to you."

"I couldn't buy something like that," Siegel said.

"Maybe you could. I'd guess that it's worth, oh, five, six thousand dollars. You could have it for five, six hundred, whatever you could afford."

"You really mean this?"

"Of course," Carmody said. "It's the least I can do for an old friend." The smile broadened, showing most of his good teeth. "Even if I can't remember who you are."

Siegel sighed. It was a sigh of regret. He reached into his pocket and took out his wallet. He opened it lengthways to show Carmody something else that glittered, even if dully. It was his police badge.

"I'm a detective," he said, with genuine sadness. "I'm sorry, Mr. Carmody, but I'll have to place you under arrest."

Carmody's facial muscles gave a twitch of surprise. He groaned slightly, and put the "diamond" bracelet into the ashtray. He was plainly distressed, but he forced himself to restore a shadow of his lost smile.

"Of course," he said. "*Now* I remember where I know you from."

Meet Mr. Murder

by Morris Hershman

Roy Worth said, "That's a lot of nonsense! Do you expect your own husband to believe in the supernatural?"

"It's true." Edie Worth put a hand to her heart, as usual when her judgment was disputed. "The man stood in front of Dr. Arbuckle's house all night, and on the next day he died."

"Arbuckle was sick. He'd had a heart condition for years. Sooner or later he was sure to die, only sooner in his case. So was that old Mrs. Culp, who suffered from an aortic aneurism."

"But *he* stood in front of the house."

"You mean the man called Gray because he always wears gray. All you know about him is that when he stands in front of a house somebody in it dies very soon."

"Yes, and you know where that man is right now."

Roy pushed back his chair from the kitchen table and stood up. "I could understand your getting excited about it if we lived in Africa, for instance, but this sort of thing doesn't happen in Lakevale."

"Look outside," Edie suddenly whispered, both hands around her heart area. "You know how sick I am. Don't argue with me, Roy. Just look."

He walked over to the window. A man stood across the road, facing them. The swiss-cheese colored full moon lighted him so that it was possible to see him leaning against a pole with his legs crossed. He wore a gray topcoat, a gray pair of pants, and a hat to match.

"Do you want me to call the police? He's loitering, after all, and I suppose he can be arrested for that."

"Go see Hugo Bradford," she insisted. "He's on the police force. Maybe he'll know what has to be done."

"It's late at night to be disturbing neighbors."

"Please," she said in a choked voice.

Roy glanced angrily at his wife, noticing how much her figure had run to fat. The once lovely bosom had started to sag, the legs had become much thicker, and nobody could have called her face a youthful one any longer.

He shrugged and strode over to the phone.

She said quickly, "Hugo only lives across the street, Roy. I don't want the whole town to know about this."

Glumly he nodded. She wouldn't quit pestering him, he knew. He had been married to her for twelve years.

"I'll be all right here," Edie said. "And please go out the back way so *he* won't see you."

"I'm going out the front way. It's my house and I can do that much if I—"

She said hoarsely, "My medicine, Roy. I need my medicine."

"You always do need it when I want to do one thing and you want me to do another."

But he brought it all the same, along with a teaspoon and a half-filled water glass. Edie swallowed an orange pill from the bottle and settled back.

He went to the closet and put on his coat, jacket, and fur-lined gloves. He was still muttering about a heart condition being used by some patients to get their own way as he walked out the back door. Wind made his skin tingle.

Roy's jaw jutted out when he passed in front of the man called Gray, having changed his route on purpose; Gray didn't look to the right or left. The Bradford doorbell was answered by Hugo Bradford himself, who invited Roy to the living room for a drink. Bradford was a tall, muscular man who'd been decorated for bravery during the Korean war and was now a police sergeant.

"I can guess why you're here," Bradford said, "and I advise you and your wife to take no notice of the man and help smash his racket."

"Racket?"

"Gray has established himself as sort of a harbinger of doom. What he now does is determine who in town is sick and phones the head of the house at work, if at all possible, and asks for two thousand dollars to stay away. You'd be surprised how many people pay up."

"Well, he's varying his method with us," Roy said promptly. "He just appeared and that's all."

"Maybe you'll get a phone call tomorrow, when your wife is more thoroughly scared," Bradford said. "I'll call the boys to take him away, but it'll bring you some publicity, heaven knows. And he'll only come back when he gets out of jail.

"There's really nothing that can be done. No one wants to testify against him. We only heard about his real racket by accident. One of his victims has a nephew who's a stenographer at the courthouse."

"You'd better have him taken away," Roy decided. "For Edie's sake. She really does have a heart condition, you know."

"Okay," Bradford said. "We'll try to scare him out of town, but it won't work with anybody like that guy, you know. He'll come back and take up his stand where he left it."

"I'm tired of being pushed around by him or by—well, never mind. Good night, Hugo. Give my best to Miranda and the kids."

Roy was muttering under his breath when he left Bradford's house. He wondered if it would settle Edie's mind to tell her the truth. Probably not. She had decided on what she wanted and was too stubborn about having anything but her way.

Roy walked to the curb till he was directly in front of the man Gray. It only took a minute. As he passed by he said: "You wasted those phone calls you made to me, buddy, so do the worst to my wife that you can. The very worst."

Roy Worth remembered to wipe the smile off his face as he let himself into his house.

Co-Incidence

by Edward D. Hoch

I first met Rosemary when I joined the editorial staff of Neptune Books, last summer. The job was my big chance, because prior to that time my editing experience had been confined mostly to the pulps and a chain of true crime magazines. For me, Neptune Books was a dream come true—a job with an unlimited future in a fast-growing phase of the publishing industry.

I suppose everyone is familiar with Neptune Books, those dollar ninety-five reprints with a picture of a smiling King Neptune as their trademark. They say in the business that the reason Neptune is always smiling is that he's just seen the latest sales figures. And if it's true, he has plenty of reason to smile.

For in three short years Neptune Books have risen to the top of the field. Their sales are beyond belief, and even their own officers shake their heads in pleased amazement as the money pours in.

The cause of it all, as everyone in the publishing business knows, is Rosemary. At twenty-eight, she is already the brains behind Neptune's smile. The simple fact is that she is a mathematical genius, not just in the usual sense, but in a very unusual sense.

My first meeting with her came, as I've said, the day I started work at Neptune. She was in her tiny office, where she spent most of her time, poring over a list of sales figures from cities all over the country.

She looked up when I entered with Mason, the vice president of Neptune, and as soon as I saw her I knew that the stories about her had not exaggerated.

Sphinxlike, with a somewhat bony face, she was nevertheless attractive—especially when she came out from behind those horn-rimmed eyeglasses. She had the look, the sound, the manner of power. And I sensed then that she was a very unusual woman.

This intuition increased as the weeks went by, and I became one of Rosemary's few good friends. Whenever I could snatch an hour, I'd sit there in her office, discussing new titles we were planning to reprint and listening to her unfailingly brilliant advice. I was even beginning to feel a romantic inclination toward her, but she never indicated any such feelings toward me. I kept my own emotions in check.

But it was in the distribution end of our business that she proved her devotion and fantastic skill. Neptune handled all its own distribution, which meant shipping books to several hundred wholesalers scattered throughout the country. Rosemary had risen to the post of Circulation Manager, a rare job for a young woman and perhaps the most important position in the whole company.

She would sit at her desk for hours, scrabbling over calculations, and then come up tired but triumphant with the solution. "Increase Salt Lake City's draw to 5,000 on this title," she'd order. Or, "Transfer a thousand Westerns from Dallas to Kansas City." I'd look at her in amazement, and sometimes I'd think she was over-reaching herself, but they always did what she said—and Neptune kept smiling on all those covers.

When I'd ask her about some fantastic bit of luck by which she'd transferred the right books to the right place at the right time, she'd simply sigh and say: "Oh, I heard they were having a convention out there, and figured they could use another thousand of that title."

After the first few months I got used to this wizardry, and like the others I stopped asking her. I just read books and helped decide which ones to reprint, and watched the money roll in.

There was only one thing about the job that was unpleasant. And that was Mason, the vice president. The real owner of Neptune Books was some midwest Croesus, whom no one ever saw; for all practical purposes, Mason was the big boss.

We were on the third floor of an ancient building on West 47th Street, and space was at a minimum. Not that the place wasn't big enough to start with; but with billing machines, bookkeepers, files, and the other necessities of distribution taking up so much room, we didn't have an awful lot of floor left for the executive end. Mason had solved his problem by erecting a partition ten feet square and declaring that the space inside the wall was his private office. He was a big, overbearing boor about a lot of little things, and he kept getting under my skin.

About once a week he'd hold what he called a strategy meeting. We'd all crowd into his private office. He'd do most of the talking, outlining company policies and telling us about his foggy future plans. Rosemary, at least, was entitled to a chair at these boring lectures. But I, being the youngest of the editorial staff, usually found myself sitting on the thick green rug that covered the floor.

It was obvious to me from the start that Rosemary and Mason hated each other. Rosemary hated him because he was the only person who stood between her and a place to which she could advance. Mason hated her because he knew her feelings and desires for the vice presidency of Neptune Books. Of course, he couldn't fire her. By that time, Rosemary's word was gospel and her every decision went unquestioned. It was the old law of the jungle: Eat or be eaten.

We all knew that Mason was waiting for her to make just one mistake, but she never made it. The sales figures kept climbing and Rosemary kept on with her necromancy on paper at her desk. Pretty soon it got so that even a poor title sold a half-million copies—and a million-copy sale was considered just average. Rosemary would dash into my office holding a hard-cover edition of some cheap novel that hadn't sold three thousand copies in the trade edition—and she'd insist we reprint it in soft covers. We'd argue that it hadn't sold well at all, but she'd simply say: "That's all the more readers left for us." Of course, we'd finally agree; and, of course, the book would sell around two million copies.

By the time I'd been there six months, my friendship with Rosemary had increased to the point where I was taking her to lunch a couple of times a week. It was at one of these luncheon dates, in a little French place off Fifth Avenue, that I finally persuaded her to tell me the secret of her fantastic skill.

"Well," she said, "I've never told this to any of the other vultures, but somehow you're different." I thanked her quickly and she went on: "It's all done by figuring the percentage of incidents. It took me nearly five years to work out a sort of slide-rule mathematical equation. I've discovered that it's mathematically possible to cause any two objects to meet at a given time and place, provided you know enough about these objects and can exercise enough control over one of them. I aim one angle of incidence to meet another angle of incidence. Result? Co-incidence!"

It sounded even more fantastic to me, but I didn't interrupt.

"In the case of distribution," she went on, "I figure out just where and when the supply and demand will meet, I send books to that spot—and people buy them. It's that simple."

I shook my head and asked for more details.

"Look," she said, "figuring mathematically that five hundred people in Chicago will want one of our new mysteries next Tuesday, I see that that many books get out there. That's all; my equation works it all out for me. It means getting the books to exactly the spot where the consumer is when he decides he wants that certain book."

Her eyes drooped as she added ominously: "I can do the same thing with any two objects, knowing enough about them."

"Why did you choose publishing?"

"I knew it was the best way for me to get to the top fast. The big drawback in publishing has always been, it seems to me, that the books aren't around at the exact instant that most people want to buy them. By the time they see the book they wanted, the purchasing desire has decreased. Put the books into their hands when their purchasing desire is at its peak, and you've got sales."

"And you say you can do this with other things as well?"

"Certainly. Did you ever stop to think that when a man gets hit with an automobile it's because both of them have come together at exactly the same time and place by a chain of events? Think of the millions of events, all unconnected, that have resulted in their coming together."

"And you claim you can control some of these events."

"*Some* of them. I can make calculations. If I can control some of the fractional events, I can bring man and book, or man and automobile, together."

She looked so serious that I laughed a little. "With that sort of power, you can control destiny."

She didn't laugh. "Yes, I suppose I could . . ."

The conversation ended there. Going back to work, I pushed the incident to the back of my mind. We had to line up some strong sellers—five-million-copy sellers—for the big Christmas trade, and I was busy fighting with publishers for rights.

It was one afternoon around four that Rosemary and Mason had their last big fight. It was over a policy matter, concerning exactly what type of books we should concentrate on; and Mason, for once, wouldn't listen to Rosemary.

"I'm still in charge here," he told her sharply. "You haven't got my job yet. And if I have anything to do with it, you won't get it either; I'll keep it if I have to live to be a hundred."

Rosemary's bony face looked frostbitten. She said nothing in return; she simply retreated to her tiny office. I thought that the whole thing had blown over until, a few days later, I happened to walk in and found her gazing out the window, making careful notes on a memo pad. When I asked her what she was doing, she was too absorbed to reply. But I had seen enough to know, anyway.

Rosemary was timing the traffic light on the corner of Fifth Avenue and Forty-seventh Street and ticking off the number of cars that passed.

In the days that followed, I caught her looking out the window several times, writing figures, timing automobiles as they rounded the corner. And she began watching Mason closely, too. He always left the office at three minutes to five. He was the kind of punctual man you could set your watch by; he always walked down the two flights of stairs, rather than wait for the elevator.

Rosemary began staying late at the office, until after Mason left. Then she would run to the window and time him as he left the building and crossed Forty-seventh Street on his way to Grand Central Terminal.

I told myself it was all sheer nonsense, but still . . .

It was on a Friday night, just before five, that she stepped from her office, stood in the hall and called to Mason as he was leaving. He frowned and walked over to her, glancing at his watch; she started discussing some quite irrelevant matter about a wholesaler out in California.

I glanced at the big wall clock as they talked, and I was aware that Rosemary was watching it, too. Finally, when they'd been talking for exactly fifty-five seconds, she suddenly cut the conversation short and retreated to her office, closing the door. Hastily Mason went down the stairs to the street.

I went to my own window and looked out. Slowly but surely an odd feeling crept over me. I wanted to shout out to Mason, to warn him—but I remained numb. What would I be trying to save him from?

I watched him come out of the building and start across the street.

He was halfway across, when a taxi rushed around the corner and struck him head on . . .

Well, shortly after Mason's funeral, word came from the big boss that Rosemary was now vice president of Neptune Books. We were all happy for her, of course, but it wasn't long after that that I left Neptune and went back to my old job on a true-crime magazine.

Oh, I know the whole thing is fantastic, and that Mason's death was just a coincidence, but still I felt a chill about staying around here, near Rosemary.

Suppose I'd fallen hard for her and asked her to marry me. And she accepted. I'd spend the rest of my life wondering when she was going to stop me and talk to *me* for exactly fifty-five seconds!

Alma

by Al Nussbaum

The day Alma Southerly was sent to us, my wife Silvia and I had been caring for foster children for close to twenty years. We were in our front yard, tying vines to a trellis, when the county station wagon pulled to the curb. Mrs. Dunbar of the county probation department climbed from behind the wheel; and Mrs. Snyder of the city welfare department got out on the passenger side, pulling the reluctant Alma after her. The women were big-hipped and considerably overweight, so there had been little room between them on the seat; however, Alma hadn't needed much space.

We had been told to expect a thirteen-year-old, but Alma Southerly looked more like an undernourished ten-year-old. She was hardly more than four and a half feet of skin and bones, and her flesh was so translucent that blue veins could be seen at her temples and along her bare arms. She had large, sad eyes, like a waif in a painting by Keane, and her straight, shoulder-length hair was such a pale blonde it was almost white. Her lips were trembling and her face was wet with tears when Mrs. Snyder deposited her in front of us.

"I done wrong," she sobbed pitifully. "I done wrong," and our hearts went out to her immediately.

When Silvia and I first began taking children into our home, we had received referrals from both the courts and the welfare agencies. Soon, however, we established a record of success with delinquents, and the children sent to us were invariably wards of the courts with suspended sentences or waived prosecutions in their pasts.

It wasn't uncommon to discover that a child could lie, cheat, or steal effortlessly. Over the years, we found just about every aberration that causes maladjustment in society. Since we'd had no children of our own, we treated each foster child as though he or she were one of the children we'd never had. We gave them love, trust, understanding, and a taste of genuine family togetherness which many had never experienced.

As a result, we became expert at breaking through the facades of even the most hardened offenders, and we did it without reference to their prior records. We seldom read a child's file. We believed that whatever a child had done in the past was unimportant. We didn't feel we had to know of what devilry a child might be capable. If we had a fear, it was that we would someday be sent a child we couldn't help, a child like Alma Southerly.

Silvia and I bent to comfort the little girl and, surprisingly, instead of turning to my wife as the younger children always did, she turned to me. She stood in the circle of my uncertain arms and pressed her tear-streaked face against my side.

"I done wrong," she said between muffled sobs. "I done wrong, an' I awful sorry."

From her manner of speech, it was apparent Alma had spent most of her life in the hills of West Virginia or Tennessee, but if it hadn't been obvious, we would never have known it. Except for confessing she had "done wrong" and professing repentance, she volunteered no information. At the end of two weeks we knew as much about her as we had known a few minutes after her arrival. We hadn't been able to stop her tears and didn't even know how to try.

"Tom," my wife said after breakfast one morning, "you'd better drive down to the Youth Bureau and read Alma's file."

"Yes," I agreed. "I had better . . ."

Alma was on hands and knees, scrubbing the kitchen floor, when she heard her father call, "Al-mah! Al-mah!"

She stood up and wiped her hands on the hem of her dress. Then she hurried into the front room where he was sitting on the couch. He was wearing only his shorts and a sleeveless undershirt; but he seldom dressed during the daylight hours, so Alma thought nothing of it. That morning's newspaper was spread out before him on a low table.

"Come here, child," he said, indicating the seat beside him.

She went to him and sat down. She got along well with her father. He was usually laughing and in a good mood. He was more fun to be with than her mother, who was seldom home, and Alma liked the smell of tobacco and whiskey that clung to him like a sticky cloud. She knew he would have helped her with the housework if he weren't always feeling poorly.

"Yes, Papa?"

He cleared his throat. "Your ma ain't comin' home no more, child. We all alone now."

Alma didn't know what to say. She looked around dumbly for an explanation but found none. The newspaper was open to a story about an unidentified woman who had been found dead from an overdose of barbiturates in a motel room, but that had nothing to do with her ma.

Alma climbed onto her father's lap and put her arms around his neck. "I don't understand, Papa. She just went on a date, like always."

He cradled her in his arms and began to rock her back and forth the way she liked him to do. "There's nothin' t' understand, child. She just ain't comin' home no more, an' we gonna have t' find some new way t' make money."

"Papa, I betcha I could get dates," she offered brightly.

He paused in his rocking, as though considering the suggestion, then shook his head. "No, you're too little. It'll be another couple of years before you'll be big enough for dates. Till then, I'll just have t' think o' somethin' else."

"Maybe we could go home?" Alma asked hopefully.

"No, cain't do that. They just waitin' for your ol' pa to show his face back there. Don't you worry, though. I reckon I'll think o' somethin'."

True to his word, within the week he had thought of something—robbery. Alma listened to him explain her part as he drove his rust-spotted old sedan to the Tall Towers apartment complex in the center of the city. Each apartment tower was twenty stories high and almost self-sufficient. Their bases held laundries, markets, restaurants, and most necessary services. The parking garages were on the third level, and self-service elevators operated from there.

He drove his car up the ramp to the parking area and left it in a space reserved for visiting clergy. Alma followed him, carrying a small, battered case that had once held roller skates, as he led the way to the elevator and pushed the button marked *Roof.*

"Now, remember what I tole you, child. These be all rich folks live here. Why, the newspaper said it costs at least a thousan' dollars every month t' live in these apartments, an' the higher up you goes, the more it costs. We should get enough money tonight t' last us for two–three months."

Alma followed close at his heels to the edge of the roof. She looked fearfully down while he tied a loop at one end of a length of dirty rope and placed it under her arms.

"You see that little balcony jus' below us?"

"Yes, Papa."

"Well, that's where I gonna put you. When you're down, see if the glass door's locked. It prob'ly won't be if the people is home. Then slip outta the rope and wait a couple o' minutes before you slide open the door. Move real quiet across the room, an' open the door t' the corridor for me."

Without further preliminaries he picked her up and dropped her over the edge. Alma swung precariously at the end of the rope for a few seconds, then landed on the balcony below, skinning her knee. She sat on the cool concrete, trying to control her fear, until he shook the line from above to remind her to check the door. It was unlocked. She wouldn't have to swing to another balcony, seeking an unlocked door. With a sigh of relief, she took off the rope loop.

She waited a couple of minutes, listening. Then, shaking with apprehension, she carefully slid the glass door open and paused. She could hear only the ticking of a clock, so she tiptoed across the deep-pile rug to the corridor door. In a moment she had removed the chain latch and quietly eased back the bolt.

Her father pushed open the door and brushed past her. He set down the case he'd used to carry his rope and took his pistol from beneath his jacket. With his free hand he reached out to touch her cheek. "You a good girl, Alma. You did jus' fine," he whispered.

Then he went to the door of the apartment's only bedroom and opened it. Alma followed and was beside him when he clicked on the light.

There were twin beds in the room, and a middle-aged couple had been asleep. The woman awoke when the light went on and sat up, clutching the bedclothes around her. She stared wide-eyed at Alma and her father; then her gaze focused on the large black revolver he held, and her mouth started to open.

"Jus' keep you mouth shut, woman. Don't you say nothin'," Alma's father ordered, and moved forward, holding the pistol ready.

It took only a few minutes to wake the man and tie and gag the pair with strips torn from a sheet. When he was finished, they were lying on their sides with their arms and legs drawn up behind them and bulky gags covered their mouths. All they could do was watch while he and Alma searched the closets and dressing table for valuables.

Alma and her father took turns carrying their loot to the car in the parking garage. Each carried an armload of clothing, a suitcase stuffed with linen, or a small appliance—nothing that would be worthy of notice if they were seen, and which could be explained as donations if they were challenged. He saved the color television for last.

"Alma, honey," he said. "I gonna tote this-here television to the car." His pistol was gone from sight, and he now held a long, thin carving knife she'd seen him pick up in the kitchenette. "There's only one thing left for you to do here, honey, then I want you t' meet me at the car."

"Yes, Papa."

"You 'member how I use' t' butcher hogs back home? I'd hang 'em by their heels an' cut 'em quick an' deep?" He made a pantomiming gesture with the knife.

Alma wet her lips and hugged herself to keep from trembling.

"Yes, Papa."

"Well, I want you t' go into that-there bedroom and do for those folks. If we don't shut them up, they'll tell on us quick as you can spit. They'd have your ol' pa in prison for sure. You don't want that, do you?"

"No, Papa."

"That's my girl," he said, wrapping the fingers of her right hand around the handle of the knife. He gave her a gentle push toward the bedroom doorway. "I'll meet you at the car. You'd best hurry . . ."

"Oh!" Silvia broke in. "How horrible! No wonder the child feels so terribly. After butchering those helpless people, even if her worthless father *did* tell her to do it, it's no wonder her conscience won't let her rest."

I put my arms around Silvia to give her strength. "You don't understand," I said. "Alma's father was identified by the robbery victims and is serving a long sentence in the state prison. When Alma entered the bedroom with the knife in her hand, the people whimpered and cried for mercy behind their gags. She wasn't able to force herself to kill them as she'd been ordered to do. She let them live. *That's* what she's sorry about."

Grand Exit

by Leo R. Ellis

Brett Delane left the key in the front door lock as he hurriedly stumbled down the darkened hallway. Upon entering the study he snapped on the desk lamp. The shaded glow revealed a figure crouched against the wall, the figure of a man, a man who held a gun.

Brett gasped. He opened his mouth to speak, but instead he groaned and fell back against the desk, half doubled over, clutching his middle.

The intruder moved out of the shadows and became a

man, barely out of his teens, dressed in tight pants and a soiled jacket. Scraggly hair hung around his ears. He held the gun pointed.

Still doubled over, Brett worked his way around the corner of the desk and slumped into the leather chair. He reached for the desk drawer.

"Don't go for a gun, dad," the man said.

"Medicine—my medicine." Brett ignored the gun, thrust across the desk, as he feebly lifted out a vial and fumbled off the top. He placed the vial against his lips and swallowed a tablet with effort. Brett collapsed back in the chair, his eyes closed, his face a deadly white.

The man stared at the slight, silver-haired Brett behind the desk. The gunman's trigger finger tightened but there was no shot; instead, the man looked back at the open window. His eyes swept across the pictures on the study wall, photographs of Brett Delane in many of the character roles he had played on the stage.

A moan brought the gun muzzle back across the desk again. Still the man did not fire. He brushed his hair back in a nervous, unsure gesture.

Brett's eyelids fluttered open and his eyes focused across the desk. "What do you want?"

"Loot, man—loot."

"Take what I have then and get out."

The man shook his head. "It don't work out that way now, dad. I figured to blow when I thought you were gone, but you messed things up by coming to life again. Now I've got to blast you."

Brett sat upright. "You can't mean you're going to kill me!"

"You get the idea real good. I don't like witnesses—witnesses get a guy pinched." The man raised the gun and Brett collapsed in the chair. "Cut the faking," the man said angrily. "You ain't dying. I saw you take your medicine."

Slowly Brett opened his eyes. "But I am dying," he said in a low voice. He reached out and touched the vial. "This medicine has kept me alive so far, but someday, someday—poof." He gave a sardonic chuckle. "Perhaps it would be a blessing if you did shoot me. It would be sudden, no drawn-out suffering."

"This ain't meant as no favor, pop."

Brett nodded slowly. "Death is something to dread when it comes slowly. But murder, now that would be a more fitting climax to the career of Brett Delane." Brett leaned forward and pulled himself to his feet. "Yes, then I would have headlines for my obituary—Noted Actor Dies in Mystery Slaying. Very nice."

The man backed away. "Man, you're a nut."

"No, I'm an actor. It is highly important to an actor to make a grand exit, you see." Brett raised his arm. "I want my final scene dramatic, packed with emotion and suspense." Brett dropped his arm. "No actor could ask for more, and since I am to die anyway, I feel that murder would serve as an excellent vehicle in which to frame my passing."

"Man, you are a N-U-T, a real, genuine filbert." The man's gun had drooped, but now it snapped back up as Brett started for the door. "Stand where you are, dad. You ain't leaving."

"But I insist this scene be done right. I'll need the proper wardrobe and I want to get my maroon dressing gown. I don't suppose you would allow me time for a shower first?"

The gunman jabbed the gun while he clawed at his face with his free hand. "You *can't* be that nutty," he yelled. "Nobody could be nutty enough to fix up for his own murder." He stopped and his eyes narrowed. "I get it, you're pulling a fast one. You've got this setup rigged somehow." His eyes darted around the room and stopped at the desk. "A tape recorder—you're putting this down on tape." The man dashed across the room.

"I use that machine to study my diction," Brett said calmly. "You'll find it quite empty."

The gunman shoved the recorder to the floor. He made sure the telephone was firmly in the cradle, then ran back to run his hand over the wall. "I got it now, the room's bugged. You're trying to stall me until the cops get here." He whirled and pointed the gun. "It won't work, I'm going to blow your head off right now."

"Please, not the head. Shoot me in the body. And there are no hidden microphones."

The young man's mouth worked as he tugged at his long

hair. "You're trying to sucker me into some kind of a trap. You *want* me to kill you, but I'm too smart for that. I'm not buying any murder rap." He ran to the window and threw one leg over the sill. "You'll have to die a natural death on your own, dad." The man slid outside and disappeared.

Brett Delane had finished the second of his two telephone calls when the front door opened and his wife entered. Brett kissed her on the cheek. "Frightfully sorry I had to leave the dinner so abruptly, dear. I should have known that blasted curry would tie my stomach into knots, and I had left my ulcer medicine in the desk drawer."

Brett helped his wife with her coat. "We had a prowler," he said. "It was quite a dramatic scene, and I gave a magnificent performance. You'll hear all about it when the reporters get here. Now be a good girl and hold them while I shower and put on my maroon dressing gown."

Hunting Ground

by A. F. Oreshnik

It had rained earlier in the day. Dark gray clouds filled the sky and seemed to press ominously close to the ground. Gusts of chill northern wind chased dead leaves across the damp grass. Without exception, the wire frames that had been set up to hold floral wreaths at some grave sites had been blown over, spilling dying flowers and brightly colored satin and nylon ribbon onto the wet grass or muddy, raw earth.

Wilson Block stood with the collar of his dark topcoat turned up and the brim of his black hat turned down against the cold. The weather was terrible, but even on sunny days cemeteries were cheerless places. During his sixty-three years, Wilson Block had buried over forty wives, so he was an expert on cemeteries. Mount Calvary outside Buffalo, St. Louis' Oak Grove, San Diego's El Camino, and a few dozen others had received business as a result of his activities.

There had been a time when almost every grave had an elaborate headstone or piece of statuary sitting atop it. Now that was seldom permitted except in the older sections. One was allowed to mark a loved one's location in the new areas, of course, but the stones usually had to be small and flush with the ground. Grass-cutting equipment could then be driven directly over the graves, thereby reducing maintenance costs to the minimum. It was all very unfeeling, and Wilson Block was repelled by it. Although he was a multiple murderer, he was not insensitive.

He held a silver-mounted, ebony walking stick in one gloved hand. He had owned it for over thirty years. There was a time when he had strolled jauntily along the boardwalk at Atlantic City, spinning the stick like a baton. When he had gone to New York City to visit his broker he had liked to stride purposely through the financial district, gripping the head tightly and reaching out to tap the sidewalk every fifteen or twenty feet. Now, however, the stick had become less of an ornament and more of a necessity. He would never walk anywhere unless he had the stick to lean upon and furnish support.

The woman was standing beside a fresh mound in the next section. She was about forty, five-foot-two and weighing a rounded and matronly 130 pounds. Her long, dark hair had a streak of gray. Because of the ban against large markers, Wilson Block had a clear view of the woman despite the fifty yards that separated them.

This was her fourth visit to the grave site in a week. She always came alone and never seemed to know what to do with herself. Sometimes she'd stand, shifting her weight from one foot to the other; sometimes she knelt and pulled out the weeds that were taking root.

After seeing her for the second time, Block had waited until she left, then approached the grave. There was no marker yet, but he was sure she had lost a husband. The woman's nervous activity was the tip-off. He had noticed that women stand quietly beside children's and friends' graves, but seem driven to movement by a dead spouse.

Perhaps it was because they were merely spectators of the lives of children and friends, while the loss of a husband left a giant void in their lives that had to be filled.

Block had no way of knowing how accurate his theory was, but its application had made him extremely wealthy. It was a tool that worked for him and that was the only test that mattered.

When he had committed his first murders forty-odd years before, he had found his victims through lonely-hearts advertisements in newspapers and magazines. Soon, however, this became both time-consuming and dangerous. Many amateur fortune hunters and inept murders began to compete with him for the more promising victims. This was hardly satisfactory, so he was forced to look for something different.

He found his next method of selection by chance. He had moved to a new city—immediately after a funeral—and had wanted to establish himself as a young widower as quickly as he could. There was a church a few blocks from the home he had rented, so he began attending services. Within a month he had been introduced to half a dozen widows and twice that many spinsters. All he had to do was choose.

Churches made an excellent hunting ground; nevertheless, they still fell short of being perfect. For one thing, the women he met were seldom wealthy or even comfortably well-off. The spinsters were invariably almost destitute; and the widows, even those who had collected modest insurance claims, as often as not had spent the money before Block got to them.

Despite the weakness of churches, Block might have continued to use them if it hadn't been for the invention of the computer. Before computers, it had been a simple matter to give himself a new name and insure his wives, carefully selecting a different insurance company each time; but as soon as electronic data-processing became widespread, the companies began to pool their claims information and investigate beneficiaries more carefully. It was no longer possible to change his identity every time he moved, and it was no longer safe to collect the insurance of his wives. If he did either, the new electronic marvel would quickly single him out for human attention.

He could no longer marry a woman for her own insurance money, so he had to do it for her former husband's. What better place to find a fresh widow than a cemetery? He figured, and that's where he began to stalk them. If a woman had an insurance policy of her own, and most of them did, he always had her sign it over to a charity or close relative, thereby alleviating the possibility of suspicion later. He took whatever real estate, stocks, or cash there might be and considered the loss of the woman's insurance money as a necessary operating expense.

The woman at the grave in the other section straightened her shoulders and seemed to take a firmer grip on her handbag. Wilson Block had wondered how long she was going to stand there. He was chilled to the bone. He turned and started down the walk toward her at the same moment she left the grave and began to walk in his direction. He timed it so that they reached the intersection at the same time and turned toward the entrance together.

The woman seemed a bit startled to find him walking beside her. She glanced up at his face and then quickly away.

"You do not have to be frightened," Block said. He had a very deep and mellow voice that women had always found comforting. "I have been visiting my wife."

The woman nodded without saying anything, but she made no effort to increase her pace. Then, as they reached the entrance, she blurted, "My husband is buried here," and hurried away.

Wilson Block watched her go. As first contacts went, that had been about average. What was unusual, however, was the fact that he had found her very attractive. No woman had stirred him quite so much since he was in his twenties. Another positive factor had been the woman's clothing. Her coat, shoes, and handbag had been new and very expensive, but they hadn't been so new that they could have been purchased with sudden, recent insurance wealth. She had been used to comfortable living even before her husband died.

The following day Wilson Block exchanged a few more words with the woman, including their names. She was Mrs. Elizabeth Ayer and her husband had been dead a month. So far, so good.

Within a week, Block was riding back to the city in her car instead of using a bus or taxi. He had a perfectly fine sedan of his own, but he never used it at times like this unless his target didn't have transportation.

He invited her to lunch one day and she accepted. From then on, his progress was swift. Block had always been able to fascinate women. He played whatever role they seemed to need. He prided himself that all of his wives had died happy. Soon there was no more "Mr. Block" and "Mrs. Ayer." It became Will and Betty.

He found her to be a thoroughly charming woman. Unlike all of his previous conquests, she didn't exert a silent pressure to be entertained, and she didn't whine about her misfortune, or try to play upon his sympathy. She held up her end of every conversation with ease and seemed to make every effort to have him feel comfortable.

The day Wilson Block took her hand in his and said, "Betty, I love you and want you to marry me," he meant every word. He always did. Acting is believing.

Neither of them had relatives or friends, and they had only a few acquaintances. There was no need to delay the wedding for the sake of appearances. Betty never even suggested it. Wilson had already filled the void left by her dead husband. He was sure she saw marriage as the next logical step.

Wilson also told her he'd like to move to another town. This way, as he explained it, they could leave the past behind them, and their honeymoon cottage would also be their new home.

"A wife's place is wherever her husband wants to be," she answered and kissed him.

More from habit than design, Block checked to see if the new community had a medical examiner. He found that it did. Had he been planning an immediate murder, that would have been a problem. He far preferred cities and towns with elected and untrained coroners. A coroner will often diagnose brucine or strychnine poisoning as a heart attack, but no trained medical examiner would. For a medical examiner, Block had always had to arrange carefully staged accidents, something he found extremely bothersome.

Happily, for once in his life he wanted a wife more than a funeral. Betty was everything his other wives had never been, and he suddenly realized she was everything he needed. He was sixty-three. He had all the money he would ever need. It was about time he retired, and he couldn't pick a better time. Betty hung onto his every word, catered to his every whim. He'd never had it so good.

He found himself enjoying domestic life. If his first marriage had been half as satisfying, he might never have hastened its end. Betty had absolutely no faults. She cooked to rival a *cordon bleu* chef. She kept a spotless house, but never nagged him for his sloppy ways, and she baked well enough and often enough to keep a constant stream of neighborhood children at the rear door.

The only household duties she reserved for him were the ones that traditionally fell to the male: he fixed leaky faucets, replaced blown fuses, and carried out the garbage at night.

One evening three months after they moved into their new home, he picked up the bag of kitchen scraps and took it outside. He carefully descended the concrete rear steps, but placed his foot on a child's roller skate that had been left on the walk. His leg flew out from under him, the bag of trash soared high, his arms went wide and he toppled backward. His startled cry ended abruptly when his head struck the edge of a concrete step with a sickening thump.

Betty stood at Wilson's grave and felt very unhappy. She hated cemeteries. During her forty-one years she had buried over fifteen husbands, so she was an expert on cemeteries—but she didn't like them.

The Big Trip

by Elsin Ann Graffam

This was the part of the day that Nancy liked best. Dishes done, place straightened, time to rest in bed, sip a cup of tea, watch TV and have a cigarette.

Being alone wasn't such a bad thing, she'd come to think. No man to order her around, no children to cause her grief. Just two aloof cats, a small apartment, and her TV. The last of life for which the first was made. She was alone the first part, she'd be alone the last part. And that was fine with her. One thing she had come to treasure was her independence. Other women her age had ties. Not Nancy. Her life was her own, every minute of it, and that was exactly the way she wanted it.

Carefully, frugally, all these years she had saved her money for the Big Trip to Europe. It had become a joke at the office, the extent to which Nancy would go to hang on to her money. Once she had heard June say, "If old Nancy can't take it with her, then she's not going!"

Let them laugh, she thought. When they were old, living on a pension, they would remember her—Nancy and her Big Trip Around the World. Yes, let them laugh, they who had no thought for the future, who lived from day to day, spending their money as fast as they got it.

Now she was having the joy of planning the trip, going to travel bureaus on her lunch hour, deciding on the clothes she'd buy. Oh, the countries she'd see! Switzerland, for sure. And Spain, the Netherlands, England, Italy—the world would be hers!

Retirement in two short months—and then the fun would begin! The money was ready, safely tucked away in her mattress, hundreds and hundreds of dollar bills. Just two months to wait!

She shut her eyes, smiling, thinking of the moment she'd get on the airplane, when the Big Trip would finally begin . . .

"What's she blabbering about now?"

The other woman shrugged. "Same old thing. How she's going to go to Europe and see everything. I kinda feel sorry for her, you know?"

"Uh, uh. Don't go feeling sorry for them, Joan. You gotta harden your heart or you'll go crazy working here, you should excuse the expression."

The woman laughed. "Yeah. Anyhow, I guess she's happy enough. I mean, look at her, off in that dream world of her own."

"Funny thing about her," the woman mused. "I was here when they admitted her, ten years ago. Seems she was just as normal as you and me until one night she fell asleep smoking in bed. Neighbors got her and her cats out in time. She wasn't burned much at all, but by the time the firemen got there, her apartment was ruined, every bit of furniture burned to a cinder. You wouldn't think that would make someone go insane, would you?"

Dutch

by William F. Nolan

Dutch got the idea when we were in Beverly Hills. It was late, almost midnight, and the whole town was quiet as a grave. All the fancy stores were dark and we could hear our own footsteps like clapped hands on the pavement. Me and Dutch and Rosa. She was one of his chicks. Dutch had plenty others.

Rosa was seventeen, a real little doll, like you find on the shelf of a toy store, all in blue and pink. She always dressed real nice when Dutch asked her out.

Dutch was eighteen and he looked like a movie star. I mean, handsome in a dark, curly-haired kind of way. The chicks flipped over him. Rosa, for instance.

Me, I'm Eddie Conners, and in the looks department I don't score. Year younger than Dutch; short, with thick glasses. Dutch always used to tell me that my eyes looked like two crazy fish swimming around behind the lenses. The chicks pass me by, and I guess I don't blame them any. Sometimes Dutch would fix me up with a cute chick, but she'd spend more time looking at him than she would me when we double-dated.

Anyway, on this particular night Dutch got the idea we should cop a couple of new irons and have ourselves a little dice over Mulholland Drive.

"Me against you, Eddie," he grinned. "You game, boy?"

"Sure," I said. "Why the hell not! Only let's be sure we get two alike. You could walk away from me in some souped-up short."

"Then let's start lookin' around."

Rosa put up no objections. What was okay by Dutch was okay by her.

We found a couple of new Fords near Martindale's bookstore. Dutch was a real cool operator when it came to a deal like this. He told us to wait over in the building shadows and keep our eyes open while he got the cars started. Dutch didn't need keys, not the way he worked. In about two shakes he had both engines purring like a pair of big cats. We were all set to go.

"Now, listen," he said to me. "You follow my iron over Coldwater to Mulholland. Then, we'll line up even for a run. I claim by the third turn you'll be outa sight behind me!"

"We'll see, Dutch," I said.

Rosa got in front with him and they glided away from the curb with me in the other Ford right behind. I sure like the way a new car feels—powerful and ready to do anything you want it to.

I felt pretty great tooling along smooth and easy, like some big high-class banker maybe, or some big office president out for a spin in his new car. My folks are tramp-poor and everything I make at the warehouse goes to the family. I couldn't afford a car of my own.

Then I pretended that Rosa was sitting next to me instead of next to Dutch. Real close, with her head on my shoulder. That was damn nice. I could almost smell that sexy perfume she wore and see her smile just for me. Yeah, Rosa was a real gone chick, and no mistake.

We were taking it easy around town because we didn't want any cops on our tail. Beverly Hills is lousy with cops at night. I saw the turn-indicator blink on in Dutch's Ford; he was swinging into an all-night gas station. What the hell was wrong with the guy, anyhow? Why risk being pegged in these hot buggies? I was plenty sore when I got out.

"You *nuts?*" I demanded, keeping my voice down. "What's the lousy idea?"

"Tires," he said. "What if the tires are low when we hit that cliff road? Hell, boy, we'd go on our heads for sure. You check 'em while I hit the can. Thirty-two all the way round should be okay."

I waved the station guy away and began to check pressures.

Rosa stayed in Dutch's car, fixing her face, touching lightly at her hair. She was always primping around Dutch, trying to look prettier than she did already. She didn't need to. Rosa looked plenty good to me all the time. She had natural blonde hair and a hell of a figure and she *really* knew how to walk.

"How were they?" Dutch asked me.

"My left rear was low," I said. "Good thing we checked."

"Damn right. I just don't like taking chances is all."

We climbed back in the Fords and got going. As long as we kept it at twenty-five we were okay. We'd done this before, taken a couple of hot irons out for a joyride. No dice then. Just a ride. Afterwards we took 'em right back where we found 'em and nobody knew the difference.

I snapped on some dance music. Rosa was sure a wonderful dancer. Once, in Gardena, when Dutch was pooped, Rosa asked me to hoof it with her. I remembered how light and airy she felt in my arms that night, how soft and warm she'd been. *Damn!*

We'd crossed Sunset, taken the long climb up Coldwater and I got ready for the sharp right-hand turn onto Mulholland. Easy to miss if you're not on the ball. I followed Dutch around, taking it slow. He waved me up, and I pulled my Ford alongside his.

"This is it, Eddie." He was smiling in that handsome crooked way of his. "We dig on three. Rosa will do the counting."

"Wait a minute," I said. "Rosa's weight adds better than a hundred pounds to your iron."

"So?"

"So I don't want any advantage. Either we start equal or it's all off."

The road stretched away ahead of us, narrow and treacherous and misted with fog.

"Okay, okay." Dutch reached across and opened Rosa's door. "Wait here for us, baby. We'll make the run down to Laurel Canyon and back."

"Right, Dutch," she said, sliding out. "But, be careful, hon."

Her voice was soft and husky and I figured she must practice talking that way, knowing how sexy she sounded.

"Nervous, Eddie?" Dutch asked, grinning at me from the open car window. He jazzed the Ford's mill and it was mean. Real mean.

"Hell, no," I snapped, lighting a cig. I was lying. Sure I was nervous. Who wouldn't be with a set-up like this?

Rosa was standing to one side, her arm raised, ready to flag us off. She looked like a little pink doll in the bright glare of our headlights.

Dutch was grinning, the way he always does when he's real sure of something. He was sure he'd cream me on this stretch. Mulholland is a bitch at night, with the fog hanging low over those hairpin turns, and a long drop waiting for you if you goof. He'd driven it a lot more than I had, and he knew the road pretty well. He was used to irons, too; he could stomp through the turn and broadslide like a pro. Sure I was nervous.

"Get ready, fellas," Rosa shouted.

I stubbed out my cig on the Ford's dash and tried to relax. I juiced the engine to make sure she was firing right and got all set behind the wheel.

"One . . . Two . . ."

I could feel the sudden sweat on the palms of my hands. God, but I wished it was all over! The whole thing was crazy and unreal.

"Three!"

We were off like twin jets, engines screaming, our tires sliding on the damp asphalt. I gave the Ford all the pedal she'd take in first and held Dutch, but when I snap-shifted into second he was by me and moving for the first turn. It was a fairly rough one and I eased off a little, watching Dutch throw his car in. He fishtailed like mad and his Ford was all over the road. He was really pushing.

I got through without much trouble and we headed for the next turn. He pulled away from me on the short straight and I let him go. Hell with it! No use risking my own neck on this kind of road.

The second turn wasn't bad at all—just a bend really—but the one coming up was a lulu. I remembered I'd almost gone off there once myself in my cousin's Chevy—and I hadn't even been dicing then.

Dutch was going like a crazy man, booming through the bend, ragged and swaying with speed. I knew he'd never make it through the hairpin.

And he didn't.

The whole rear end of his car broke loose and slid sideways. I could see him fighting the wheel, but it didn't help. He was in the kind of a slide that ends only one way.

Dutch went over.

I saw his Ford jump the little raised hump at the edge of the road, hover for maybe a split second in the air, like it couldn't make up its mind which way to go, and then drop out of sight.

I'll never forget the long roar it made going down, bumping over rocks and brush and trees, clear to the bottom.

Pulling over, I cut the engine and got out.

I was trembling. I snapped loose a cigarette and lit it; the smoke felt good. I began to relax.

Dutch was dead. That was for sure. Nobody, but *nobody*, could live through one like this. Besides, I could hear a dry crackling sound, like cellophane being crumpled up, and I knew the car was burning down there. Yeah, Dutch was finished all right.

What really got me was how dumb he'd played things. When he made that first rough turn and felt the whole car going he should have known something was haywire. But, he wouldn't stop in the middle of a dice, not Dutch. The fever was in him, and that's what I'd counted on. Anything to beat me. In racing or in pool or with chicks. Beat ole Eddie. Make him look like a damn fool.

Well, Dutch, this time *you* lost. Because not even you could corner at speed with only fifteen pounds of air in your back tires!

I killed the cig and fired up the Ford. I'd better hurry.

Rosa would be wondering what had happened.

Loaded Quest

by Thomasina Weber

Tony Graybill stepped out of the bus, his joints stiff from the long ride. It was eight-thirty on a warm July evening, but the Florida air was pleasingly fragrant after the air-conditioned atmosphere of the bus. The cigar smoker who had been his seatmate for the last two hundred miles had not helped matters.

Reclaiming his duffel bag from the luggage compartment, Tony headed for the motel he had noticed a few blocks from the depot. The night was young and, after cleaning up, he would still have an hour or two to look for Millie.

The room he was given was clean, but far from luxurious. Compared to where he had been, though, it was paradise. He never wanted to see another jungle. He relished the hot shower, letting gallons of water revitalize his weary body. He wondered if he would ever feel rested again.

He still had not grown accustomed to the fact that he was his own man, with no more orders and living with filth and death, grateful every time a bullet whizzed past his ear to a less fortunate target. Now he could do exactly as he pleased. At the moment, he had one goal in mind, the goal that had kept him alive, day after hellish day.

Maybe that explained ghosts, he reflected, as he locked his motel room door behind him. They were probably dedicated persons who had died before achieving their goals. It seemed logical. Death would not be strong enough to quench *his* fire. He could readily picture himself as a dedicated ghost. A smile touched his lips and it felt strange, like something he had forgotten how to do.

The main street did not look familiar to him, but he had been away a long time, and towns change. People change too, he mused grimly. You can't blame a town; but a person, that's different. A faithful, worthwhile person does not change, not the way Millie did. So what did that make Millie?

Other wives waited, even though it wasn't easy. It wasn't easy for the men, either, but knowing they had someone to go home to made it bearable. Millie hadn't even given him that. He should have known something was wrong when her letters stopped coming. When he finally did get a letter, it was not from Millie but from her lawyer.

Before the ink was dry on the divorce papers, Millie had married again. That was all he knew. He did not know whom she had married, but he was willing to bet it was someone with money. When Tony and Millie had married, they had less than fifty dollars between them. At first Millie had thought it was a lark, sitting on a plank laid on concrete blocks and eating off lap trays. Rent and food, those were all his wages as a gas-pump jockey supplied.

The novelty soon wore off, for Millie was not the grin-and-bear-it type. Millie was strong, but in Millie's life, Millie came first. Her parents were well-to-do, and she was used to an easy life. When Tony was drafted before their first anniversary, he had the feeling Millie was happier than she let on at the prospect of moving back into her parents' home. His only consolation was that even if he had not gone off to war, chances are their marriage still would not have survived.

So her new husband must have money. It followed, then, that they would live on the wealthy side of town. Every town had its Snob Hill, so he headed in that direction.

It was a waste of time, he discovered half an hour later. The houses were set well back from the streets and many of them were unlighted. The Party Set, of course. Those families that were at home had discreetly drawn their drapes. He would have to come back tomorrow, when it was daylight. Just as well; he was tired.

Next morning he had breakfast at The Diner and no one recognized him, but that was not surprising. He did not recognize them, either. It was probably under new management. Businesses were always changing hands, and waitresses never stay in one place very long. Besides, these waitresses looked as though they had still been in school when he went away.

He set out once again for Snob Hill. Refreshed by a good night's sleep and a satisfactory breakfast, Tony covered the neighborhood systematically. Another man might have been discouraged by the apparent futility of his quest, for very few people showed themselves, but Tony was determined to find Millie. He knew beyond a doubt that the intensity of his feeling would flush her out. It was his belief that by concentrating on what he sought, he emitted electromagnetic waves which attracted electromagnetic waves emitted by the object sought. This would bring them together.

Whether that was the case or not, Millie did emerge from a $200,000 house just as he was walking by. Thanks to the distance between the house and the sidewalk, she did not see him. Averting his face, he hurried on. He was not yet ready to confront her. He would know when the time was right.

He watched her for a week. He saw her in shorts, in slacks, in mini-skirts, in suits, in every sort of outfit money could buy; all expensive, nothing but the best. Millie had had a good figure, but it had never looked that good in the clothes she wore when she was married to Tony. He remembered with a pang how he used to run his fingers through the long red hair that was now bleached blonde and piled on top of her head so elegantly. His Millie—the same Millie—yet so different.

There were no children, he was glad to see. He didn't think he could have endured his Millie being mother to another man's children. It was bad enough that she was another man's wife. He wondered vaguely if her husband had done his part to defend his country. Probably not; money like that does not have to fight.

He wondered what she would say when she saw him. Would she cry? Back there, squinting through sweat and grime, he had thought he could not possibly wait another day to see her. Now that they were practically together, he could afford to wait. Everything had to be just right; he would not allow haste to spoil it. He would approach her when he was ready, and not a moment before. He had all the time in the world.

He watched her sunning in the yard and swimming in her pool. He followed her when she went shopping, even took a seat a row behind her in a movie one afternoon, watching her profile instead of the film. Her husband must have been out of town, for one evening a cab delivered a big, well-dressed man carrying an attaché case. She opened the door for him and he enfolded her in his arms. Tony watched the house all night; the man did not come out again.

The husband was about what Tony had expected—close to fifty, showing the effects of too much rich food, with a way of carrying himself that indicated years of commanding bellhops, porters, and other lesser mortals. Money must have meant more to Millie than he realized.

It was toward the end of the second week that Tony knew the time had come. Apparently her husband had gone off on another business trip several days before. It was early evening, not quite dark, although the full moon was already visible. Millie came out of the house wearing a gold bikini. Concealed behind the hibiscus that ringed the pool, Tony followed her with his eyes as she seated herself on the edge of the pool, swinging her legs in the water. Hands flat beside her, she gazed downward into the green depths. Soundlessly, he came up behind her.

"Hello, Millie," he said as he grasped her shoulders and pushed. He had to go in with her, for, fighting wildly, she started to scream. That would have spoiled everything, but she didn't scream long. He left her there, a shimmering stone on the bottom of the green pool.

Tony Graybill stepped out of the bus, his joints stiff from the long ride. It was nine o'clock on a hot August evening, but the Texas air was refreshing after the air-conditioned atmosphere of the bus.

Reclaiming his duffel bag from the luggage compartment, Tony headed for the motel he had noticed on the way into town. The night was young and, after cleaning up, he would still have an hour or two to look for Millie.

Hand in Glove

by James Holding

"The man was a blackmailer," said Inspector Graves, wrinkling his nose in distaste. "There's nothing nastier. Therefore, in my opinion, the person who killed him deserves a vote of thanks, not censure and a possible prison term."

Golightly, standing with his back to the fireplace and jingling his change in his trousers pocket, looked at the inspector with surprise. "A blackmailer?" he inquired. "The newspaper report of the murder made no mention of that."

"Naturally not," said the inspector, "since it was one of the few clues we had to work with in the case. Releasing it to the press would have complicated matters enormously."

"I can understand that," said Golightly. Then, curiously, "What I *can't* understand is how you concluded Clifford was a blackmailer."

The inspector said, "Quite simple, really. We found a list of his victims in a wall safe behind a painting in his bedroom—with the amount of blackmail each one had paid to Clifford, and at what intervals. It was a very revealing document."

"I daresay." Golightly nodded agreement. "It also answers a question that has puzzled me ever since you knocked at my door a few moments ago, Inspector."

"Why I am here, you mean? Yes, Mr. Golightly, your name is on Clifford's list. He was into you for a rather staggering amount, wasn't he?"

"You could say so." Golightly looked bleakly about his once luxurious flat. Everything had a slightly shabby and uncared-for look now. "I make no secret of the fact that Clifford's murder made me a happy man."

"As it did every other victim on his list," acknowledged the inspector. "And all have admitted it readily, once they realized we were onto Clifford's dirty work. We have, of course, contacted them all. They comprise a ready-made list of suspects, as you will appreciate."

"But you have not been able to discover the murderer?"

"Each of Clifford's other blackmail victims has an unshakable alibi for the evening of Clifford's murder, as it happens," said the inspector sadly. He gave Golightly an expectant glance. "Are you also provided with one, Mr. Golightly?"

Golightly seemed taken aback. "For last Saturday evening?"

"Friday evening. From ten to midnight, approximately."

"Friday, yes, let me see." Golightly frowned in the act of memory, then smiled. "As it happens, I, too, have an alibi, Inspector. I would prefer, however, not to give you her name except in the ultimate extremity. She is what Clifford's blackmail demands on me were all about. I can tell you this much: she is a lady of high station and—thus far—unblemished reputation. Do you see my dilemma?"

The inspector sighed. "Perfectly," he said. "Yet if our other line of investigation proves a dead end, we may very well come to your ultimate extremity, Mr. Golightly. It is only fair to warn you."

"Thank you." Golightly bowed. "You do have other clues, then?"

"Only one. A full set of bloody fingerprints on the sill of the rear window by which the killer made his exit from Clifford's home."

"Bloody fingerprints, you say?"

"Yes. As the newspapers reported, Clifford was stabbed with a paper knife, a letter opener. There was a great deal of blood about."

Golightly looked baffled. "Perhaps I am dull," he said, "but if you have a set of fingerprints to work with . . . Aren't they infallible in establishing identity?"

The inspector nodded. "If they are clear and unsmudged, they are infallible. But our bloody fingerprints were far from clear, I regret to say. They were badly smeared. Even without the smearing, they presented certain difficulties."

"What difficulties, Inspector, may I ask?"

"Whoever left bloody fingerprints on Clifford's windowsill was wearing gloves."

Golightly started. "Gloves! Then no wonder it was impossible to learn anything from the prints."

"I said difficult, not impossible," murmured the inspector. "As a matter of fact, I was able to deduce certain basic information from the prints, even though the fingers that made them were gloved."

"I shall never cease being astonished at police technology," said Golightly. "What could you possibly deduce from prints made by gloved fingers?"

The inspector ticked off his points on his own fingers. "One, I deduced that the gloves worn by Clifford's murderer were of a type that would be very expensive. Under high magnification, the prints showed that the gloves worn by the killer had been string gloves—you know, the woven or knitted type. And not just knitted of the ordinary kind of cotton, but of fine silken thread. Two, some seam stitching showed quite plainly in one of the glove prints, and it was so fine and so carefully contrived that our laboratory had no hesitation in pronouncing that the gloves had been handmade; custom-made, if you prefer. And by a very expensive glove-maker."

"You astound me, Inspector."

"I sometimes astound myself," the inspector said comfortably. "In any event, these and other characteristics of the glove smudges indicated to us that they might provide a feasible, even a fertile, field of inquiry."

"And you followed it up?"

"Just so. I, myself, after a city-wide search, unearthed a custom glover in a byway off Baker Street, Mr. Golightly, who admitted to producing gloves of this particular kind. His testimony is available if needed."

"He must have made such gloves for scores of clients," Golightly suggested.

Inspector Graves shook his head. "Such was not the case. This glover had made only a single pair of gloves like the ones I described to him. One pair only. Several years ago. Yet by great good luck, his records still contained the name and address of that client."

"Indeed?" said Golightly. "That *was* good luck, Inspector. For you, if not for me." He shrugged his shoulders. "I suppose," he went on with a wry smile, "that your investigation's success now depends rather heavily upon a show of hands, does it not?"

Inspector Graves nodded regretfully. "If you please, Mr. Golightly."

Golightly stopped jingling his coins. Slowly he withdrew his hands from his trousers pockets and held them out for Graves' inspection.

His right hand had six fingers on it.

The Slantwise Scales of Justice

by Phyllis Ann Karr

Were I five years younger, Hal, I had killed myself for bringing such shame upon your memory. But now, let me be content to set all down in this paper, and bury it in the earth above your grave. And pray you, also, be content with this much, for here has been enough of bloodshed.

That your father was a hard man, my husband, who should know better than you? Had his lordship your father been willing to lay aside his quarrel with Camden, this six years past come Shrovetide—had he bethought himself that it was his only son's life which hung in the balance, and summoned Camden who was the nearest surgeon—but no, having sworn to ruin Camden's repute, he must needs send to Saltash for Trevane, for sottish, worse-than-useless Trevane—and that when your pressing need was for physic that same night! So now we lie apart, with cold earth and sod and stone between us, when you might have been still in my bed.

I pray you, Hal, do not judge me in haste. I have a horror

of judgements which can not be undone. This present disgrace took its root when you and I were little more than children, in 1616 when your father sued and won his unjust judgement against Thomas Penhallow; and when Penhallow would have appealed, the Justice replied to him in the words King James had used to the Star Chamber, that "it is better to maintain an unjust judgement, than ever to be questioning after sentence is passed." So that Penhallow was ruined, losing house and lands and all, and it was rumoured his child starved and his wife left him because of this, too. He had reason enough to hate your father, Hal, but he dropped from sight, and for fifteen years his lordship had no thought of him save to gloat now and again over those words of his late Majesty, which could be turned to such convenient use.

Only, some while after you were buried, your father went to work at Master Carnsew and Sir Edward, and by wearing them down and wearing them down he was able, last year, to buy out both their shares in the Wheal Nancy. But one day going to see his new mine, he stood there looking on whilst the men were drawn up out of the shaft, when up came one who, on stepping into the light of day, stood and stood looking back at his lordship. Then your father, peering more closely, saw beneath the grime and ore dust and coating of years, and knew this man to be Thomas Penhallow.

We searched and made enquiry (for after Master Harkness refused to stop longer in Wilharthen House, your father had made of me, though a woman, a sort of secretary; a clever economy it was for him, seeing he need pay me no more than food, gowns, and chamber in Wilharthen, which he must have provided me in any case; nor could I leave him, having no where to go). But all we learnt was that Penhallow had been three or four years in the Wheal Nancy, working as a tributer, for a share of the ore he brought to surface, and a good man for finding out new lodes; and the mine captain thought he had come from the Great Pelcoath when it filled with water, but how long he had been at Pelcoath, or where he lived before that, the captain could not say. Your father privately fed a hope that Penhallow, now he had seen his old and powerful enemy, would leave of his own will, but when Penhallow did not do so, his lordship began to cheat him of his earnings: your father had learned well enough, Hal, the arts of juggling accounts and corrupting assayers. To my shame, I also helped him cast up his columns of false figures—there are so many little persecutions a man may put upon his daughter-in-law day by day, she living alone under his roof. But Penhallow did not leave, only his pile of ore grew less, which diminished a little your father's profits from the mine. Then, in the next fortnight there was a cave-in that shut up the new tunnel, and although no men were trapped therein, yet no ore could be got from it for three days while they dug it out again. At the last, his lordship went again to see how he might have more tin out of the miners, when Penhallow's core, having come up after their morning's time below, and playing at quoits, a quoit flew astray and narrowly missed your father, who would believe no otherwise but that it had come in malice from Penhallow's hand.

Whether indeed Thomas Penhallow meant your father some bodily mischief, or your father merely chose to believe it was so, his lordship now made up his mind he must see to the man he had wronged fifteen years ago, before that man saw to him. There was a certain worthless fellow called Ned Curnow working at the Nancy, or rather signed on to draw his month's pay, for little ore he ever brought to surface. They said that by some traces in his speech and bearing he must be some gentleman or gentleman's son fallen into low estate, and scarcely a day passed but Curnow was in mischief of some sort, and often serious mischief. The mine captain pointed him out to your father, that same day of the quoit, remarking he wished to turn this Curnow out of the mine. His lordship questioned the captain more closely, and ended by telling him to have the fellow come round to Wilharthen House.

He did not come round until two mornings after, and being let in by Bosvannion (our new steward, Hal; old Parsons died a fortnight after you, of a kick he had from Thomson's jackass), and finding us in the parlour, Curnow bowed, and looked at me as a man looks at a woman, past my thirtieth year as I was, and still in the mourning I have vowed never to lay aside. Then taking an apple from the bowl on the table, he sat in the oaken armchair, which had used to be your favourite, and put his feet on the settle. Three weeks before, this vagabond had been whipt through the streets of Saltash, and had stood in the pillory, and cared not who knew it, and yet he bore himself as if Wilharthen were an ale-house, and your father his drinking companion. Only to me, Hal, did he shew respect. I sat on and sewed. Your father had brought me far enough into his confidence that, though he did not tell me in so many words all that was in his evil heart, he cared little whether I went or remained.

His lordship told Curnow of certain enquiries he had made. "It was only by the grace of Sir Edward Chilwidden," said he, "that you were not banished to the galleys when you would not say the name of your home parish, and it is only the lightest thread holds you from the Stannary Gaol now."

"Send me up, then," said Curnow, "to galleys or gaol, whichever you will." The rogue had, I think, washed his face before coming up, and perhaps even his hair, which fell long and golden on his shoulders; but his beard was untrimmed and the rags he wore left the dust of the mine on all they touched, and he was like a man who has lost all joy and desire and hope, so that he no longer cares how long he lives or when he dies.

I too, Hal, I had lost all joy, all desire and hope, and there have come lines into my face, and silver hairs in with the chestnut. I would look very seldom in my glass, but that it was your gift to me.

So your father talked for some minutes to Curnow, sounding him, as I have seen him sound the mettle of a mare before buying, or the honesty of a judge before bribing, whilst Curnow sat and ate his apple. The colour of Curnow's eyes was between green and grey, and he looked at your father as I think he might look at a long deep shaft in the mine. At length his lordship came to the point, and offered Curnow fifteen pounds to do away with Thomas Penhallow.

Curnow put back his head and laughed. "So I am to murder a man," he said, "and be paid for 't too. How if I were to go to the magistrates with this tale?"

His lordship replied that "I have the magistrates in my purse, and judges too."

Curnow threw the core of his apple into the fire. "I misdoubt that," said he, "if you pay them in proportion as you offer to pay me."

Then they haggled over the blood money as if Penhallow had been a pound of fish or a pile of ore, and at length Curnow settled for thirty pounds. His lordship gave him ten, and told him to return when he had done the thing, and to come at night. Curnow bowed to me again in leaving us, and looked once more into my eyes, as a man looks at a woman. I dropt my eyes to my seam. (Your father had money enough, Hal, I could have sewed with good thread, that was not forever knotting and breaking.)

I had no power to stop this thing, Hal, but what great difference was there, after all, between how your father had dealt with Thomas Penhallow fifteen years ago and how he would deal with him now? In any case, whatever we keep hid from outsiders and strangers, it is no life to go about in ignorance and suspicion of those under the same roof with you, those on whom you depend; and I judged it better I should know, than only suspect.

This was why I sat up with your father into the night, to see the play run out to its end. His lordship had sent the steward on some errand to Launceston, and ordered Betty to her room an hour before sunset, to stay there all the night as punishment for some pretended fault in sweeping her kitchen. All so that we would be alone; and I much thought he meant to settle all likelihood of Curnow ever telling what he had done.

There had come no word nor even rumour from the mine during the day, and we did not know whether Curnow would return on this night or another—or indeed, I thought, ever. Your father sat and studied over his accounts. You remember how he loved his accounts, Hal: as others love their coin, and more, for there was ever the hope of catching some mistake I had made in casting them up, for which he might take me to task. I nodded over my book, and as the hours passed I rose to pour out a glass of wine from the silver bottle which had been your mother's pride.

"I would advise you against it, Margery," said your father.

I smelled the wine. It was hippocras, sleep-heavy with many spices. I brought back the glassful and set it at his elbow, rather than my own, and saw that he did not drink. "Why did you not find some means of killing Penhallow by your own hand?" I asked.

"Penhallow would not have trusted himself near enough my hand," said your father. "Nor would I have trusted myself near his."

"Perhaps Ned Curnow will not trust himself near your hand again, neither," said I.

"I took the man's measure," said his lordship. "There is twenty pounds in the balance. He will come."

I thought that your father had but applied his own scale to Curnow, while that insolent man with neither hope nor desire nor fear in his grey-green eyes had likely taken better measure of his lordship. But I did not speak this thought, and so we waited. Somewhat after midnight a storm broke, and, thinking Curnow would not come, I might have sought my bed, but every moment I delayed would lengthen out into another moment, and yet another, and so I sat on, scarce thinking, with my book open in my lap. Your father had laid aside even his accounts, and all was still, excepting only the thunder and rain without. A mouse ventured into the middle of the floor. Your father said, "We must find another cat," and at the sound of his voice the mouse scurried away.

Close on to one, Curnow came, knocking at the door in the pattern they had arranged. His lordship sent me with a rushlight to bring in his hireling. Curnow was wrapped in a ragged sodden cloak, and trailed mud and filth wherever he stepped, yet on seeing me, he gave me a greeting which shewed he had indeed had gentle breeding once.

When we were come again into the parlour, his lordship stood already with the silver bottle in one hand and a fresh glass in the other. "Have you done it?" he asked.

Curnow unwrapped the cloak and tossed it down on the bench. Beneath it he carried in one hand his miner's pickaxe of iron. The rain had wetted him through cloak and all, but had not utterly rinsed away the blood and bits of hair from the flat-headed end. Curnow stepped forward to shew it his lordship at closer hand.

His lordship looked shrewdly at the blood, and nodded. "There is your twenty pounds, safe in the purse," said he.

"But drink you a glass of hippocras before you go, to warm you against the weather."

"Tom Penhallow told me much about you before he died," replied Curnow, "and there is one thing which I owe his soul." And turning the pickaxe to the sharpened end, he drove it into your father's skull. The poisoned wine mingled with the blood and streams of filthy water, and the silver bottle took a great dent as it fell.

Curnow let fall the pickaxe with your father's corpse, and turned to me. He smiled. "Here is enough of murder for the day, my lady," he said. "But do not follow me, lest you take a chill in the storm."

I smiled at him then as a woman smiles at a man. "There will no one come until the morning," I said. "Time enough to take off your clothes and dry them by the fire."

Hal, your father never did but one good work in the whole of his life, and that was the begetting of you, and that he undid again the night he let you die for his stubborn heart. Yet he was your father, and my father-in-law, and murdered, and he had at least the bowels to leave me better provided for by his death than he had in his life. Let his slayer go out into the night and the storm, and by morning was it likely they could find so much as his trail?

Forgive me, Hal, my husband, my love, but how else could I keep Ned Curnow until the morning, when he could be taken, save in my bed?

Child on a Journey

by Fred S. Tobey

The big jet had scarcely lifted off the runway at Los Angeles Airport before the passengers began to busy themselves with the things that would pass the time on the long flight to Boston. Some turned their eyes to the TV screen, waiting for the movie; others took out books and magazines. A Hollywood actress drew a script from her handbag and began leafing through it. Two elderly men opened a pack of cards and started playing rummy.

Dr. Gordon Prince, sitting by himself in a window seat in the coach section, waited until the airliner was well above the clouds before he took his nearly completed treatise on medieval history from his briefcase and laid it on the little table that he had lowered from the back of the seat in front of him. The lengthy document, on which he had labored for weeks, was to be published in a distinguished journal, and the youthful professor of social science meant to spare no effort to perfect the syntax and punctuation. By great good luck, the two seats beside him had not been sold, and he was taking an almost sensual pleasure in the thought of the quiet hours of undisturbed concentration that would be his. He thought he might even pass up dinner, and work right through.

Midway through page two, as Dr. Prince raised his eyes to ponder a fine point of grammar, he became aware of a small figure standing in the aisle beside his seat. He brought his eyes into focus and saw that it was a girl of seven or eight. She was staring at him steadily with large blue eyes. A pair of auburn pigtails hung primly down the front of her blue denim dress.

"Hello," she said. "My name is Suzy. Are you busy reading?"

Dr. Prince was a very literal man. "Not exactly," he said. "I'm writing something."

The child's eyes grew even bigger. "Oh, that must be wonderful," she said. "I'm going to write when I get older. Do you write for movies?"

"This is a different kind of writing," the professor said. He supposed it was not surprising that a writer boarding in Los Angeles should be suspected of turning out froth for the screen. "This is history. Important things that really happened."

Suzy dropped into the aisle seat. "I guess I'll sit here a minute," she said. "Unless you don't want me to."

"Well . . ." Dr. Prince began; then, rather lamely: "Won't your mother be wondering where you are?"

"Mummy—" Suzy paused and looked appraisingly at Dr. Prince, as if wondering how much she should confide in this stranger. Then she shook her head. "Mummy's dead," she said. "Mummy and Daddy were killed in a car accident, and Uncle takes care of me."

Dr. Prince looked at the child with increased interest. What a shame that one so young should lose her parents! The professor was not married, but he expected to marry someday when he found time, and if there were children he hoped they would be like this one: bright, neat and well-spoken.

"My big brother was killed, too," Suzy offered. "He was driving the car and he and Daddy were having a big fight about money, and he went too fast and hit a tree. I was lucky because I was in the back seat and only got hurt a little, and I went to the hospital but I'm all right now."

"Well, you poor kid." Dr. Prince looked around. "Where is your uncle sitting?"

"Uncle didn't come with me. He said he was too busy."

"You mean you're traveling by yourself? A little girl like you?" He knew that children sometimes were handed over to the care of stewardesses, but to his conventional thinking it seemed a strange way of life.

Suzy nodded. "Uncle put me on the airplane and went home to get drunk."

Before Dr. Prince had a chance to respond, a stewardess who had been watching came toward them.

"Is the little girl being a bother?" she asked. "I said I'd try to keep her amused, but we've been kind of rushed today. But if you're busy—" She nodded toward the manuscript on the table in front of him.

"Oh, no, it's all right," Dr. Prince said.

The stewardess smiled, patted Suzy's head and went away.

"Who is going to meet you in Boston?" Dr. Prince asked.

"Uncle said his brother will take me home to stay at a mansion and give me a maid all for myself, and I can go out on a big yacht whenever I want. But I don't believe him. I don't think anyone is going to meet me at all."

"Oh, come, Suzy! Of course someone will meet you. Your uncle wouldn't say so if it weren't true."

"Yes, he would. Uncle Lucifer wants me to get lost and die, because he wants my money. When Uncle gets drunk he always says, 'I hope you die, you little brat, and then I'll get your money.' "

The information was coming too fast. "Lucifer?" said Dr. Prince. "His name isn't really Lucifer, is it? What do you mean, he wants your money?"

"Of course his name is really Lucifer! Uncle says there's always been a Lucifer in the family. Daddy left tons of money for me, but I can't have it until I'm eighteen, and Uncle can only spend little bits of it to take care of me, so he wants me to die and he will get it."

Dr. Prince looked speculatively at the little girl. How much of this was fantasy? She did seem an imaginative sort. On the other hand, of course, there certainly *were* people like the uncle that Suzy was describing. Dr. Prince made a mental note to watch and make sure someone *did* meet Suzy in Boston. Meanwhile, of course, there was his manuscript, which was being sadly neglected. He turned back to it and picked up a page, hoping Suzy would take the hint.

"I wish I had my teddy bear," said Suzy, sighing.

Dr. Prince thought he saw an opportunity. "Why don't you go back and sit with Teddy for a while, then?" he said. "I think they're going to serve dinner now, and you ought to be with Teddy when you're having dinner."

"His name isn't Teddy, it's Smoky, and he didn't come with me. He was in the suitcase but Uncle Lucifer took him out and put in a box of candy instead, because he said there isn't any candy in Boston."

"That was a foolish thing to say. There's all sorts of candy in Boston, even some famous candies . . ."

Suzy nodded. "Uncle lies to me all the time. Anyway, it isn't all candy, I know. There's a clock."

"A clock?"

Suzy nodded again. "I heard it going 'tick, tick' in the box when Uncle went out of the room for a minute, and I told him I heard it, but he just said, 'Shut up, you little brat!' and locked the suitcase."

Dr. Prince felt a prickling at the back of his neck, and it seemed to him his forehead had suddenly become moist. He took a handkerchief from his pocket and dabbed at it.

"Listen to me, Suzy," he said. "Where is the suitcase now? Is it back at your seat?"

Suzy shook her pigtails. "Uncle gave it to a man at the airport and the man put a little tag with my ticket and said I could get the suitcase with it when I got to Boston."

The public address system of the airliner came on with a sharp click. "This is your captain speaking," said a confident, pleasant voice. "We have leveled off at our cruising altitude of thirty-six thousand feet. We have a good tail wind, and our ground speed is six hundred and—"

Dr. Prince cast a furtive glance around the plane. *All these innocent people!* he thought. *How could anyone be so utterly unscrupulous!* Fighting panic, he thought incongruously of his precious manuscript, saw, in his mind's eye, the pages gliding and fluttering down, like autumn leaves, toward faraway earth.

Pull yourself together, you fool, he thought. *With luck, you've found this out in time. There must be an airport we can get down to in a hurry.*

He saw a stewardess in the service area, ten rows or so ahead, and he scrambled over Suzy and started up the aisle toward her. Then, turning back, he grasped the child's hand and pulled her along with him. Better to have her there to repeat the story.

As they reached the service area, Suzy pulled her hand

out of his grasp abruptly and went to sit down in a seat just ahead, in a rear row of the first-class section.

"I guess I'll stay here a while," she announced.

The frightened professor hurried toward her and tried to take her hand again, but the child pulled away and shrank toward the woman in the seat beside her. It was the Hollywood actress.

"Dammit, Suzy, honey!" said the woman, putting her manuscript down with a gesture of exasperation. "Where in hell is that stewardess who was going to keep your busy little mind occupied for a while? I *told* you all about my new movie, *Uncle Lucifer.* Now can't you leave Mummy alone for a *minute* to study the script?"

The Witches in the Closet

by Anne Chamberlain

Except for the witches in the closet, Catharine was the wife John had thought she would be. She was companionable and neat, she played an expert hand of bridge, and she was really interested in cooking. She liked, or pretended to like, the movies, the magazines, and most of the people he liked. It did not occur to him to worry about the witches until some weeks after his marriage. He did not think of them, in fact, until he and Catharine were looking for their first apartment.

"Remember, darling," she said, with a chuckle at her own foolishness, "we must find one with the proper bedroom closet."

John had to think a moment before he did remember. The problem had not come up in the hotel where they had been staying, and John had almost forgotten the evening when Catharine had told him about the witches. He recalled how she made a small point of telling him, soon after they were engaged, and of how at the time he had thought tenderly of what an innocent child she was. He had not been uneasy at all because, with the telling, she gave a plausible explanation.

"You see—" she had pressed his hand confidingly. "I really must warn you before we're married. It wouldn't be fair not to warn you about my phobia."

"Every smart person has at least one phobia these days."

Catharine mused, resting a small bright-tipped finger on her lips.

"Maybe it isn't a phobia; I'm not sure about those terms. Anyway, when I was ten years old I was real sick with a high fever and chills and all, and one night I woke up and saw three witches in the bedroom closet. I screamed and screamed—really, I did!" She smiled reminiscently. "I was such a silly thing, and you know we had a big bedroom closet in that house, a big, deep dark one. Well, I saw three witches there. Well, since then . . ."

"You're always expecting to see them again," he interrupted, not because he was uneasy but because he thought they had more important things to say.

She clasped her fingers.

"Brace yourself, darling. I was going to tell you. As a matter of fact, I do see them. I still do see those witches once in a while." Her eyes narrowed, as though she were pondering an irritating puzzle. Then she laughed and shook her head. "Of course, a good deal depends upon the closet."

That was all that they said about the witches until they were looking for their first apartment and Catharine demanded brightly that they find one with a closet that was small, shallow, and had a light in it. They made a little joke of this, telling each other that the landlords probably thought they were finicky bores for inspecting the apartment so carefully. When they had rented a place that exactly suited Catharine's specifications, John almost, but not quite, forgot about the witches again.

"You're not the imaginative type," he observed lazily the evening after they had moved. "It's funny you think you see such things. Of course, it's a business of hallucinations." He looked at her and laughed. She was sitting on the edge of the bed, brushing her fine black hair. In a few minutes she would meticulously tuck a hairnet around the curls, cleanse her face with a thick white cream, step out of her yellow kimono, and turn out the light. She looked to be the last person in the world to have hallucinations.

"Oh, I know that," she said, a bobby pin between her teeth. "I know it's perfectly silly, and probably a good psychiatrist could explain it all away. But then he might not."

"I can see myself telling the office that I'd just dropped my wife at a psychiatrist's."

"It's nothing to worry about," she answered casually. "I hope there's enough breakfast cereal; I forgot to buy some."

"You haven't seen anything of them since we were married, have you?"

"Oh, no," she gave her little smile. "No. I imagine I'll tell you when I do."

"Maybe it all had something to do with sex."

Catharine giggled.

"I bet that's what a psychiatrist would say." Her eyes were suddenly mysterious. "Maybe."

One night, seven months after their marriage, John returned late from his poker club. He had told her he would be home by one, but he did not make it until after four. He entered the apartment softly, and was surprised and irritated to find all the lamps turned on. He had thought her much too sensible to wait for him, angrily awake, and he walked from room to room, calling "Sweetheart?" in a loud, belligerent voice. When she did not answer, he stalked into the bedroom, flung off his coat, and began explaining as he undressed.

"I couldn't get out very well when I was taking everyone in the house; it went on like that all evening . . ."

He glanced toward the bed, and started. She was curled in a tight, covered hump in the middle. The hump was shivering, as though she had been crying for hours.

"Catharine!" He leaned over her, weak with remorse. "Were you that worried? You could have phoned."

She pulled an inch of cover from her face.

"Oh, darling." She sat up, suddenly cheerful. "Darling, they've been there for hours. It must have been hours ago I saw them."

"Saw what? Oh my God!"

She laughed happily.

"I really didn't mind you staying out. It wasn't that. But several hours ago I knew they would be there, so I got up and turned on all the lights. But I was afraid to turn on that light. I was nervous, you see, and I did feel so silly."

"My God," he repeated. "Is *that* what had you down?"

"Please don't think you can't stay out because of it. I would hate you to think that." She accepted a cigarette and leaned for a light. "Really, I did see them, though."

He did not know whether to believe her or not. The timing seemed too apt. But Catharine was certainly not the melodramatic type, and in his memory she had never been too possessive. She was not sly nor subtle and her gay lack of sentimentality had pleased him more than it had troubled him. When he looked at her now, suspiciously, he thought her smile seemed too honest and her eyes too strange. He spoke carefully:

"Now you look here. You've got to stop indulging yourself. You know and I know how ridiculous it is. Why, you're not neurotic, darling." He waited, and then said again, "You're not neurotic, not at all."

She was rearranging the wrinkled hairnet around her curls.

"Do you remember a Russian children's story about an old witch?" Her voice was gossipy. "And a little girl named Magda who ran and ran away from her? Well, I read that when I was little. Come to think of it though, they're more like the witches in *Macbeth*." She shivered slightly. "Only it's 'when shall we *four* meet again.' "

"Some women would invent a thing like this to keep their husbands at home. What'll you do when I'm drafted? What'll you do then?"

She patted his hand.

"Don't worry, please don't worry. I got along by myself for years." She shrugged. "They don't do anything, you see. They just appear." Sighing, she leaned close to him. "Maybe I shouldn't have told you about them. I won't tell you next time."

He clutched her shoulders harshly.

"Yes, you will. You'll tell me every time; you've got to tell me. And for heaven's sake," his voice grated, "get that funny look out of your eyes!"

He suggested the next morning that they move to another apartment. In the small sunlit kitchen, the conversation seemed so incongruous that he could not help smiling when he said:

"We don't need a psychiatrist at all. All we need is a place without a bedroom closet. Let's look for one today."

Catharine smiled back as she poured the coffee.

"Wouldn't that be hard to find? Besides, if they weren't in the bedroom, I don't know why, but I'm sure that they would move somewhere else."

The thought of sending her to a psychiatrist stayed with him. He hated to suggest it seriously. He was afraid she would be hurt, or angry, and would behave as though there were no real provocation. When several quiet weeks had passed, he began to think that the problem was absurd. Some men he knew hated spiders, and since a fall when he was four years old, he had always secretly feared unlighted stairways.

He did not got out often in the evenings. When he did, he always turned on the light in the closet just before he left, and he did not allow himself to think of the witches while he was away. But he went out less and less often. He dropped the poker club, and Catharine observed:

"I thought you liked to play, darling. And it's nice for men to get out by themselves once in a while."

"It was something to fill a bachelor's evening." He looked at her closely, and was sure that she did not realize why he was staying home.

They entertained or went out together, and the evenings they spent alone were relaxed and companionable. She was fond of sewing, and he liked to watch her, over the edge of his magazine, as she neatly whipped the needle in and out. The weeks stretched into months. The draft crisis passed when John was rejected because of a compound skull fracture that was not too solidly healed. He had forgotten about the boyhood accident, but now he could not help being glad of it. They said patriotic things and settled down to a smooth married life. Then John was obliged to go on an overnight business trip.

He did not think of the situation as an emergency until, well-settled on the train, he remembered that he had not turned on the closet light. He resolved immediately to return at the earliest possible hour, putting the other thoughts out of his mind. He did not even tell himself why he was boarding the train the next morning at the unbearable hour of five.

When he opened the door of the apartment, he was trembling and sick. His heart bounded with relief when he found the lights turned out, the morning seeping softly through the dusky rooms. He tiptoed into the bedroom and dropped his coat on a chair. Humming softly, half hoping that his voice would wake her, he walked over to the bed.

A chill crawled up his spine. At the foot of the bed, completely covered, the curled-up lump of her body shuddered convulsively. In a fury, he whipped off the blankets.

"Catharine!" he shouted. "What the devil's wrong?"

He seized her wrists and pulled her to a sitting position.

"Don't you feel well? What's wrong?" He repeated the question arrogantly, closing his mind to what he knew was wrong. Her eyes looked out of black circles. After a moment, she shook her head and began to rearrange her hairnet.

"Aren't you going to give me a kiss?"

"You've got to stop this, Catharine." He strode to the closet, snapped on the light, and returned. "If it means you have to go to a psychiatrist, you've got to stop. Do you hear me?"

She smiled placatingly.

"I didn't even have time to turn on the lights," she chattered. "As soon as I walked in here—it was twilight—I had a feeling it would happen. But I got into bed all right and read for a while, and the feeling went away. I turned out the bed lamp and looked up . . ."

"Don't talk. Tomorrow I'll find a good psychiatrist."

She made a sad little face.

"Darling, I'll never go to a psychiatrist. I decided that a long time ago."

He slapped her cheek. She drew back, her eyes wide between her fingers.

"Darling, please don't do that."

"We must stop it," he said gently.

"We can't," she said with equal gentleness. "You see, if a psychiatrist shouldn't be able to do anything—if it shouldn't work out, I mean—I'm sure that everything would get worse." She stared at the closet. "They might come out."

He sat for a long time on the edge of the bed. He did not know how long he sat there. The morning grew brighter and brighter in the bedroom. The light in the closet shone through the sunlight like a jaundiced eye. Once in a while, John looked at Catharine. She was wearing a pink satin nightgown with lace over the bodice; fatigued as she was, she looked fresh and darkly caressible, and her eyes met his with loving confidence.

She smiled the smile that implored him to be amused with her at her foolish whims. But she was different. He saw a wickedness about her lips, a strange glee in her eyes. He did not speak or move toward her. This morning he felt that he would never want to touch her again.

Setup

by Jack Ritchie

McNalley picked up the phone. "Hello?"

The voice was a man's. "Mr. Amos McNalley?"

"Yes."

"My name is Hamilton. James Hamilton. I am a vice-president at the First National branch bank in the Southview Shopping Center."

McNalley was tall and thin and in his middle seventies. He nodded. "That's my bank."

"Yes. Mr. McNalley, I've heard that you are a respected citizen in this community. A man who can be trusted."

"I guess so. Why?"

"I . . . *we* would like your help, Mr. McNalley. Your cooperation."

"What's your trouble?"

"We have an employee—a teller—at our bank who . . . how shall I put it . . . of whom we are . . . *suspicious.*"

"What's he been up to?"

"We think he's been doctoring his records. When a depositor withdraws one thousand dollars from his account, for instance, this teller marks the withdrawal as being eleven hundred, pocketing the extra one hundred himself."

"Sounds pretty simple-minded. Why isn't he behind bars?"

"He is very *very* clever, Mr. McNalley. Somehow he manages to cover up these shortages before we can check on his books at the end of the day. It's all very *technical,* Mr. McNalley, and would take a long time to explain. However, we—the officers of the branch and I—have decided that the best . . . the most *direct* . . . way of catching this criminal would be while he was in the *act* of committing the crime."

"I suppose so," McNalley said. "But where do I come in?"

"You have . . . let me see . . . I have your records somewhere here on my desk . . . something like $10,000 in your savings account?"

"$5,256 and some odd cents," McNalley said. "And the rest in savings certificates. Can't touch any of that but once in six months. Been thinking of putting everything into savings certificates."

"A very sound idea, Mr. McNalley. However, for the moment . . . Ah, yes. I have the records now. $5,256. And those extra pennies. But they do add up, don't they?"

"Which teller is it? There are three or four, as I remember."

"I don't think I ought to mention his name. You know how courts are these days about the silliest little thing. However, if you go to the window where you'll find a young man in his late twenties, with black hair, and a mustache . . ."

"Oh, sure," McNalley said. "You know, I never did trust him. I know you can't judge a book by its cover, but I just don't like him."

"Perhaps your instinct is more accurate than you suspect.

Now, sir, it is just after 9:00 A.M. We—the officers of the bank and I—would like you to go to this teller's window at exactly ten o'clock and withdraw $5,000 from your account."

"Five thousand dollars?"

"We are not asking you to go through all this trouble for *nothing,* Mr. McNalley. We will see that you receive two hundred dollars for your cooperation in apprehending this criminal."

"Two hundred dollars?" McNalley rubbed his jaw. There was a pause. "If I withdraw $5,000, then what?"

"You put the bills into an envelope and leave the bank. You walk to that little park in the shopping center."

"Darrow Square?"

"Yes, that's the one. Anyway, you go and sit down on one of the benches and wait for me. I should be there in five or ten minutes."

"Should I sit on any particular bench?"

"Any one will do. I'll recognize you. When I join you, you give me the envelope."

"Give you the envelope?"

"Yes, you see that is *evidence* and we will need it."

"But . . ."

"You have absolutely nothing to worry about, Mr. McNalley. Our bank is *bonded* to cover the entire amount. It's just a *technicality* to satisfy the law, but we need the money when the police make the arrest. I will return the money to you immediately after. The whole operation shouldn't take more than half an hour. And remember, we'll give you *two* hundred dollars for your cooperation. Not bad interest for the loan of $5,000 for half an hour, now is it, Mr. McNalley?"

"You want me to stay in Darrow Square until you come back with the money?"

"Exactly, Mr. McNalley. You stay there until I get back."

In the phone booth, the man who had identified himself as Hamilton waited exactly three minutes and then dialed McNalley's number again.

McNalley answered. "Hello?"

Hamilton had a talent for disguising his voice. "Is Bill there?"

"Bill? There's no Bill here."

"Isn't this 674-4778?"

"No. This is 674-4779."

"Sorry, I must have dialed the wrong number."

He waited another three minutes and then dialed McNalley's number once more. When he heard McNalley's phone ring, he hung up.

Good. The line hadn't been busy either time he dialed.

If the suckers didn't phone the police within the first five or six minutes, the chances were that they had been hooked.

Hamilton went back to the bar and ordered a whiskey and sweet soda.

Sitting on this particular stool, he could watch the front of McNalley's three-story apartment building. He always liked the extra insurance of being able to do that. More than once he'd seen the squad car draw up when the pigeon got suspicious later and phoned the police.

Hamilton sipped his drink.

Why did they fall for it so often?

Ignorance, stupidity, old age. Sometimes all three?

Yesterday, Hamilton had spent the morning in the lobby of the First National branch in the Southview Shopping Center. He had kept an eye on the deposit window. It was the second day of the month and that was usually a busy time, what with pension and social security checks being deposited.

He had selected Amos McNalley.

McNalley fitted the pattern. In his seventies or more. Good clothes. Neatly groomed.

Hamilton had followed him when McNalley left the bank.

McNalley covered four blocks at a brisk pace before he turned into the three-story apartment building.

Hamilton, one block behind, found himself puffing when he entered the small foyer and studied the names on the glassed mail compartments.

Evidently the mail had just been delivered. There was mail in all the slots except one. Amos McNalley had apparently picked up his before going up to his apartment.

Now Hamilton glanced at his watch as he saw Amos McNalley leave the apartment building and begin walking toward the shopping center.

Hamilton quickly downed his drink and followed. He was

puffing again when McNalley entered the First National branch building.

After approximately ten minutes, McNalley came out of the building. He blinked for a moment at the green square and its park benches. He sat down on one of them.

Hamilton waited another five minutes and then approached. "Mr. McNalley?"

McNalley looked up. "Hamilton? The vice-president of the bank?"

Hamilton nodded. "You have the money?"

McNalley took an envelope from his inside coat pocket. "You said something about two hundred dollars?"

"Of course." Hamilton brought out his wallet and removed two one hundred dollar bills. "Here you are, sir. And the bank wishes to thank you for your assistance."

Hamilton glanced into the envelope. The money was all there. "Now I'll go back to the bank and we'll get after that scoundrel immediately. I should be back in half an hour."

He took a dozen steps before he felt a tap on his shoulder. He turned to face what instinct told him were plainclothesmen.

The taller of the two spoke. "You are under arrest. You have the right to remain silent. If you do not choose to . . ."

Hamilton closed his eyes and listened to the bitter end.

McNalley joined them and spoke for Hamilton's benefit. "I waited *fifteen* minutes before I used the phone." He grinned. "I spent forty years on the force before I retired and the last ten were as head of the Bunco Squad. I think I learned a few things about Pigeon drops in that time."

Hamilton sighed. Every five years or so he had a day like this. It made him wonder if it was really all worthwhile.

A Very Rare Disease

by Henry Slesar

Spiro got to the restaurant first, and sat silently on a plump semicircle of leather cushions, sipping a cold, dry martini and listening to the lunch talk. Big talk, little talk, deal, deal, deal; it was just like the talk he'd heard in every restaurant in every city where the selling business had taken him and his black suitcase. But today, the talk jarred. Today, Spiro had big worries.

O'Connor showed up at 12:30. He said: "Welcome home, Joe. You knock 'em dead in Chicago?"

Spiro edged over for his lunch partner and picked up a spoon. "Yeah, I knocked 'em dead, all right." He rapped the spoon against a glass and rang a clean sweet bell that made the waiter look in his direction. "You want a martini, right?"

"You got it," O'Connor grinned. "Tell you the truth, Joe, I kind of think you're lucky. I hate being stuck behind a desk. Me, I like to travel."

"I like it all right," Spiro said.

"Then what's wrong? You look worried."

"I am."

"Bad trip?"

"No, good trip. Best three weeks on the road since last year. It's no business worry. It's a health problem."

"No kidding? You having trouble, Joe?"

Spiro slumped in his seat.

"No, not me. It's Katherine."

"Your wife?"

"Yeah. I guess the worst is over, but she really had me scared for a while. I been through hell these past three days—"

"Well, what happened?"

"It must have started a couple of weeks ago, when I called her from Chicago, just to say hello. She complained of a headache, some dizziness, nothing very serious. But that's the way this thing is—hardly a symptom at all. That's what's so frightening about it."

"About what, for Pete's sake?"

"About this disease. I forget what it's called exactly—mono, monotheocrosis, something like that. It's a very rare disease, one of those medical freaks that show up once in a hundred years. The symptoms are practically nonexistent; the doctor told us some people don't realize a thing until it's too late."

O'Connor's jaw slackened. "Until it's too late? You mean this thing's *fatal*?"

"That's right. If you don't catch it in time—" Spiro snapped his fingers crisply, "—that's it."

"But she's okay now? You found out in time?"

"Yes, thank God. It was pure coincidence that saved us. My doctor came to our house on Thursday night to play some bridge. I told him about Kathy's cold, and he looked her over. He thought she was looking funny, so he decided to take a blood sample; that's when he found this crazy bug. It's a damn good thing he did—for both of us."

"How do you mean?"

"This monotheocrosis—it's catching as hell. A couple of nights more, and I would have had the damn thing in my system, too."

O'Connor's drink arrived, and he gulped it gratefully.

"But what did you do about it? Is there a cure?"

"That was my first question, too. My doc was a little baffled by the whole thing, but luckily he remembered the name of a man who made a study of the disease. A Dr. Hess, on the third floor of the Birch Building. We shot right down there and saw him, and he was very comforting. He said they might not have been able to do anything ten, twelve years ago, but now they had drugs that could do the trick. I was so relieved I almost cried."

"Boy! No wonder you look so beat. That was quite an experience."

"It sure was," Spiro said, downing the rest of his drink.

They left the restaurant at two, and Spiro said good-bye to O'Connor on the corner of Fifty-eighth and Madison. Then he stepped into a cab and gave the driver the address of the Birch Building.

He was there in ten minutes. In the lobby, he stopped at a newsstand and bought a pack of cigarettes. He lit one, and entered the elevator. "Three," he told the operator.

The corridor was bustling with people settling back into the afternoon work routine. He lounged near the elevator for another ten minutes, and the hallways emptied.

At 2:30, O'Connor stepped off the elevator, looked up and down the hall, and then headed left.

Spiro called out: "O'Connor!"

O'Connor whirled, looked bewildered, and then walked up to his friend.

"I just wanted to be *sure,*" said Spiro, "you son of a bitch." Then he drew back his fist and drove it into O'Connor's cheek. O'Connor yelped and fell sprawling to the marble tiles. Spiro, feeling better than he had in a long time, pressed the Down button.

Two Small Vials

by Elsin Ann Graffam

He awoke at 6:55, five minutes before the alarm was to sound. Turning on his side, he gazed with dispassionate interest at the woman who lay sleeping beside him.

Such a cow, he thought, When he thought of who he could be sleeping next to—

Sighing, he sat on the edge of the bed and pushed the alarm button in.

"Is it seven already?" Joanne asked sleepily. "I'll get breakfast. Hotcakes O.K., honey?"

"Sure," he said, not looking at his wife.

Her banal chatter at breakfast was almost suffocating.

"And this woman who won the jackpot was rich, from Great Oaks—can you imagine! How come poor people never win?"

Cow, he thought, rising. "I'd better get going," he said, slipping on his topcoat.

The ride to work was pleasant. Peaceful, after a breakfast with Joanne.

He tuned in his favorite FM station and drove slowly, thinking of Chris. Chris, with her long golden hair, her youthful figure, her blue eyes.

"You'll get over her, Bill," Joanne had said a hundred times, humoring him, forgiving him. The placid, long-suffering wife. Cow! he thought.

He turned the car into the immense parking lot of the Willsin Chemical Plant and parked at the spot marked MR. REED.

It was nice, he thought, to be only twenty-seven years old and a production manager with his own private parking spot. Willsin Chemical Plant was relatively new, but growing fast. Maybe in five years, ten at the most, it would be rated Triple-A, Dun & Bradstreet.

He'd had the best—college, good connections, looks, ambition; everything but the right wife.

He could never have his colleagues and their wives to dinner. They'd sit down to one of Joanne's insipid dinners—tuna casserole, say. She'd open her mouth and say, "And this woman who won the jackpot was rich, from Great Oaks—can you imagine!"

Wincing, he locked the car and headed for his office at the front of the plant.

I could have bought her off, he thought. I could have given her money and seen her through an abortion. But not Mr. Nice. I marry her.

And she loses the baby. And I'm stuck. With a *cow*! A—

"Good morning, Mr. Reed."

"Morning, Susan," he said to the bookkeeper.

"We're getting a rush of orders for that new explosive. Harper Construction Company, Mideast Construction, Fallstaff." She flipped through a stack of orders.

"Well, it's good, cheap, does the job."

"And you have to use so little of it," she said.

Suddenly he felt light-headed. He sat down.

"Is something the matter?" she asked.

"No. I just thought of something, that's all."

Joanne glanced at the skillet clock on the kitchen wall. Five of ten. In a few minutes her TV programs would begin. She poured herself a glass of soda and padded to the living room to turn on the set. Drawing her fuzzy-slippered feet under her, she settled down.

In seven hours Bill would be home. Maybe. The week before he'd come home late three nights in a row. How late, she hadn't known; she'd been asleep. He no longer bothered to call to say he'd be working late. He simply wouldn't show up. In frustration she'd eat her meal—and his. All fifty-five of her overweight pounds, she reflected, were his fault.

She was willing to put up with his tomcatting. Someday he'd settle down and realize what a comfortable, homey place she'd created for him. Realize, more importantly, that he still loved her as he once had. He'd come to his senses. All she had to do was wait.

The first show, *Mister Dollar,* was on. Leaning back, she immersed herself in the program.

"You're tense tonight, honey," Chris said, drawing on her robe.

"I've got a lot on my mind."

"Poor Lumpkin."

"It's just—a lot of pressure at work."

"Well, I've got my problems too."

"I know, I know." Bill lit a cigarette. Sometimes she nagged him a little too much for comfort.

"I mean, I don't want to wait so long for my ship to come in that my pier collapses."

He smiled, despite his mood. "It won't be much longer. One of these days Joanne'll see the light and give me a divorce."

"And one of these days I'll win the lottery."

"Oh, come on, Chris. Be patient. We still have each other, haven't we?"

"Sure," she said. "How about a drink?"

He nodded. His mind returned to the two small vials tucked into his jacket pocket. Getting them that afternoon had been absurdly simple. Now all he had to do was figure how to combine the two chemicals.

The telephone rang.

"Damn," she said, going to answer it. "I'll bet it's Mother, *again.*"

The alarm went off at 6:30. Quickly he reached over and silenced it. Joanne was still asleep, he saw, relieved. Easing himself out of bed, he tiptoed from the room and went down the carpeted stairs to the kitchen. The two vials were at the back of the cutlery drawer where he'd left them the night before.

The beauty of the new explosive was not only that such a small amount was needed to do the job, as Susan had said, but that just the slightest vibration—like the ringing of the telephone—would set off the explosion. Apart, the two chemicals were inert. Combined, he guessed most of the downstairs would be blown to a powder. And Joanne with it.

He knew that she sat down fatly on the sofa at ten in the morning to start watching her precious TV shows. The telephone was on the end table next to the sofa. At ten-fifteen he'd dial his home number. The vibration from the ring would be more than enough to do the job.

For a moment he clasped his hands together to stop their trembling. Then, the phone cover removed, he placed a drop of dioxorb and one of riantrin on the bell.

Did he hear her coming down the stairs? Holding his breath, he listened. No, it was just the thumping of his heart. Gently—*gently*—he replaced the cover of the telephone. There. It was—

She'd been thinking about him and his "Be patient" all night, unable to sleep, more infuriated with each passing hour. He had been stringing her along for far too long. How was she supposed to explain her time to her mother, her sisters, her brother, her friends?

Well, an early call *at home* should let him know how serious she was! *When* her call finally got through. She raised her finger from the cradle button and dialed again.

Sweet Remembrance

by Betty Ren Wright

"I blame those dreadful books for his death," Miss Mackey told the sergeant. "Indirectly, of course, I'm liberal in my thinking, I assure you, but I do think that publishers have a responsibility. Have you *seen* the kind of trash being sold in every drugstore and supermarket at this very moment?"

She didn't look like a liberal. The sergeant watched her thin white hands, expert among the tea things, and felt nostalgia for an age he had never known. In the short hours of their acquaintance he had become very fond of Miss Mackey, and he could not understand why. Certainly she was nothing like his mother—his noisy, moody, cheerfully vulgar Ma—nor like any of his noisy, cheerful, vulgar sisters and aunts. Perhaps that was it, he decided, forgetting for a moment the dreary purpose of his visit in the pleasure of watching her pour tea into pearly cups. Perhaps he loved her because she was the other side of his moon, the unresolved, even unrecognized dream of what a female should be.

"Now, about Mr. Higgins," she said with endearing directness, after he had taken his first sip of tea. "He is a simply heartbreaking example of what I mean. If he didn't read those books—if he didn't think those thoughts!—I venture to say he would be alive at this moment."

The sergeant set his cup back on its saucer. "I don't see—" he began gently, but she was quite ready to explain her theory.

"He always had one of those dreadful books in his overalls pocket," she said. "You know, the ones with the *covers.* He was always snatching a moment to read them—

I've seen him—and all that nastiness aroused his prurient curiosity. Prurient curiosity, young man." She passed him a plate of tiny cookies, which he refused. "Why else would he have been lurking behind my draperies?"

"Robbery, perhaps," the sergeant suggested, but Miss Mackey would have none of it.

"Nonsense! As the janitor of this building he had keys to every apartment, and he knew that I go to my book club every Tuesday afternoon without fail, and buy my groceries every Friday morning, so he had plenty of opportunity to come in if he simply wanted to take something." She shook her little white head decisively. "No, Sergeant, carnal appetite was his problem, and guilt was what did him in. When I saw him and screamed, he turned and climbed out of the window as though he had taken leave of his senses. He was the very picture of a guilt-ridden man."

It was one more delight that Miss Mackey saw nothing strange in Mr. Higgins choosing to spy on her instead of on one of the younger women who lived in the building, the sergeant decided. He put aside the tea regretfully. "Well, I won't bother you any longer," he said. "You've been very kind and helpful, and I'm sure you're tired after your bad experience. Thank you for the tea."

She followed him to the door. "You are not at all the way one usually imagines a detective to be," she said. "You're very young. And you have a certain—grace."

The sergeant stiffened for a moment. How his parents would have roared at that, how his brothers and sisters would have jeered! *Grace,* he thought, and then decided he liked the sound of it as long as no one else had heard.

Westerberg was waiting in the lobby. "Well?" he asked.

"An elegant old lady."

"Who pushes janitors out of windows."

The sergeant led the way to the car, feeling very much on the defensive. "So a few people heard her scolding him for reading dirty books," he said grumpily. "So this makes her a killer? She admits she spoke to him about it—for his own good. She thought she was doing her duty."

"She threatened him," Westerberg said patiently. "He told people in the apartment about it, thought it was a joke. She told him he'd be punished if he kept up his sinful ways, that his evil thoughts were showing in his face. She sounds like a nut."

"She's a nice old lady trying to set the world straight," the sergeant told him. "Anybody who wants to magnify that into a criminal act is going to have his hands full."

He thought about Miss Mackey while he shaved, mentioned her guardedly to his date at dinner, and that night he dreamt he was fighting a duel under an oak tree that was festooned with Spanish moss.

In the morning there was a report on his desk at the station, and Westerberg was waiting in the chair by the window, a cup of coffee in his hands. When he had finished reading the report, the sergeant sat for a long time staring at the crack that marred the brown-egg wall in front of him.

"I was never as young as you are when I was as young as you are," Westerberg said finally, when the coffee was gone and the silence had become too oppressive to be borne. "Do you want me to go get the old lady while you patch up your shattered illusions?"

"Go get her!" the sergeant repeated sharply. "Why should you get her? You want to send her to the chair because this damn sheet says someone died in the last apartment she lived in, too?"

"Not just *someone.*" Westerberg set the coffee cup on the windowsill, adjusting its position slightly to coincide with the stains already there. "A window-washer; a wholesome, clean-living fellow who supported a wife, a mother, a sister, and the sister's two kids. Been washing windows for seventeen years, and there was never a complaint about him not minding his own business until Miss Mackey moved into the building. She reported him twice as a peeping tom—and the third time he was doing her windows he fell seven stories to the ground and broke his neck."

The sergeant slouched in his chair and thought of gallantry in the shade of a giant oak. "You can't arrest a nice old lady for being around when two people died," he said, "whether she happened to like them or not."

"Tell me one thing," Westerberg said with irritating gentleness. "Did the nice old lady mention the window-washer to you? Did she tell you Mr. Higgins was the second man to leave her elegant presence in a great big hurry?"

The sergeant looked at him with something close to hate. "No," he said. "She didn't happen to mention it. She probably assumed we'd look at it the same way she did—as a nasty coincidence."

"Good grief!" Westerberg said, but he didn't go on with the discussion.

They spent the rest of the day talking to residents of the apartment building. Most of them had known Mr. Higgins casually; none of them had thought there was anything odd about him, though they all agreed that he had been seen with lurid paperbacks in his hands and was always well-informed about, and eager to discuss, the latest sensational murder. Three residents reported having received anonymous letters in the last couple of months: a bachelor who had a painting of a nude delivered to his apartment; a model who had posed in a bikini for a slick magazine; and a young actress who had been accused in her letter of letting a man stay overnight in her apartment. Each of the letters had been a warning of punishment to come; none of them had been taken seriously. The recipients remembered that they were written on pale gray, tissue-thin paper in fine script.

As he looked over his notes, the sergeant wondered why he found it impossible to believe anything bad of Miss Mackey. Who was to say, actually, that her righteous innocence did not become a twisted, perverted passion behind those bright blue eyes? His mind simply would not accept it. He moved angrily through the long day, and at the end of it he visited her again, wondering at his own sense of homecoming as he sat down in the parlor.

Parlor, he thought. The word prompted a picture of plush and velour and china figurines; a Seth Thomas clock; books bound in muted leather, stillness tucked protectively around every object. Then he remembered that when he was twelve he had asked his seventh-grade teacher a question about Browning and, in an ecstasy of gratitude—how many seventh graders had ever asked her about Browning?—she had invited him to stop in at her home that evening and pick up a book.

The house was a treasure of towering gingerbread where she had lived first with her parents and then alone. The boy had entered into a dream when he stepped through its door. The crowded kitchen, center of life at home, had faded from his consciousness as if it had never been, and with it the bursts of laughter, the slaps, the curses, the tears that were the music he lived by. Dignity, dry wit, and, most of all, orderliness were what he found in the teacher's old house, and he had gone back again and again making mental lists of subjects to ask about the next time as his eyes moved over the ceiling-high shelves of books.

"You look tired, Sergeant." There was a tiny crease of concern between Miss Mackey's eyes. "I don't think I'll offer you tea this time. I have a better idea." She crossed the room to a glass-doored cabinet and took from its glittering depths a crystal decanter and two glasses on a tray. The glass was like a small bubble in his hand; he held it gingerly and let the brandy restore him.

"How is your case developing?" she asked as he settled back in his chair. "Have you learned what you needed to know about that unfortunate man?" She might have been asking about the weather, or his indigestion, or where he was going to go on his vacation.

"Well," he said, "it seems to be getting more complicated instead of less so. We're beginning to wonder whether there's some connection between Mr. Higgins' death and another one that occurred some time ago."

She took a tiny sip from her glass. "I don't understand."

"Your theory," he told her, "may be the right one."

She leaned forward with a tiny smile of triumph. "Twisted thoughts," she said. "Evil influences lead men to do things they would not otherwise do."

"Twisted thoughts," the sergeant agreed. "Of the murderer, however, rather than the victims'. There's someone living in this building, Miss Mackey, who is very mixed up indeed."

She watched alertly as he put down his glass and went to the window. "I hate to keep going over this," he said, "but I have to be very sure of the facts." He opened the window as far as it would go. "Now," he said, "when you came into the room you saw Mr. Higgins standing there, partly hidden by the drapery. You had no idea till then that he was in the apartment."

"That is correct," Miss Mackey said, and the sergeant seemed to hear again his seventh-grade teacher's voice.

"You're sure you didn't call Mr. Higgins in to fix a window?" he went on. "Some of your neighbors report having heard voices in the hallway minutes before Mr. Higgins fell."

"Certainly not," Miss Mackey said.

"When you caught sight of him, you screamed and ordered him to leave," the sergeant went on.

"Exactly." Miss Mackey put down her glass and came over to the window. "He seemed to panic. He crawled out on the sill, looked back over his shoulder at me, and then he fell forward and was gone."

"Like this." The sergeant then climbed cautiously onto the sill and crouched there, balancing himself with his fingertips. He looked back in time to see her small, reproachful face close to his shoulder, and then he felt her hands on his back, pushing with great purpose, and he was hurtling out into space.

"Like that," he heard Miss Mackey say very closely behind him.

It was an astonishingly long way down. The sergeant thought of his Ma, and of the cheerful, sometimes ribald girls he had loved as he grew up. He saw, in kaleidoscope, the dark places of his life and the churning colors, the chronic grand disorder of being alive. When he landed, bouncing twice in the great lap of the safety net, it was as if he had resigned himself—committed himself—forever to the way things actually were.

Westerberg helped him down.

"You want to go up or should I?" he asked sympathetically.

"You go," the sergeant said.

He waited in the dark courtyard until Westerberg had disappeared into the building. Then he straightened his coat and went around the side of the building to where the patrol car was parked. He took out his pipe. He knew they wouldn't be down for a while. Miss Mackey would want to wash the brandy glasses and put them away, powder her nose, and close the window before she went to the station.

A Dip in the Poole

by Bill Pronzini

I was sitting in a heavy baroque chair in the Hotel Poole's genteel lobby, leafing through one of the plastic-encased magazines provided by the management, when the girl in the dark tweed suit picked Andrew J. Stuyvesant's pockets.

She worked it very nicely. Stuyvesant—a silver-haired old gentleman who carried a malacca walking stick and had fifteen or twenty million dollars in Texas oil—had just stepped out of one of the chrome-and-walnut elevators directly in front of me. The girl appeared from the direction of the curving marble staircase, walking rapidly and with elaborate preoccupation, and collided with him. She excused herself. Bowing in a gallant way, Stuyvesant allowed as how it was perfectly all right, my dear. She got his wallet and the diamond stickpin from his tie, and he neither felt nor suspected a thing.

The girl apologized again and then hurried off across the padded indigo carpeting toward the main entrance at the lobby's opposite end, slipping the items into a tan suede bag she carried over one arm. Almost immediately, I was out of my chair and moving after her. She managed to thread her way through the potted plants and the dark furnishings to within a few steps of the double-glass doors before I caught up with her.

I let my hand fall on her arm. "Excuse me just a moment," I said, smiling.

She stiffened. Then she turned and regarded me as if I had crawled out from one of the potted plants. "I beg your pardon?" she said in a frosty voice.

"You and I had best have a little chat."

"I am not in the habit of chatting with strange men."

"I think you'll make an exception in my case."

Her brown eyes flashed angrily as she said, "I suggest you let go of my arm. If you don't, I shall call the manager."

I shrugged. "There's no need for that."

"I certainly hope not."

"Simply because he would only call me."

"What?"

"I'm chief of security at the Hotel Poole, you see," I told her. "What was once referred to as the house detective."

She grew pale, and the light dimmed in her eyes. "Oh," she said.

I steered her toward the arched entrance to the hotel's lounge, a short distance on our left. She offered no resistance. Once inside, I sat her down in one of the leather booths and then seated myself opposite. A blue-uniformed waiter approached, but I shook my head and he retreated.

I examined the girl across the polished surface of the table. The diffused orange glow from the small lantern in its center gave her classic features the impression of purity and innocence, and turned her seal-brown hair into a cascading black wave. I judged her age at about twenty-five. I said, "Without a doubt, you're the most beautiful dip I've ever encountered."

"I . . . don't know what you're talking about."

"Don't you?"

"Certainly not."

"A dip is underworld slang for a pickpocket."

She tried to affect indignation. "Are you insinuating that *I* . . . ?"

"Oh come on," I said. "I saw you lift Mr. Stuyvesant's wallet and his diamond stickpin. I was sitting directly opposite the elevator, not fifteen feet away."

She didn't say anything. Her fingers toyed with the catch on the tan suede bag. After a moment, her eyes lifted to mine, briefly, and then dropped again to the bag. She sighed in a tortured way. "You're right, of course. I stole those things."

I reached out, took the bag from her and snapped it open. Stuyvesant's wallet, with the needle-point of the stickpin now imbedded in the leather, lay on top of the various feminine articles inside. I removed them, glanced at her identification long enough to memorize her name and address, reclosed the bag and returned it to her.

She said softly, "I'm . . . not a thief, I want you to know that. Not really, I mean." She took her lower lip between her teeth. "I have this . . . *compulsion* to steal. I'm powerless to stop myself."

"Kleptomania?"

"Yes. I've been to three different psychiatrists during the past year, but they've been unable to cure me."

I shook my head sympathetically. "It must be terrible for you."

"Terrible," she agreed. "When . . . when my father learns of this episode, he'll have me put into a sanatorium." Her voice quavered. "He threatened to do just that if I ever stole anything again, and he doesn't make idle threats."

I studied her. Presently, I said, "Your father doesn't have to know what happened here today."

"He . . . he doesn't?"

"No," I said slowly. "There was no real harm done, actually. Mr. Stuyvesant will get his wallet and stickpin back. And I see no reason for causing the hotel undue embarrassment through the attendant publicity if I report the incident."

Her face brightened. "Then . . . you're going to let me go?"

I drew a long breath. "I suppose I'm too soft-hearted for the type of position that I have. Yes, I'm going to let you go. But you have to promise me that you'll never set foot inside the Hotel Poole again."

"Oh, I promise!"

"If I see you here in the future, I'll have to report you to the police."

"You won't!" she assured me eagerly. "I . . . have an appointment with another psychiatrist tomorrow morning. I feel sure he can help me."

I nodded. "Very well, then." I turned to stare through the arched lounge entrance at the guests and uniformed bellboys scurrying back and forth in the lobby. When I turned back again, the street door to the lounge was just closing and the girl was gone.

I sat there for a short time, thinking about her. If she was a kleptomaniac, I reflected, then I was Mary, Queen of

Scots. What she was, of course, was an accomplished professional pickpocket—her technique was much too polished, her hands much too skilled—and an extremely adept liar.

I smiled to myself, and stood and went out into the lobby again. But instead of resuming my position in the baroque chair before the elevator bank, or approaching the horseshoe-shaped desk, I veered left to walk casually through the entrance doors and out to Powell Street.

As I made my way through the thickening late-afternoon crowds—my right hand resting on the fat leather wallet and the diamond stickpin in my coat pocket—I found myself feeling a little sorry for the girl. But only just a little.

After all, Andrew J. Stuyvesant had been *my* mark from the moment I first noticed him entering the Hotel Poole that morning—and after a three-hour vigil I had been within fifteen seconds of dipping him myself when she appeared virtually out of nowhere.

Wouldn't you say I was entitled to the swag?

Doctor's Orders

by John F. Suter

The pain, the pain is everywhere. No, not everywhere. But I throb in places where there is no real pain. And now it is only an ache and a tired feeling. It seems as if there is no time, no space, nothing but this. But I am a little stronger than I was. So little. But I *am* stronger. I have to get well. I intend to get well. I will get well.

"Mr. Shaw, I think she'll come out of it all right. As you know, it was either your wife or the baby, for a while. But she's improved, I know that. Of course, there will always be the weakness. We can't correct that."

"I understand. Just to have her well again is all I care about."

I had better open my eyes. Jeff isn't here. I can't sense him. But I can stand the white room now. I no longer have a wish to die. No, even though he didn't live. I could cry and cry about it. I wanted to when Jeff first told me. But there is no strength in those sorts of tears. I will get well.

"You did tell her that the baby died?"

"Yes, Doctor. It was hard for her to take at first. Very hard. Then I told her that it had been a boy. That pleased her, in spite of—of what happened."

There. The world is back. So much sunshine in the room. So many flowers. I wonder if Jeff—

"Did you tell her that the child is already buried?"

"Not yet. If you're sure that she's stronger, I'll tell her today."

"You don't think she'll hold it against you, Mr. Shaw? For going ahead with the funeral, I mean."

"Jessie is very level-headed, Doctor. She'll understand that we couldn't wait. And—if you don't think it's out of style to say so—we love each other."

I'm sure Jeff has done whatever is best. If only it—he—had lived until I could have seen him. . . . How long have I been here? Where is Jeff? Is he being sensible, as I begged him to be? Is he at work? I hope so. The job is so important to him. Oh, I do love him! And I do so want to give him fine children.

"Perhaps, then, Mr. Shaw, it would be better for you to tell her the rest of it. Better, I mean, than for me to do it. It might be easier for her to believe someone who loves her. Sometimes people think they know more than doctors do."

"That part won't be easy."

I hope the children will look like Jeff. I'm not ugly. But I'm so—plain. Jeff has the looks for both of us. That's one of the reasons they all said he was only after my money. But he's refused to let me help him. He's independent. He keeps working hard managing the sporting-goods department. And why? He wants to support us. Neither of us would ever have to work again, if we didn't want to. I must get well, for his sake. I will get well.

"Easy or hard, Mr. Shaw, it has to be done. Someone has to tell her. It will come best from you. She must never try to have a child again. Never. It will kill her. Make no mistake about it—having another child will kill her."

"I'll take the responsibility, Doctor. You needn't say a thing to her. I think I can convince her. Perhaps I can even persuade her to move away for a while. A room's all set up for the baby. Those things shouldn't keep haunting her."

I'm glad I made my will before I came to the hospital. I'm glad I made it in Jeff's favor. He doesn't know about it. And it wasn't necessary, as it turned out. But I'm glad. He's been so good to me that now I'm sure of him. . . .

The door swung inward, silently. She turned her head, slowly. A tired smile crept across her white face. A tall young man with crinkled blond hair was in the doorway.

"Jeff."

He was at her bedside, kissing her hand. "Jessie."

When they both could speak, she gripped his fingers. "Jeff, I've been lying here thinking. Everybody has troubles of some kind or other. We can overcome this. I'm going to get strong, fast. Then we're going to have another baby. Just as quickly as we can. Aren't we?"

He smiled proudly. The truth was exactly the right answer.

"We certainly are, sweetheart. We certainly are."

Mrs. Twiller Takes a Trip

by Lael J. Littke

Old Mrs. Twiller ran a gnarled finger over the inexpensive wrist watches on the display card and smiled tremulously at the salesgirl.

"Could I try that one on, Miss?" she said, her voice quavering a little. "The one with the pretty brown band?"

"Why, certainly," the salesgirl said, smiling back at Mrs. Twiller. "These are very nice watches for the price." She strapped the watch on Mrs. Twiller's frail wrist.

"Now, isn't that pretty?" Mrs. Twiller said, stretching out her arm and twisting it around to admire the watch from all angles. She cleared her throat. "How much is it, my dear?" she asked hesitantly.

The salesgirl beamed. "Would you believe it? They're only $9.98. A special, this week only. Shall I wrap that one up for you?"

"Oh, mercy, no," Mrs. Twiller said. "$9.98? Oh, mercy." She fumbled at the buckle on the wristband, trying to undo it.

The salesgirl looked perplexed. "It's very reasonable," she said. "Really, it's a bargain for the price."

Mrs. Twiller looked up brightly. "Oh, it's just lovely," she assured the girl, "but with everything so dear these days—oh, my, I couldn't possibly spend all that on a watch. Thank you anyway, Miss."

The girl blinked a little as she helped undo the watch. "I'm awfully sorry, ma'am."

"That's all right, dearie." Mrs. Twiller patted the girl's hand. "It's just that a body can't help wishing now and then." She held the watch in her fragile hand and gazed at it with one last sympathetic look as the girl turned to another customer.

With a quick motion, Mrs. Twiller dropped the watch into the large shopping bag at her feet.

There, she thought. With the transistor radio and the electric shaver she already had in the bag, that should be enough for one day. The money Mr. Simpson would give her for them would feed her army of stray cats for several days.

As she stooped over to pick up her bag, Mrs. Twiller noticed a man watching her from two counters away. A floorwalker, no doubt. She grasped the handles of the bag and straightened up, tottering just a little not so much as to make the floorwalker come to her assistance, but just enough to make him think tenderly of his own dear old mother. She fluttered a hand to her chest and saw the suspicious look on his face fade away and be replaced by a benign smile.

Well, that took care of him. Now if he saw her drop something into her bag he would merely chalk it up to her absent-mindedness, which was certainly forgivable in a lady of her age.

It was time to leave, but first Mrs. Twiller wanted to visit the basement floor and pick up a few more plastic bowls for the new cats who just that week had found out about the private welfare center she ran. They did so appreciate their own dishes, and she liked to afford them that small dignity.

On the way down the escalator she checked her coin purse to see that she had the necessary cash. She wouldn't think of filching anything like the dishes. That wouldn't be ethical. She only took the other things because she just couldn't stretch the tiny check she received weekly from her son—certainly could not stretch it to cover all the cat food she put out each day. Besides, her son kept close account of how she spent the allowance he sent her.

Actually, she thought, the department store would probably be quite proud of the humane project they were supporting, if only they knew.

Suddenly Mrs. Twiller realized she had been on the escalator for some time. She should be down to the basement floor by now. Maybe the escalator was broken. No, it was still moving. Then why was it taking so long?

Mrs. Twiller squinted into the darkness. Darkness? Why was it dark? Was there another power failure like the ones in 1965 and 1977? No, the escalator would have stopped if that were the case.

For a moment Mrs. Twiller was alarmed, then she breathed a sigh of relief when she saw a glimmer of light far down in the mists at the bottom of the escalator. Mists? Mists in a department-store basement?

The light became brighter as she descended toward it. The mists began to look more like smoke and she could detect a faint sulfuric smell. In the distance she could see what looked like vast fires. And then she caught sight of a colossal gate, topped by a spectacular sign whose flaming letters spelled out: HELL. Underneath was a smaller sign which read: Entrance.

"My stars," marveled Mrs. Twiller aloud. "So that's where it is, right here under the Hardware Department."

She didn't have much time to wonder about it because she was about to be met by an uncomfortable-looking individual who appeared to have a bad sunburn.

"Follow me, lady," he intoned without introducing himself, which Mrs. Twiller regarded as especially bad manners. But then, she reasoned, what else could you expect in Hell?

She decided she had better follow the man since it seemed safer than trying to escape into the smoky terrain that stretched out on all sides. He led her into a seared building beside the imposing gate, and Mrs. Twiller found herself in a large room decorated sumptuously in vivid colors—scarlet, tangerine, and blood-red, among others. There was another fiery-looking individual seated behind a huge table which Mrs. Twiller took to be a reception desk, but when she headed toward it her guide said curtly, "Sit down," and disappeared through a crimson door.

Mrs. Twiller chose a cherry-colored sofa and sat down heavily, jarring her poor old bones until they rattled. Despite its soft appearance, the sofa was hard as a rock—which was only logical, Mrs. Twiller thought, since on closer examination it turned out to be made of petrified lava. She settled herself as comfortably as she could and glanced at the man behind the desk; but he was occupied with some business of his own involving a large book into which he seemed to be burning notations. Since he seemed in no way hostile, she relaxed a little and let her gaze roam around the brilliant room.

Mercy, she thought, it was a nice place to see but she certainly wouldn't want to live here. Not that it wasn't beautiful, in its own fashion, with its startling colors and stunning art objects scattered casually about. But to Mrs. Twiller's way of thinking it was overdone and even rather vulgar, as if the owner were trying to impress someone by displaying the valuable things he owned. Still, she caught her breath as she leaned closer to examine a small gold figurine of an imp which reposed on an obsidian table next to the sofa. There was also a ruby statue of indeterminate shape and a small vase studded with huge diamonds. She was admiring a solid platinum Mt. Vesuvius when a deep voice addressed her.

"Mrs. Twiller."

She turned quickly to see an elegant dark-haired gentleman attired in a shiny-black cutaway coat with a copper-red vest and tie, and striped trousers. He wore a well-trimmed goatee and managed to look distinguished in spite of being a brilliant shade of red.

Mrs. Twiller gulped, then stiffened her back. "How do you know my name?" she asked, standing up and eyeing him belligerently.

"I make it my business to know the names of people like you," he said, smiling sardonically.

Mrs. Twiller clutched her shopping bag in both arms, it being the only familiar object in this frightening situation. "What do you mean, people like me?" she demanded somewhat weakly.

The fiery-faced gentleman shrugged. "I hate to apply so harsh a term as thief to so lovely a lady. Shall we say pilferer?"

"I don't know what you mean," Mrs. Twiller whispered, her voice trembling. She let her left hand flutter to her throat in the gesture that never failed to make strong men turn squishy with concern and sentiment.

The red individual raised his hand. "Please, dear lady," he said, "spare me that. I am well aware of your wiles and I also have a record of every item you have ever appropriated for your—ahem—worthy cause."

Mention of her project gave Mrs. Twiller new courage. "Who would feed all those starving cats if I didn't? I'm just trying to do a little good in the world the only way I know how." She blinked her eyes and tried her best to squeeze out a tear or two.

The man in the cutaway, which had turned wine-red, strode to a window whose black shade he raised to reveal a landscape of fire and smoke. "Dear lady," he said, "you seem to forget where you are. We are not concerned with the good you do. Quite the contrary!" He turned and pointed a slender finger at her. "You are running up a very bad record, Mrs. Twiller, and I have brought you down here this time just for a warning. Mend your ways or you may end up down here for good—or rather, I should say, for bad."

"This time?" Mrs. Twiller was cheered. "You mean I'm not really here to stay?"

Her companion gave a short laugh and turned back to gaze out of the window at his domain. "I hope to frighten you enough so that we can burn our records on you, Mrs. Twiller. What would happen if we started taking in little old ladies like you down here? In a short time we'd have frilly curtains at our windows and sweet daffodils all around our fire pits." He swung around. "This is a last warning, dear lady. No more stealing from department stores or you'll wind up down here, and none of us would like that now, would we?"

Mrs. Twiller's courage had returned. "Oh, I don't know," she said, running her hand over an emerald statuette of the god Pan. "It doesn't seem to be that bad down here."

"You've noticed my collection," the scarlet man said, a note of pride creeping into his voice. "Of course there are compensations to this job or no one would want it, not even me. I can truthfully say that I own the most priceless objets d'art in existence." He stopped and sighed. "The hell of it is, there's really no challenge to getting them. All I have to do is wish for them and they're mine."

"Oh, that is too bad," Mrs. Twiller clucked sympathetically. "Takes all the fun out of it if you can't outsmart someone."

"Yes, it does," grumbled the fiery one.

Mrs. Twiller made a small cooing sound and patted his arm, which made him jerk it angrily away.

"Now cut that out!" he bellowed. "See what I mean? Get a sweet little old lady down here and within ten minutes she has me all soft and mushy. I won't have it, do you hear?"

"Oh, mercy, yes," Mrs. Twiller said, retreating a couple of steps. "I hear."

The man's eyes glowed crimson. "Swear, then, that you won't take any more merchandise from any store up there."

Mrs. Twiller swallowed. "I swear. Oh, my, yes."

"Then go," roared the Master of Hades. "And see that you don't have reason to come back."

Mrs. Twiller went, clutching her shopping bag and scuttling along toward the escalator as fast as she could. She had a moment of panic when she discovered that the escalator moved only down, but she did find a narrow, almost unused stairway which she ascended as quickly as she could; and she didn't stop until she reached the department-store's street floor.

"Missed the basement again," she puffed, but decided against going back down. She was already late for her weekly appointment with Mr. Simpson. She could pick up the cat dishes somewhere else, although she did like to give this store her business.

As she hurried toward the door, a display of silver flatware caught her eye. It was always easy to slip a few pieces of flatware into her shopping bag. But after a moment's hesitation she walked on past. After all, a promise was a promise. She would miss these shopping trips, though. There was something decidedly heady about seeing what she could get away with. But of course there would really be no need for any more forays. Oh, mercy, no, not with what she had in her shopping bag.

Just before entering the revolving door, Mrs. Twiller paused long enough to peep into her bag at the platinum Mt. Vesuvius, the ruby statue, the diamond-studded vase, and the emerald Pan. If she was any judge of value, her cats would be well taken care of for the rest of their combined nine lives.

Humming softly and a little breathlessly to herself, she closed her bag and hurried from the store. Mrs. Twiller had had a good trip.

Such a Lovely Day

by Penelope Wallace

Little Treddington is the prettiest village you could hope to see. It nestles in the Cotswolds and the guide books describe the Church of Saint Andrews as "a little gem," as indeed it was.

I well remember the first time I saw the village. My late husband, the Reverend Charles Framley, drove me down to see his new parish. The departing vicar, Mr. Wyland, showed us the Church and pointed out all the tourist attractions. (I am afraid that he was rather a worldly man!) He also showed us the postcards and booklets which were on sale in the church porch, but I could see that poor Charles did not approve, and so could Mr. Wyland, for he very tactfully led us across to the Vicarage. He was a bachelor but I must say that he provided a splendid tea and the house and garden were quite beautiful.

I so looked forward to living in this beautiful place and moving from the rather depressing Manchester suburb where Charles had his present parish. The thought of seeing, everyday, green fields and those neat golden cottages instead of dirt-grained houses, sustained me during the drive back to Manchester. It would almost be like going home; for I had been born and brought up in the soft lands of Surrey and to me the North would always be "alien corn".

That was ten years ago.

We moved to Little Treddington in the autumn and soon it was the Carol Service and Christmas and taking sherry with Lord and Lady Dawson at the Manor House; then Easter and Whitsun, and then every waking minute getting ready for the Church Fete. It was always held on the second Saturday in August and opened, of course, by Lady Dawson so it had to be between the time she returned from the Riviera and before they went to Scotland—Lord and Lady Dawson are both excellent shots. I remembered that the Vicar (Mr. Wyland that is, not my husband for he never made a joke!) had said Lady Dawson really chose that day to mark the last appearance of her second-day Royal Ascot hat! Fortunately, Charles did not hear.

There was so much to be done for the Fete and so many little jealousies to be sorted out, but I do pride myself on being rather good with people, and really I felt I could take quite a lot of the credit when I looked around the Vicarage garden and saw so many happy faces behind the stalls and all the children—such a happy day for them—with their pennies and sixpences clutched in one hand while they threw coconuts or delved in the lucky dip, and Lady Dawson most beautifully dressed . . .

And then—quite without warning—down came the rain! I was sure that Lady Dawson's hat was quite ruined, but she took it very well and we all ran as fast as we could into the Vicarage.

The rain stopped as suddenly as it had started and back we all went to the garden—except for Lady Dawson who had "called it a day" (as she put it) and driven home. Of course, it was rather muddy round the coconut shies and the bran in the lucky dip was a little squelchy and poor Mrs. Wills was very upset because young Millicent had left her "guess-the-weight cake" in the rain and all the icing colours had run! But there, I always say, "These little things are sent to try us."

Poor Charles is not so philosophical and he was most upset, and the following year he started to worry about the weather long before the Fete. That year there was no rain and I thought all would be well, but it made no difference—sometimes it rained and sometimes it was fine—but every year for two weeks before our "D-Day" on the second Saturday in August, Charles would study the Weather Reports.

"Oh, I do hope it will be a fine day for the Fete," he would say (so gloomily too), and then for the last week before the Great Day he would stand in the Vicarage doorway scanning the skies.

I remember once Dr. Brown (such an amusing man, but very irreligious I am afraid) asked him whether he was looking for rain clouds or a sign from the Almighty! My husband was not at all amused and when Dr. Brown went on, "The Devil sends sin and the Lord sends the weather and I should have thought He could have arranged one fine afternoon in return for all the work you do for Him," poor Charles was really most upset.

"Charles," I would say (I would never have called him Charley for I think these abbreviations are such a pity), "Charles, why do you worry so much about the weather? If it is wet we can always hold the Fete in the Village Hall." But his answer was always the same.

"No, Maude," he would say in his sad voice. "You know how that upsets Miss Gosling; she has such a job afterwards getting it ready for Sunday School the next morning." And indeed it was true that on the one occasion when we did use the Hall, Miss Gosling complained for weeks!

Even after Miss Gosling died, quite suddenly, at the end of July three years ago, it was as if her ghost haunted him for he still insisted that the Fete be held out of doors.

Day after day he would open *The Times* and read the Weather Report (before he'd even cracked his boiled egg). Day after day he would "Tut Tut" and say, "Oh, I do hope it will be a fine day for the Fete." Day after day he would scan the skies . . .

He died suddenly, last year—just four days before the Fete.

Dr. Brown was most surprised—but I cannot say that I was.

They tried to say that I was mad—wasn't that silly of them! I am glad to say that they didn't succeed. (And luckily no one found out about poor Mother.)

Because, you see, there was Miss Gosling too; at the time they thought she was what they call "natural causes", but after my husband's death they dug her up! (Such a distasteful practice, I feel.)

They said that my husband was well-insured; but that was not the reason at all, as you can imagine!

Today is such a lovely day for a Fete—or a hanging.

Matinee

by Ruth Wissmann

"It isn't my fault I fell in love with you," Carla said. She placed her elbow on the pillow, her chin in her hand and gazed at the man on the bed beside her. "I didn't want to. I really didn't want to become involved like this. It just—happened."

He smiled and rumpled her hair. "But you aren't sorry," he said. "I know you aren't."

She sighed, sat up and swung her legs from the side of the bed and, after a moment of quiet reflection, said, "No, I'm not sorry, Alan, but I'm not happy either."

"It's one of those things, baby," he said. "You'll get over it—the worry, I mean. That's what you're referring to again. Right?" She nodded.

"Sometimes," she said, "I look at Tom and get the most God-awful feeling that he knows about us."

"I should hope not! Aw—he *couldn't*."

A frown shadowed her face. "I know. At least, I don't see how . . ."

"We've been careful." He spoke in a relaxed, contented tone of voice.

"Yes. Careful and foolish and selfish and—"

"Come on now. No self-contempt, please."

Looking around the motel room, Carla said, "I'm always afraid someone I know will see me driving in here. I've even had nightmares about it—and about being followed, too."

"Let's hope you don't talk in your sleep." An amused smile played around his lips and eyes.

"Oh, lord! I should hope not. Alan, aren't you ever worried about Lisa finding out about *us*?"

He laughed and shook his head. "She'd kill me, baby. I don't let myself think about it. This is a chance we have to take, honey. But I believe that everything is chance. Life itself is a chance. What the hell! We can't worry all the time about what *might* happen. It would spoil these afternoons for us—these matinées."

"True." She sounded uncertain as she stood up. Then, frowning at her wristwatch, "It's getting late. We'd better shower and be on our way. I have to get home in time to cook dinner and . . ."

"Okay, my sweet. If you have to, you have to."

It was Carla who opened the shower door. It was Alan who gasped and clamped a hand over her mouth before the scream really exploded. What they saw would be stabbing their minds for the rest of their lives.

The limp form lying there stared at them with sightless eyes, a bullet hole in its forehead. Here was a deathly white, bloody red shock dressed in black trousers and a gray shirt. Carla was not conscious of Alan's closing the shower door, but he had. Yet she could still see the grotesque, gruesome body. There was no stopping the wave of hysteria that surged to the surface.

Above the torment wracking her mind she heard his words. "*Please! My God!* Someone will *hear* you! Be *quiet!*" He held her to him while his eyes circled the room quickly as if looking for an escape route where there was none. "*Jesus!*" he said with disbelief. "What'll we do? What in hell are we going to do?"

She was shaking and crying, and he felt her skin turning cold and clammy. "Get dressed, Carla," he said in a voice that had become tense and sharp. "We've got to get the hell out of here fast as we can."

"I know," she sobbed. "I know, I know!" When he released her, she found that her arms and legs seemed to have turned to water, her fingers to icicles. "It's so *awful!* So ghastly! That—that *man!*" Her heart was thrashing inside her chest, her throat, her ears. Her face was without color. "Alan—I—I think I'm going to—faint."

"Listen to me," he said, gripping her shoulders in his cold hands. "This is no time to black out. We've got to run for it, and don't panic. Just don't panic."

"Yes, but—" she stared at him with tortured eyes, "—shouldn't we call the police—or someone?"

He looked at her incredulously as he reached for his clothes. "The police?" he said. "You've got to be *crazy!* I don't think you realize the jam we're in."

"But, Alan—that man's been *murdered*! He's been shot in the head!"

"Oh, *God!*" He turned his eyes toward the ceiling. "I know you're not overly bright, but—just get yourself dressed and hurry." He paused and frowned at the shower door, his eyes dark with apprehension. "We've got to think," he said as though speaking to himself. "Yeah—wait a minute. We . . ."

"We can think later," she told him as she tried to brush at her tears and fumbled with the zipper of her skirt. "After we get away we can—"

He shook his head. "It's not that simple. We *can't* just leave here. We can't just walk out and leave a dead body behind us to . . ."

She swallowed with effort and the horror of their predicament began to twist in her mind. "*Alan*!" she gasped. "We'll be *caught,* won't we? And it'll all come out about us. The manager of this place will tell, and the police will come after us, and there'll be questions, and Tom will find out, and then—"

"Shut *up*! I've got to *think.* I can't think when you're talking."

"But Alan, I've got to get *out* of here. I don't want to get mixed up in a murder. I don't want Tom to—" Then the tears flowed again and she heard Alan speaking, and there was no sympathy in his words.

"What about *me*? You think *you're* in trouble—what's this kind of publicity going to do for me at the studio? Let alone with Lisa and that temper of hers."

Now his eyes seemed to be looking at Carla without seeing her. Watching the lines that fear was etching in his face, she said, "You're scared. I don't like to see a man scared. Oh, Alan! Think of *something*! We have to get away from here—from that . . ." She swallowed with difficulty and found her throat had become dry and nearly paralyzed, that it was difficult to speak.

He shook his head and finished dressing in silence.

"Alan, whoever was in this room before us must have killed that man, so why don't you just go to the office and tell the—the manager the truth. Tell him what we found and—"

"Good God!" He spoke with disgust. "Why do you think he'd believe me?"

"Well, I don't know—but he'd have the name of the person who checked into this room before we did, so—"

"Names, hell! Probably as phony as the one I've used. Oh, why? Why did *we* have the stinking luck to find that stiff?"

She shuddered and reached for her sweater. "Alan, I'm going home. I *have* to be there before Tom arrives. I—I'm leaving."

His face darkened quickly. "You just wait one damn minute," he snapped. "You're not going to walk out of here and leave me with *this* on my shoulders. You're in this jam as much as I am, you know."

Her eyes widened with alarm. "But I *can't* stay here!" she wailed.

"Keep your voice down. These walls are thin. Someone will hear you."

Carla looked at the room around them as though it were a prison. Seeing Alan pace the floor like a caged animal, she croaked, "We're trapped, that's what. We're trapped in this ugly place with that—that—"

"Shut up. I'm trying to think of everything—of every angle."

"Like what?"

He turned on her with narrowed eyes. "Well, suppose—just suppose Tom does know that you've been with someone, and—"

"*No!* Don't *say* that. I won't listen. I just *won't*!"

"You'll listen and you'll listen good. How do you know you don't talk in your sleep? How can you be sure that he hasn't followed you here? Maybe he thought that . . . Look, suppose he came here and found that guy in this room and thought he was me—thought *he* was the one you've been meeting here."

"*No!* Oh, *no!*" She shook her head quickly.

Again Alan paced the floor. Then he walked back into the bathroom, opened the shower door, grimaced and closed it again. "Jesus! That's horrible! Whoever did that was goddamned mad—insane." Now he stood still, frowning thoughtfully and hitting a fist against his open palm.

A long, agonizing moment of silence followed before he walked back into the bedroom, took a deep breath and said, "There's only one thing we can do. It's a hell of a chance, but we've got to take it."

"Leave here?" she asked. "Just get into our cars and drive away?"

"How can you be so stupid?" he said, spitting out the words. "The manager here would recognize us anytime, anywhere, because we've been here so often."

"But he doesn't know your name."

"This," he said, pointing to his face. "This he'd recognize, describe. Yours too. No doubt he's taken a good look at you more than once. He could identify our cars, too. Did you ever think of that? He may have our license numbers."

She was trembling again. "I want to go home. I have to get out of here. I wish I'd never come here in the first place, I wish . . ."

He dropped into a chair, closed his eyes and rested his chin on clenched, white-knuckled fists that looked like marble. Then he finally nodded. "Yes, all I know is to wait until dark, put that stiff in the trunk of my car, take him somewhere and dump him."

She caught her breath and then said, "You're right. Yes—you do that. I'll leave now, and after it gets dark, you—" She saw him cast her a long and thoughtful stare. "Don't look at me like that, Alan. You make me feel guilty."

"Do I?"

"Alan—I *have* to leave here. I can't help it that soon Tom will be home, and that he'll be worried about me. He'll wonder where I am. He'll call the neighbors and our friends. How can I ever explain where I've been? It'll be late and dark and—"

"Funny," he said, "but suddenly I'm thinking about a rat leaving a sinking—"

"What do you expect me to *do*?" she cried.

"Nothing."

"But, Alan, you know I can't wait any longer."

He watched her silently as she walked to the window, parted the Venetian blinds a little and looked through. "The sun's going down," she said. "In winter, you know it gets dark early. You won't have long to wait."

"Thanks. That's most encouraging."

"Alan, where will you—put him?" she asked in a tight little voice.

"On your front porch. Where else?"

"Oh, Alan! You can't blame *me*. You can call Lisa and tell her you've been delayed, but I can't. There's no logical reason for me to be late. Tom would—"

"Look, he said, pointing a finger at her. "If I'm caught dumping that body . . ."

"Dammit," she said. "What do you want me to do?"

"Testify for me if I get caught," he told her. "That's what you can do."

"But you didn't kill that man, so they couldn't . . . *Could* they?"

"You think not? Carla, if I get caught dumping this body—or if his murder is traced to me—you're going to have to come forward and swear that we arrived in this room at exactly the same time. Understand? I don't want anybody to know that I got here before you did. Remember that."

"But then Tom will . . ." She stared at him while perspiration trickled down her forehead. "I can't believe it," she said. "I can't believe that all this is happening to me. Alan, if you cared for me, you wouldn't want me dragged into this horrible mess. You would try to protect me, keep my name out of it—if you loved me."

The air thickened with the heavy silence, and then he said, "Carla, whatever made you think that I did?"

"*Alan*!"

"For God's sake, what does that matter now? What does anything matter but to get ourselves out of this jam? I mean—we're in *real* trouble."

"It matters," she said slowly.

"Jesus! There's a dead man in that shower. There's no one to pin the blame on but us. *Us!* You and me!"

Carla's cheeks had turned from white to a fiery red, and

her voice rose as she said, "I'm getting out of here. Alan, don't call me. Don't try to contact me—ever—in any way. I'll never help you. You should have told me that you didn't love me. Do you know what I hope? I hope you burn in hell!"

She was gone, and he was staring at the door she had slammed behind her. He heard her start her car, kill the engine, start it again. He stood like a stone pillar as she drove away. Then he went outside, looked around swiftly and, seeing no one, opened the trunk of his car, pulled out a raincoat and hurried back into the motel room.

He went directly to the shower, reached inside, and dragged out the lifeless form. Hastily he wrapped his coat around it as he said, "We've done it again, good old George. Now it's back to the prop department for you."

Big Mouth

by Robert Edmond Alter

Hardesty had just got his eggs going well in the bacon fat with the three bacon strips crackling around them, when his old enamel-chipped coffee pot leaped off the rock and spilled itself, grounds and all, in the sand. Then he heard the flat *whap* of a rifle.

He sprawled in the sand beside the bullet-drilled pot and raised his head. About a hundred yards up the slope, west of his camp, was a hardwood ridge. He figured a good rifleman could get a clear shot at him from there. He hunched up his knees, preparing to crawl to his tent for his Winchester.

The second slug hit the smoking frying pan and sent it into a spin. Hardesty ducked his head away from the spattering fat. His eggs went all to runny goo when they hit the ground, and for a moment the pool of hot fat continued to sizzle and spit in the sand. He looked around as his canteen jumped with a *toomp* and started to bleed a silvery guzzle of water through its bullet wound.

Figured he missed me on that first shot, he thought. *But a man don't miss another man with a rifle three times running—not and hit a coffee pot and a frying pan and a canteen. Fella up there knows what he's doing.*

Hardesty knew what he was doing, too. Nothing. He was pinned down proper and there was nothing he could do except stay that way and wait his turn.

His enamel drinking cup was on his tin plate on top of the packing box he used as a table when he wasn't using it for something else, and he watched the cup spin away as the hidden rifle *whapped* again. *That was a good shot,* he thought. *A damn good shot.*

A tin of peaches, standing on the box next to the place where the cup had been, fell over with a moist *thop.* Next, a really sweet shot sent the tin plate skimming off in a crazy oblique, and finally a hole appeared in his dishwater-gray tent.

There was a sense of hesitation as he stared at the opening in the tent. Abruptly, the fore pole snapped in two and the forward section of the tent crumpled like a skirted old lady falling to her knees.

Figured so, Hardesty thought. *That lick he gave the tent flap was the first time he missed. Takes some shooter to pick off a tent pole at that distance.*

He craned his head to the left and looked down an alley of scrub at Shingles, his mule. *If he goes to drill her,* he thought, *then I'll kill him. Don't care what it takes, I'll get him.*

He started crawling towards the tent. He thought he had it figured now. It wasn't a killing; it was a joke, western style. Most of the Indians and the gunslingers and all the rest of that lawless bunch were long gone now, but occasionally you still came across a rowdy who was a hangover from those old ripsnorting badmen days—one of that wild restless breed who hadn't quite been able to make the transition from the nineteenth to the twentieth century.

They, the restless ones, went drifting across the plains daydreaming about the Kid and Jesse and Earp and, in the monotony of their frustrated loneliness, a sort of simple-minded, outraged madness gripped them, and they figured the only way they could assuage the fury was by busting loose. That's what the fella on the ridge was doing now, busting loose, giving himself a good laugh.

Thing was, though, Hardesty wasn't a joking man, had no sense of humor at all. He crawled up to his baggy tent as a bullet went *phut* in the sand right in his face, and he blinked and spat, and crawled on under the canvas and reached for his Winchester.

But the game was over. He could hear the muted *clack-clack* of hooves moving off down the stony draw beyond the hardwood ridge. He went over there, anyway, just for a look around. Didn't discover anything, though; no clue as to who had shot up his camp. The few U-shaped hoofprints in the sand told him nothing. And the prankster had had enough sense to gather up his empty cartridges.

Hardesty went back to camp to change to his town trousers and shirt and jacket.

He went to Stag, which he and all his isolated neighbors called "town." But it wasn't. It was simply a ramshackle landmark whose existence depended solely upon the needs of the men of the desert. It sold; it did not give. It did not have a church or any civic buildings or any homes. You either brought money to Stag or you stayed away. It had that much honesty.

Hardesty went into the store which had the sign "Post Office" tacked on it and answered, "Um-hm," when the storekeeper said, "Hello, Hard. How's the pickings?"

"Want a new coffee pot, pan, canteen, cup—"

"Getting yourself a new outfit, hey? You must've struck a pocket out there," the storekeeper said without a hope of an answer, because he knew Hardesty was an uncommunicative, if not inarticulate, man.

"Tent pole, too," Hardesty said, and he put down some money and turned on his heel and went through the open doorway into the adjoining saloon where four or five men were playing poker at a table.

They said, "Hello, Hardesty," and "Want to sit in?" and he nodded, saying, "Um-hm."

It was a quiet game, because that was the unintentional

influence the tall, gaunt, mute, mildly angry, deliberate man had on people. He had very little to say during the game. Sometimes he said, "A card," or "Check," or "Call," or "Raise."

The game shuffled and chipclicked through the coyote night and the black morning and the chill dawn, and then it broke up. Hardesty's luck had been in. He pocketed nearly $200. He didn't have anything to say about it.

He went over to the little hotel and said, "Want a room," saying nothing when the Mexican clerk said, "Joe tells me you got yourself a new outfit, Hard?" He went upstairs and gave himself a bath and a shave and went to bed.

It was dusk when he returned to the saloon. He bought himself a steak and a bottle and, for about an hour, he sat off in a shadow-pooled corner by himself and worked on the bottle. He left the saloon without any visible alteration in his taciturn disposition.

Hardesty hung around Stag for three days, nursing a few pints, playing a little poker. Then he paid off the hotel, collected his gear from the storekeeper, and he and Shingles went back to his claim.

Hardesty was hunkered over his fire and he had his eggs going, with the bacon fat popping around them, when he heard the *thup-thuppity-thup* of a rider coming. He looked up and watched the distant man and mount for a moment, and reached behind him and picked up his Winchester and leaned it against a rock near his right hand. After that, he shifted his gaze from the eggs to the rider, until the man was near enough for Hardesty to recognize. Then he ignored him.

It was Tope Jenkins, a young wrangler from over the ridge west of Hardesty's claim. The cowpoke slowed his bay to a dainty step and let her pick her way into the camp. He smiled amiably at Hardesty.

"Hidy, Hard. Coffee smells good."

"Um-hm."

"Hear you had some trouble last month, huh?" Tope said. "Stag folks tell me some joker shot up your camp for a laugh. Bet a quart it was one of them sheepmen south of the valley."

Hardesty had nothing to say. He lifted his crackling pan

from the fire and set it on a flat rock. Then he removed his hat and placed it crown down on the sand and picked up his Winchester and levered the cartridges into the hat. He leaned the empty rifle against the rock again, picked up the hat and scooped all the shells out of the hat and put them in his jeans.

Tope sat up there with his hands folded one on top of the other over the saddle horn, and watched him with a blank expression. Hardesty walked over to the bay and reached for Tope's rifle with a smooth, seemingly unhurried movement; drew it from the boot and stepped back and began levering the shells into the sand.

"Hey! What're you doing?"

Hardesty said nothing. He took the rifle by the barrel and raised it over his head and swung the stock against a rock. Then he pitched the barrel into the scrub.

"You crazy coot! What the hell you—" Tope shut up as the tall, gaunt, mute, quietly angry man walked back to him, rubbing his work-grained palms on the sides of his jeans. All at once those hands flashed upward and outward and caught Tope by the belt and levered backward and to the left, hauling him clear of the saddle and dumping him head-and-shoulders into the sand.

Hardesty slapped the nervously stepping bay with the flat of his hand, saying, "Git," and the bay bolted out of their way, rearing its head and backrolling its off eye.

Tope, outraged, spitting sand and wet curse words, got up on one knee and started accusing Hardesty of a vivid and varied list of vice.

Hardesty hit him in the face and nearly somersaulted him into the fire. He went after the wrangler, getting him by the front of his corduroy jacket and hauling him to his feet and planting a left deep in Tope's wind, jack-knifing him, and then straightened him up with a right uppercut and followed that with a left-cross, and Tope went into the sand again.

"You crazy old bastard! Why you poundin' *me*? What I ever done to *you*?"

"Because I never *told* nobody, damn you!" Hardesty cried, losing his temper at last. "You hear me, big mouth? I never told *nobody*!"

The Weathered Board

by Alvin S. Fick

Why they dug their pit at the base of the little hill I don't suppose we will ever know. Maybe it was because there was a scrub pine which provided a bit of shade, a rarity in this section of Wyoming range country where the land starts to rise in anticipation of making the mountains which divide the continent.

Perhaps they were just riding along and stopped to rest the horses. Or they might have been arguing for days, and this spot of dry and seared plains with its greasewood and black sage happened to be where the talk erupted into something more deadly. The territories were not tranquil places.

It could be they sat and smoked in the taciturn manner common to range hands, each hoping for a cooling of blood. But it was not to be. In the end they dug the pit in the loosest soil they could find, probably loosening it further with a piece of pointed rock and throwing the soil out with their hands. They both worked at it, shirts off and the sweat drying almost as soon as it surfaced on the skin. The wind blew little dust devils off the top of the pile of dirt beside the pit.

The sun was low and the shadows were long when they finished. The horses, restless now and eager to move on, nickered and pulled at the reins looped around a branch of the pine.

When the pit was chest-high in depth and oval in shape, they stopped digging. It is likely they climbed out to rest and smoke. When they got back in, they fought with knives, silently.

Only one man crawled out. He slid back in twice on top of the other man, for he was grievously hurt. The smell of blood spooked one of the horses. With a wild tossing of head and rolling of eye it broke loose. The man watched the spurts of dust rise from each hoofbeat as the mount ran off.

Some weeks later a rider drew rein at the spot where a small mound of stones, wrenched from the rib cage of the hill, marred the otherwise featureless aspect of the plain. He dismounted slowly, tethered his horse to the pine, and took down from the back of the saddle a board attached to a stake.

He worked with one hand. His right arm hung down, and swung loosely when he walked. A raw scar the color of fresh liver began at his temple, ran down the side of his jaw, under an ear, and disappeared beneath his collar. From time to time he stopped to rest, hunkered on his heels with his good hand pressed to his side under the nerveless arm. He had to prop up the stake with stones in order to drive the sharpened stake with a piece of rock held in his left hand.

When he was finished he rolled a cigarette, spilling two papers of tobacco down his shirt front before he succeeded. It hung unlighted in his mouth. He fished for a match but found none. It took him a long time to reach into his right-hand pants pocket with the good arm. The unsmoked cigarette still dangled from his lips when he rode off.

The section of the Wyoming territory where the men dug their pit is on the edge of the upper Sonoran continental life zone of North America. It is dry country, but it is almost on the verge of the Transitional zone. Sometimes rain washes the sage and the air has a clean sharp bite in the nose. You might come on the grave in the morning after just such a spring rain. Small bright blossoms of wildflowers will spangle the brown sod between the jagged rocks of the hillside.

Wood seldom rots in this dry land. If you ever find this lonely spot, you will still be able to read the legend carved into the weathered board nailed across the stake:

LAFE THOMAS
1882
HE LOST

Before you leave, be sure to notice how the drops of water on the needles of the little scrub pine catch the sunshine, breaking the light into glass-like shards which pierce the eye, even as a knife might pierce the heart.

Lot 721/XY258

by R. L. Stevens

It takes more than hatred to make a murderer.

William Willis had hated his wife almost from the day of their marriage seventeen years ago, but the thought of murder had never once crossed his mind. He was quite content to live out the days of his life without complaint, driving to the office each morning, returning each evening, and simply shutting his ears to the constant drone of her voice.

In her late thirties, Constance Willis had lost almost all the youthful beauty that had first attracted Willis to her in college. She was flabby of body and mind, hardly ever bothering to read a newspaper or pick up a book. Her days were spent in random shopping excursions with girl friends, at a weekly bridge club, and in countless hours on the telephone. But for all his hatred, William Willis had never thought of murder. In fact, he did not even think of divorce until he met Rita Morgan in the apartment downstairs.

Willis and his wife had no children, so they'd remained for many years in the pleasant garden apartment close to the downtown expressway. It was convenient to his office, and the surroundings had taken on the comfortable feeling of home. The apartment was one of the few things in their marriage that William and Constance agreed on.

When Rita Morgan moved into the apartment below

them, Willis' evenings and weekends immediately perked up. Rita was a twenty-five-year-old schoolteacher with long blonde hair and the sort of quiet beauty that couldn't have passed unnoticed even among her fifth-grade pupils. Willis helped her move in, carrying a few cartons of books up from her car, and they became friends immediately. She was everything he'd seen in Constance seventeen years before. But more important, she was intelligent and witty.

"Were you down in Rita's apartment again?" Constance asked one Saturday afternoon.

"One of her faucets was leaking," he explained. "It only needed a new washer."

"There's a janitor to take care of those things."

He sighed and opened a beer for himself. "You know she'd have to wait a month before he'd get around to it."

Constance grunted, but he knew she was unhappy about his attentions to Rita Morgan. She need not have worried quite so much, for Rita was a virginal young lady—at least as far as Willis was concerned—who treated him only with neighborly good will.

Nevertheless, it was Rita's presence on the scene that came first to Willis' mind when he read in the afternoon paper about the food contamination. A twelve-year-old boy had died of botulism in Chicago after eating canned peaches that had been improperly sterilized. As a rule, peaches were rarely affected by botulism, but these had been processed in a special manner, making them more susceptible to the deadly spores.

Reflecting on the blind fate that had killed the boy, he could not help speculating on a similar fate befalling Constance. Driving home that night, his recent daydreams of divorce and marriage to Rita shifted focus. Now he imagined Constance dead, killed by some trick of fate like an automobile accident or contaminated food.

Constance did not mention the news of the botulism scare, and it passed from his mind for the night. She kept up so little on current events that he'd often had to explain at length some happening on the foreign scene or some new face on the political horizon. Her interest in events, and in people other than her own circle of friends, had virtually ceased the day she left college to marry Willis.

But he was reminded again of the canned peaches when one of the secretaries at the office mentioned it. The afternoon paper had further details, including word that all of one lot was being recalled by the canner. Can o' Gold Fancy Prepared Peaches, lot 721/XY258.

Then the daydreams returned. He knew Constance ate canned peaches during the summer, often having them as part of her dessert. And he knew that she sometimes bought the Can o' Gold brand.

He poured over the newspapers that afternoon, even walking three blocks to a store where he knew he could buy a Chicago paper. He read more about the boy's death, and about the deadly effects of botulism poisoning, and the fantasy continued to grow in his mind. By the evening paper all Can o' Gold fruit products were being recalled, and consumers were being warned to avoid lot 721/XY258.

That evening at home, while Constance chatted on the telephone with some friend, William Willis glanced over the cupboard shelves, inspecting the canned goods. There were two cans of peaches, and one of them was Can o' Gold. His heart skipped a beat as he peered in at the lot number embossed on the lid. It was lot 721/XY258. Studying it more closely, he noticed that the can was bulging a trifle—an almost certain sign of gases produced by the bacterial activity inside.

There, standing on a shelf in the cupboard, was one of the deadly cans of peaches.

He said nothing to Constance, but that night in bed the possibilities paraded through his mind. All he had to do was say nothing, and sooner or later Constance would eat the contaminated peaches and die of botulism. Everyone would be most sympathetic. No one would suspect a thing.

And William Willis would be a free man.

He rolled over on his side and gazed into the darkness, thinking of Rita Morgan downstairs.

On his way out in the morning he saw Rita washing her car with a hose. "Hello, there," he called out. "I didn't think teachers ever got up this early in the summertime."

"I'm going on a picnic," she answered, beaming a smile his way. "Trying to get some of the dirt off this thing first."

"If I didn't have to go to work I'd help you out." He stood

chatting with her for another few moments, until he noticed Constance watching them from an upstairs window. "Gotta be going," he said finally. "Be seeing you."

That day in the office he tried not to think about it. But after lunch, while reading the latest newspaper account of the can recall, he let the idea of murder cross his mind.

If Constance died from eating those peaches, was he guilty of murder?

No, no—he refused to accept that. He had not even touched the can. Constance had purchased it, Constance would open it, Constance would eat it—possibly during the day when he wasn't even at home. How could it be his fault?

Accident. Or death by misadventure, as the British liked to say. But certainly not murder.

William Willis went back to work and tried not to think of the can of peaches waiting on the shelf for Constance.

When he got home that evening the first sight that greeted him was Constance sitting at the kitchen table eating peaches and ice cream.

"Won't that spoil your dinner, dear?" he asked a bit stiffly.

"It's too hot to cook dinner in the apartment. I thought we might just go out for a sandwich later. All right?"

On any other night he might have grumbled, but this evening he simply said, "Sure," and walked behind her back to the cupboard. The Can o' Gold peaches were still on the shelf. She was eating the other brand.

They talked very little that night and for the first time in many years he found himself getting through the hours with Constance without feeling the old hatred. When they returned from dinner, Rita came upstairs to borrow some milk, and Constance greeted her in a friendly fashion and even invited her in for coffee. Willis went to bed that night feeling good.

The feeling persisted the next day at the office and he wondered if he might be mellowing toward Constance. He made a point of buying the New York and Chicago newspapers, where the story of the botulism scare was still very much alive on the inner pages. One paper carried a detailed account of the boy's death agonies, of the gradual impairment of various parts of his brain until finally he simply stopped breathing. Willis read it grim-lipped, imagining

Constance as she might be during those long hours of dying.

He grabbed the telephone and dialed his home number, but the line was busy. She was chatting with a girl friend again.

His hands were trembling when he put down the phone, and he knew he must get a grip on himself. He'd been only an instant from warning her, from telling her of the contaminated can and thereby revealing the dark presumptions that had run through his mind. He must control himself. He was not a murderer. He was not even an instrument of chance.

And yet—if Constance died would he ever be able to look at himself in a mirror again? Would he ever be able to love Rita Morgan without the memory of Constance's death to haunt them?

He picked up the phone and dialed his number again. The line was still busy.

"I have to go home," he told his secretary. "Emergency."

He got the car out of the lot and headed for the expressway. It was nearly midafternoon and he knew she sometimes had her peaches about this time of the day. The drive home seemed longer than it had ever been at rush hours. Driving fast, almost recklessly, he imagined finding her stretched out dead on the kitchen floor—even though he knew from the newspaper articles that botulism took several hours to show its first symptoms.

He turned into the drive next to the apartment house and parked in his usual spot. The second-floor window of his apartment seemed the same, the place itself seemed unchanged. Perhaps he'd made the drive for nothing, and he'd have to explain it to Constance. And somehow get that can out of the house.

"Dear! I'm home early!"

There was no answer and he went into the kitchen seeking her. The first thing he saw was the open, empty, discarded can of Can o' Gold Fancy Prepared Peaches by the sink. That, and an empty dish, with its dirty spoon and telltale juices.

"Constance!"

She appeared then, coming from the bathroom. Her face

was pale and somehow a little strange. "What are you doing home?" she asked.

"I wasn't feeling well."

"Oh."

"Constance, did you eat those peaches?"

She glanced at the empty dish and the discarded can by the sink. Then her eyes met his and there was something in them he'd never seen before.

"Oh, no, dear. That nice Miss Morgan came up to borrow something, and she stayed and chatted, and I persuaded her to have a little snack."

Thirteen

by Edward D. Hoch

Renger looked up from the crude map on the table before him and studied the newcomer with critical eyes. "You're Hallman?"

"That's right."

"They tell me you're a good man with a gun."

"I get by."

"Then I guess you're the man we need for this job. Ever used an automatic carbine?"

"Plenty of times."

"Like this one?" Renger asked, bringing out a new Plainfield carbine very much like the standard military weapon. "It uses thirty-shot clips. All right?"

"Fine." Hallman glanced around at the five other men in the room. The only one he knew was Asmith, a part-time heroin pusher who'd been in and out of prison. He nodded to him and waited for Renger to introduce the others.

"That's Crowthy and Evans and Asmith and Galliger and Yates. A damn good team for this job. But we needed a good man with a gun—somebody who's not afraid to use it."

"That's me," Hallman said. He had earned the reputation.

"Good! We'll have smoke bombs and stuff, but I'm not kidding myself that we're going to get in there without killing a few people."

"What about guards?" Hallman asked. "And patrol cars?"

Renger pushed back his graying hair and stabbed at the map with a pencil. "The only guard you need to worry about is right here. Take him out and it's smooth sailing. Now, a patrol car comes down this street about once every hour. We're timed to miss it, but we can't be sure. All I can tell you is that Crowthy here will be covering you from across the street. If the patrol car surprises us, you'll have to deal with it."

"I understand," Hallman said.

"Your job is to take out this guard, get into the place, and fire a few shots. Create confusion. Make them think we've got a whole army out here. Then I'll toss a few smoke bombs and the rest of us will move in."

Asmith spoke up from his corner. "What about the getaway?"

"We'll leave the truck at this point and go the rest of the way on foot. Afterwards each of you will have to get back to the truck on your own. Evans will stay with the truck as a lookout. But at ten o'clock we pull out. Anyone not back to the truck by ten, we figure they're caught. Any questions?"

As they went over the plan step by step, Hallman found his attention wandering. He was twenty-four years old, and already he had the reputation of being good with a gun. Anyone who bothered to check his record would know he was equally good with a knife. The first man he'd ever killed had been with a knife, and he still remembered the expression of shock in the man's eyes as Hallman's blade slid deep between his ribs.

That was the way it had been the other times, too, though he remembered that first one best of all. Sometimes he had not even seen the men he'd killed. They'd merely been figures to be gunned down at a distance, or sometimes men to be blown up in their beds by a well-tossed bomb. And people knew that Hallman was an expert. They came to Hallman when the killing had to be neat and swift and efficient.

"All right," Renger said. "It's set, then. We go at dawn."

The men nodded silently and left the room. There was very little conversation, and Hallman was glad of that. He was not much of a talker.

The early morning was usually best for a job of this sort, Hallman had discovered. It was especially good if you could hit a place just a few minutes before eight, when people were arriving for the day's work. The patrol cars were generally off the road then, too, changing crews for the day tour.

This morning was especially good, because a light mist from the river hung over the streets of the town. Evans had parked the truck an hour earlier, and they'd come the rest of the way on foot, moving singly to avoid attracting attention. The town was quiet, with only a few people moving about, when Hallman poked his head around a tree across the street from their target.

The first thing he saw was the uniformed guard by the gate. He seemed to know everyone who entered, though occasionally he glanced at a pass when it was held out to him. The holstered revolver at his side presented no difficulty to Hallman, who could have, if necessary, killed the man from across the street.

Hallman broke from cover and walked directly toward the guard, carrying the carbine casually in his left hand, pointed at the ground. The man didn't notice him until he was almost up to him, and then the guard's hand dropped uncertainly to the holstered revolver. "You need a pass here," he said. "A pass."

Hallman smiled and kept walking toward the man, as if he didn't understand the language. When he was close enough he brought his right arm up quickly to the guard's throat, plunging his knife deep into the flesh. The man went down with the gurgling sound they always made. Already, before the guard hit the ground, Hallman swung his automatic carbine up to cover the doorway ahead of him, and that was almost a fatal mistake.

From behind him he heard Crowthy shout a warning,

and he whirled to see the patrol car traveling fast down the street. They'd already spotted him and screeched to a stop. Crowthy fired a quick wild shot and retreated toward the woods. Two officers jumped out of the car and one of them fired three rapid shots at Crowthy's retreating back. Hallman saw him topple in the dirt as Hallman brought his own weapon up. He fired a quick burst, dropping one officer in his tracks as the other dived behind the patrol car. A third man, the driver, started out his side and then fell back, bleeding from the shattered windshield.

Hallman moved backward into the building, firing as he went, and saw the second officer fall over. Then he was inside, running down a dingy hallway, ramming another 30-shot clip into the weapon. He hoped the others would be coming soon.

A man appeared ahead of him at the end of the passage, like a pop-up target in a shooting gallery, and Hallman sprayed him with bullets. Then he ran on, into the first room, firing quick shots to clear the way. He'd got the rhythm of it now, the half-forgotten feel for killing that left him at times but always returned.

In the second office a screaming woman was hunched in one corner, covering her face. Hallman paused only an instant, and then fired a short burst into her body. She slid down the wall, torn and bleeding and already without life. She was the first woman he'd ever killed, and he was surprised at how little it bothered him.

He smashed out the window in a front room, seeking the others, and saw two more uniformed guards running around the front of the building. He fired fast, cutting them both down with a line of bullets across their backs. Then he saw the others break from the cover of the trees. Renger was in the lead, running with his gun ready, and he hurled a smoke bomb as he crossed the road. Then someone on the floor above cut loose with three quick shots and Hallman saw Yates stagger and go down in the street, just before the smoke obscured him.

Hallman found the stairs and started up. A figure appeared at the top and Hallman let go with the rest of the clip. Before he could reload, a second man fell on him with a roar, toppling him backward halfway down the steps. He felt the carbine slide away from him, but he rolled over and managed to get his knife out. He plunged it into the fleshy man's side, heard his grunt of pain, and plunged it again. The man went suddenly limp, and Hallman rolled his body down the stairs.

There was shooting below him now, and he knew Renger and the others were past the gate. He made it the rest of the way to the top of the stairs, finding his weapon and then reloading it as he climbed. He burst through the door at the top landing and killed the man at the window with a sudden spray of bullets. Two others—short, frightened men—raised their hands and backed against the wall. Hallman shot them both.

He could feel the warmth of blood on his lower lip now, and he realized the man on the stairs had landed some damaging punches. But there was no pain. The exhilaration of the moment had blotted it out. He glanced out the window, but the smoke was too thick to see anything.

Leaning against the wall, he tried to remember how many he'd killed. The guard, and at least two of the three in the patrol car, and the man in the passage. And the woman. The two guards out the window. And the two on the stairs. And three in this room. That made twelve, in just under five minutes. Fast work. Good work.

He took out his knife again and made sure they were dead. He was on his last clip of bullets, so he couldn't waste any more. Then he heard someone coming up the stairs, calling his name. It was Renger, carrying two suitcases. Hallman licked the blood from his lip, savoring it, and went to meet him.

"You did a damn good job," Renger told him. "You're a regular one-man army!"

"I said I was good with a gun. How many men did we lose?"

"Crowthy and Yates. The others are all right. Let's plant these explosives and get the hell out of here!"

They did their job, working fast, and then left the building with the others.

"Damn!" Renger said as they started across the muddy road toward the shelter of the woods. "I'm going to see that you get a medal for this, Hallman!"

"Thank you, Major."

"When they hear back home how you led an attack on the enemy's forward command post and helped destroy it, almost single-handed, they'll make you a hero. How many did you kill?"

"Twelve."

"Damn good shooting!"

They passed the enemy patrol car, parked at a crazy angle on the road, and Hallman saw that the driver was still alive, gasping for breath behind the shattered windshield. He raised his carbine with one hand and killed the man with a single shot.

"That makes thirteen," he said, and walked on.

Operative 375

by Gary Brandner

When the creature walked in the office door, Gus Blattner stopped cranking the printer and stared. The apparition wore a trench coat and a thrift-shop fedora pulled low over a pair of orange eyebrows. The eyes and mouth were concealed behind purple shades and an unlikely black moustache.

"Aren't you supposed to say trick or treat?" said Gus.

With a flourish the trench-coated figure whipped off the hat, glasses, and moustache to reveal a grinning young man with orange hair to match the eyebrows. He stepped to the counter and announced, "I'm Dudley McBean."

"So?"

"This *is* the Universal Academy of Investigation, isn't it?"

"Yeah," Gus admitted.

"Well, I'm Dudley McBean," the young man repeated. "Operative 375."

Gus wiped his hands across his ink-smudged sweat shirt. "I think you better talk to my partner," he said and retreated to the rear of the office and into a plywood-partitioned cubicle. Inside, a round-faced man sat at a card table with a pile of envelopes in front of him. He was slitting these open with a nail file and removing cash and checks, which he stacked in tidy piles.

Gus said, "Secret Agent X-9 or somebody like that is out front. I've got a terrible feeling it's one of our students."

"What does he want here?" asked the man at the desk.

"How would I know? I'm just the muscle in this operation. All I do is crank the stupid machine."

"Don't sulk, partner," the other man said. "You know how important it is that we keep turning out the lesson booklets. I would gladly spell you out at the machine, were it not for my old lacrosse injury. Shoulder stiffens right up."

"I'd just like to get out of here once in a while, even if it's only to go to the post office."

"Now, Gus, the only reason I pick up the mail is because I have to be out anyway making the necessary personal contacts. That is, after all, my specialty. Besides, what difference does it make how we split up the work? The money goes fifty-fifty, and take a look at what came in just today. You never did this good sticking up gas stations."

"Ah, don't mind me," Gus said. "I'm on edge from worrying about Natalie. I think she's playing games with some other guy. If I could just catch her at it, then I could kill both of them and get it off my mind."

The other man stood up and walked around the table to clap his partner on the shoulder. "That's the curse of being married to a beautiful woman," he sympathized. "While I go out and talk to our visitor, you sit down and count some money. Maybe that will help cheer you up."

Adjusting his butterfly bow tie, the round-faced man left the cubicle and strode to the counter where Dudley McBean waited, smiling hopefully.

"Good afternoon, my friend. I'm Colonel Homer Fritch. What can I do for you?"

"Pleased to meet you, sir. I'm Dudley McBean." The young man waited for a reaction, got none, and went on. "Operative 375. From Snohomish. I took your course in how to be a private detective."

"Of course!" Colonel Fritch exclaimed. "From

Snohomish. One of our very best students. What brings you to Los Angeles, Dudley? You *do* know that our classes are strictly home study?"

"Oh, yes, sir. But now that I've completed the course, I wanted to come down in person to pick up my solid bronze investigator badge and handsome embossed diploma. I brought the extra ten dollars for handling, like it said in your ad in *Fearless Action* magazine."

The colonel searched the guileless blue eyes for a trace of mockery. Finding none, he said, "I think I can fix you up, young man." He reached under the counter and brought up a badge in the shape of a shield with an eagle perched aggressively on top. It bore the words *Official Private Investigator.* Colonel Fritch laid it reverently in front of Dudley. "Wear it with pride," he said. Reaching down again, he produced a printed sheet of stiff paper. "There wasn't time to have your name embossed on it, but if I may borrow your pen I'll take care of that. I have been told I write a very fine hand."

Dudley passed over a ballpoint pen, and the colonel carefully stroked the young man's name in the blank space on the diploma. He added a touch of rococo scrollwork and slid it across the counter.

"There you are, my boy, and godspeed back to Snoqualamie."

"It's Snohomish, Colonel Fritch, and I'm not going back."

"You're not?"

"No, sir. I figure there are probably more opportunities in the detective business here in Los Angeles than there would be back home."

"I daresay. Now, if you'll excuse me . . ."

"So I'd like to get the free job-placement assistance like it said in your ad."

"Hmm, yes, right your are. Sharp-eyed lad. Very promising. I'll take care of that right now."

The colonel tore a sheet out of a spiral notebook and wrote rapidly:

This will introduce Mr. Dudley McBean. He has my personal recommendation for a position as Private Investigator.

Col. Homer Fritch

"There you are, my boy," he said. "Just take this note to

any of the larger detective agencies in town and they'll have you out on a case before you can say Continental Op."

"I don't know how to thank you, Colonel."

"Tut-tut, lad. Good luck to you and good-bye."

With the new badge pinned discreetly inside his lapel, Operative 375 cinched up the belt of his trench coat and replaced the hat, shades, and moustache. "Lesson Eight—The Art of Disguise," he explained, and slipped furtively out of the office.

Colonel Fritch sighed heavily and headed back to the plywood cubicle. Gus Blattner came out to meet him.

"Didn't you lay it on a little thick?" Gus said.

"It doesn't do any harm," the colonel said, "and it made the boy feel good."

"How will he feel when he finds out that your name at the legitimate detective agencies carries about as much weight as Daffy Duck?"

The colonel shrugged. "I am afraid the young man will be disillusioned, but he will have learned one more valuable lesson—Be Wary of Strangers."

"That won't help much when the cops come for us."

"There is nothing to fear from the police. We have made good, to the letter, on all offers put forth in our advertisement. Try to remember, Gus, that we are honest businessmen, so stop your worrying."

"Sure, if you say so," Gus muttered, and resumed cranking the machine.

The next afternoon the colonel and Gus were stuffing handsome embossed diplomas into mailing envelopes when Dudley McBean entered their office again—undisguised this time.

"Hello, there," the colonel said coolly. "I didn't expect to see you back here."

"I think I need more assistance," Dudley said. "I took my diploma and your personal note to every detective agency in the Yellow Pages. Some of them laughed at me, and the others weren't that polite."

"I'm sorry to hear that, my boy, but I've done all I can for you."

"So I decided to go into the business on my own," Dudley continued, as though there had been no interruption.

"I see. Well, best of luck." The colonel returned to stuffing diplomas.

"I thought you might want to put up the money to get me started."

The jaws of Gus Blattner and Colonel Fritch dropped in unison, and they stared at the orange-haired young man. When the colonel found his voice, he said, "What gave you that preposterous idea?"

"It would be a good investment for you," Dudley said. "I've learned a lot about detective work. For instance, how do you think I found your office? All the ad gave was a post office box number."

Colonel Fritch started to answer, then his eyes grew suddenly thoughtful and he turned to his partner. "Gus," he said, "how about running down to the stationer's for some more of these envelopes?"

"What for? We got two boxes in the back."

"It wouldn't hurt to have two more."

"Oh, all right," Gus grumbled, and walked around the end of the counter and out the door.

When he was alone with Dudley, the colonel asked, "Tell me, my boy, how *did* you find our office?"

"Lesson Three," Dudley said proudly, "Shadowing and Surveillance. I waited at the post office until somebody—it turned out to be you—came to pick up the mail from the box. Then I trailed you, just for practice."

"Very enterprising."

"But you didn't come straight here from the post office. You stopped at an apartment on Franklin Avenue where you visited a blonde lady for one hour and twenty-two minutes."

The colonel dabbed at his forehead with a crisp white handkerchief. "Dudley," he said, "I have reconsidered and decided to finance you after all. If you will step back into my private office, we will discuss the terms."

"I sure appreciate that, Colonel Fritch," the young man said. "Some coincidence, isn't it, how that blonde lady has the same last name as your partner."

He'll Kill You

by Richard Deming

I said, "I think I'd better report Ellen missing tomorrow. If we wait any longer, the police may think it strange."

Margot's freckled face spread in the grin I had grown to love. She always laughed when I mentioned Ellen, and while I loved the sound of her deep, good-humored laughter, her jollity on this subject upset me. I suppose humor was the sanest attitude toward Ellen's departure, and I for one certainly felt no regrets, but somehow Margot's laughter indicated a lack of delicacy I would not have expected from her.

It was the laughter and the wide, unaffected grin that first drew me to Margot. When we moved to Bradford, the faculty house assigned us was next door to hers, and my study window looked directly into the broad windows of Margot's sun room, where she kept her phone. She was fond of phone gossip, and often I would see her there, her sun-freckled face animated with laughter, and one lean, strong hand making wide gestures as she talked. When she phoned Ellen I particularly enjoyed watching her, for in the hall I could hear Ellen's part of the conversation, and from Ellen's words and Margot's gestures, sometimes piece together what Margot was saying.

Almost from the first we were attracted to each other—as early as the faculty tea given in my honor as the new head of the English Department. Miss Rottell, the dean of women, introduced us, saying in her precise, inhibited drawl, "Professor Brandt, Miss Margot Spring. She's Music," and moving away to leave us together.

I remember bowling formally and saying, "An appropriate name, my dear. You have the look about you of nature's fairest season."

She laughted. Why, Professor! I do believe you're a romantic."

It started as simply as that, and grew as the months passed into a deep but quiet love. Oh, on the surface we were merely good-natured friends, for in a college town gossip can be fatal to careers, and Margot chose to accept my compliments as laugh-provoking jokes, even when no one was nearby to hear. I too was meticulously careful to arouse no comment. Not once did I even so much as kiss her on the cheek, restraining my physical love-making to an occasional accidental touch—my fingers brushing against her hair when I held her coat as she prepared to leave after a visit with Ellen, or lightly managing to touch her hand as I passed her a cup at a faculty tea.

But the depth of understanding that springs from mature love made my innocent words and gestures as meaningful to Margot as though I held her in my arms, just as her apparently joking replies had a meaning for me that a less perceptive nature might have missed entirely. As a matter of fact, it was best that no one aside from me understood her sublety, for she had a breathtaking flair for danger and seemed to love making me shudder at the risks she took. She had a trick of brazenly stating her true thoughts as though they were rather clumsy jokes, such as the time she lightly remarked to Ellen, when Ellen first began to plan her visit home, "You better hurry back again, or you may find I've stolen your romantic husband." But Ellen only laughed, and I pretended Margot's remark was a great joke.

I waited until two days prior to Ellen's scheduled departure before even mentioning what opportunities her absence would leave us, and even then I brought it up to Margot casually. But she surprised me with the blunt frankness of her reply.

"It's too bad Ellen means to stay only two weeks," I remarked.

"Ask her to stay a month," Margot said. "I'm sure if you explained you wanted to elope with your next-door neighbor, Ellen would be glad to cooperate."

Margot's habit of affixing a completely fantastic suggestion to a sensible statement was another twist her odd sense of humor sometimes took, and I knew of course she had no expectation of my explaining any such thing to Ellen.

I asked, "Would you like it if she stayed away permanently?"

"You mean bury her body in the cellar?" She dropped her voice to a conspiratorial whisper. "Is there enough insurance to finance our honeymoon?"

I said patiently, "I meant ask her to get a divorce."

"And have a campus scandal?" Somehow she managed to grin and look horrified at the same time. "No, Theodore. The safest way is the cellar." She closed one eye and made a cutting motion across her throat.

I said, "I've never even killed a chicken."

"There's nothing to it," Margot said. "Read the papers. Husbands do it all the time. I'll phone Ellen tonight and ask her to stand still."

"Now please don't make clever comments to Ellen," I told her. "I know Ellen misses the double meaning of your jokes, but it's an unnecessary risk."

But Margot disobeyed my request when she phoned Ellen that evening. From my study I could see Margot's wide smile and loosely gesturing hand, and in the hall behind me I could hear Ellen's restrained laughter.

"It amazes me that you find Theodore so excruciating," Ellen said. "I've never been able to detect the slightest sense of humor in him."

I knew then that Margot was brazenly describing our conversation to Ellen, and even though Ellen was obviously enjoying it as a joke, I was irritated at Margot for indulging her bizarre sense of humor against my specific request.

It was a week after Ellen's trip was supposed to have started that I suggested to Margot I inform the police I had not heard from her. We sat in my study sipping a Sunday afternoon cup of tea.

"You've never shown me where you buried the body," Margot said, grinning across her cup like a good-natured spaniel.

I said, "I thought you'd rather not know. However, come along. I'll show you."

I rose and led the way through the house with Margot chattering behind me. Getting my flashlight from the kitchen, I preceded her down the cellar steps.

Holding my flash on the floor behind the furnace, I indicated the freshly laid cement. "There," I said simply.

She turned toward me, a peculiar expression beginning to form on her face, and all at once she was so desirable my restraint fell away and I took her in my arms. She stood stiff but unresisting when I kissed her, and her lips were cool.

Immediately I realized it was a mistake to let down the barriers so soon, and the wisest course was to retain our surface amiability until the police lost interest in the case. I moved back a step, bowed and apologized.

Margot's stiffened face gradually drained to the color of paper. It was an interesting example of delayed psychological reaction. Obviously the sight of fresh cement for the first time fully impressed on her what we had done, and that it was not a matter for laughter.

She climbed the stairs ahead of me slowly, swaying slightly from shock. When we reached the parlor, she turned to face me and her expression was a study in terror. Without a word, she took her coat and stumbled toward the door.

From my study window I can see her talking on the phone now. But her boyish face is not laughing as usual and that eloquent hand is strangly still. Her expression is one of dull horror, and I am worried that she may transmit some of her feeling to whichever of her innumerable friends she is phoning. But she loves the phone, and perhaps a little womanly gossip will help cure the delayed shock reaction.

I wish she would grin.

Caveat Emptor

by Kay Nolte Smith

The wish first occurred to Judson Wick while he was attending the opera.

An opera box was not his normal milieu, but he could not pass up the chance to escort the elderly widow who glittered with diamonds and influence; so, masking his lack of interest and knowledge, he kept an attentive look on his handsome, if rather bland, face and bent his sleek, dark head in response to the widow's frequent nudges. It was during such a moment, when he did focus on the performance, that the wish occurred to him. He smiled ruefully and dismissed it.

It came back to him the next day, during his yearly lunch with the manager of Wick Industries. The man always recited lists of figures—this year they showed the declining value of the company's stock—and reminisced at irritating length about the years when Judson's father had built and run the company. It was Judson's practice to keep his manner aloof and unconcerned; but this time, when the manager made pointed references to "the leisurely life," the manner began to show fine cracks, like battered safety glass—until the moment was saved by the sudden return of the wish.

That evening it returned once more when, as a guest of the director, Judson attended the opening of a Broadway play and the party that followed. He ate smoked oysters and listened while the rave reviews were read aloud; over the rim of his champagne glass he watched the director, with whom he had gone to school, standing in the spotlight of success, and the wish came back so forcefully that the champagne soured in his throat and he left the party.

He barely had returned to his apartment when the doorbell rang. His spirits lifted at the thought that the red-haired actress had changed her mind about a nightcap, but the person at the door was not female, and the hair was quite gray. The suit was gray too, in both color and spirit, drooping on the man's shoulders and rounding over his knees. Everything about him seemed tired and sad except for his tie, a strip of vivid orange silk that ran down his shirtfront like a tongue of flame. "Good evening," he said. "I am advised by my firm that you have some property for sale."

"I think you've got the wrong apartment."

"I think not. You are Judson A. Wick, you are forty-one years old, and you are interested in selling the balance."

"Of what?" asked Judson cautiously.

"Last night you attended Gounod's opera and made a wish, which you have repeated twice. Therefore you are requesting an arrangement similar to Doctor Faust's. May I come in?"

Judson moved aside mechanically while his mind struggled for comprehension. "I think you're putting me on."

"Mr. Wick," sighed the man, "if I were not what I claim to be, how could I have known about your wish?"

"I don't know," said Judson finally. "But you don't look the part. Who ever heard of you as the man in the gray flannel suit?"

"But I am just a salesman, a mere servant of the firm. Call me John, if you like." The man shot his cuffs and smoothed his tie. "This is the twentieth century, Mr. Wick. We are no longer a Middle Ages barter service but a modern business corporation. Naturally we don't ask you to take us on faith. We offer, in fact we insist upon, a twenty-four-hour period in which you sample our merchandise free of charge, with no further obligation. Now, for what did you wish to negotiate? Power? Knowledge? Eternal Youth?" When Judson frowned, he added, "Then there is our most popular offer, Fame and Influence."

"Ah," said Judson. "Yes."

"In which field would you want it?"

Judson shrugged. "I wouldn't care. No, wait a minute." Into his mind bubbled the memory of champagne and rave reviews. "Make it show business. Broadway. No, make it bigger. Hollywood."

The man took out a small, gray pad, made a note, and rose. "When you wake up tomorrow, the twenty-four hours will begin. Incidentally, we'll be observing you, to insure that satisfaction is achieved. Then I return at the end of the period, with a contract for you to sign."

Judson's gaze wavered and slid around the room. "All right," he said finally. "What have I got to lose?"

Something flickered for a moment in the man's gray eyes, like matches at the ends of two tunnels. Then the orange tie dimmed out, and he was gone.

When Judson awoke at ten, he heard a voice that seemed to be located in his ear. "Good morning," it said in metallic, asexual tones. "The observation has begun. We are ready to grant your wishes." After a moment there was an odd sensation inside Judson's head: a faint, not unpleasant, echoing, rather as if someone were listening on a telephone extension. "They mean it," he said softly. "What the hell do you know about that?"

The words made him smile; he lay in bed for some moments grinning, but finally he began to consider what his requests should be. Self-consciously at first, because he was aware of the inner listener, and then with growing pleasure in the fact of an audience, he thought of some of the important film people he had met in the past, during the years when he had been married to Shelley and she had not yet catapulted to fame. He could, he thought, choose to be like any of them—to be one of those who moved on the edges of the limelight but in the center of power, or even to be an actor, perhaps the top male box office star in the country. Or the world.

The pale green phone on his nightstand rang. In a rather puzzled voice a man introduced himself as a reporter from *Variety*, said he had just heard there was an important story to be gotten from a Judson Wick, and inquired what it might be.

It took all of Judson's skill to convince the man there was a story but that it could not be divulged yet; when he hung up, he was sharply aware that the inner listener was still listening. He got into the shower and made a careful list of people he might call, narrowing it to three, one of whom was his director friend of the night before, but finally rejecting all of them. While he was shaving, the thought that Shelley was in town promoting her latest picture kept pulling at his mind. He nicked his chin, swore, and suddenly laughed aloud: why should he worry about finding an excuse to call? Shelley would call him—if he wished.

When he reached the restaurant two hours later, Shelley was just arriving in a cloud of reporters. He detached her and led her to a table, where he insisted that she talk about her new film throughout their first drink. "All right," she finally said. "I'm the one who called you, God knows why, so I must want to hear what you've been up to all these years."

He took her hand, and a deep breath; it seemed to him that the interest of the inner listener had quickened. Picking his way among the words, he said, "I'm on to something big. Very big. Something that's going to lead me straight to your town."

"Something in pictures, you mean?"

"What else do you do in Hollywood?"

"But you don't know anything about the industry."

"Shelley," he said softly, "I'll be able to do anything I want. Anything."

She studied him, her violet eyes narrowing to points of black light. "Are you serious? You're going to produce a picture?"

"Yes, I guess you could say that. Of course. That's what I'm going to do."

"What picture?"

He raised a hand for the waiter, wishing for him to come immediately, and ordered more drinks. Then he leaned back and said carefully, "Let's put it this way. I'm in the market for ideas."

"Are you? That's a coincidence." Shelley tapped her glass slowly with one mauve and perfect nail. "There's a book that Global is planning to buy for Lisa Gordon. But it would be so right for me. If someone else got it, that is. If someone else were able to get it."

"That's a coincidence." He smiled boyishly, the smile she used to say she liked. "Because what I had in mind was to make a great picture for Shelley."

When he returned to his apartment, there were eighteen

hours left of the twenty-four. Despite the successful lunch, there was a fist of tension at the back of his neck that would not uncurl. He made a martini and sat staring down at its olive eye. Then he picked up the phone and called the elderly widow whom he had escorted to *Faust*. Adopting the bantering manner she liked, he inquired about the charity ball she was staging, automatically wangled an invitation, and finally extracted the true object of his call, a telephone number.

He dialed it, adjusting his mental posture to one of deference; to the famous film critic who answered, he posed as a graduate student researching the adapting of novels to the screen. He sought the critic's opinion of several recent films, and then casually mentioned the novel Shelley had suggested. When the critic spoke of it enthusiastically, he asked, in a casual, speculative manner, which writers and directors would be most capable of translating such a property to the screen. He hung up with a half smile that could not seem to grow; he sat fingering the back of his neck, and told himself that he needed to get out.

An hour later he headed for an art gallery on Madison Avenue. The crowd at the opening was already so dense that there was no way, or need, to see the paintings; he thrust himself in among the bodies and soon had collected enough comments to deliver them to the artist as if they were his own tribute. Then he was free to turn to the real business of the evening.

Moving among the crowd with studied aimlessness, he talked to a Senator's mistress and the president of a Fifth Avenue store, telling them that he was going to make a film; the sudden interest in their eyes became a glint in his own. He told the wives of three industrialists that Shelley Garnett would be starring in his picture; the warmth in their voices became a cool assurance in his own. He told two art critics of the major literary property he was going to buy and the screenwriter and director he planned to hire; the attentiveness in their manner became a certainty in his own veins.

By nine o'clock the crowd had thinned, but its power was still with him. With the insolence of confidence, he attached himself to the painter and to the man's plans for dinner with a few influential clients.

When he got home at two o'clock, he did not know

whether his exultation was the racing of his own pulse or the throbbing attention of the inner listener. He paced the living room in wide, jagged arcs; finally he took a sleeping pill and forced himself to lie on the bed.

Around five o'clock his staring eyes closed, but behind their lids a dream began almost at once: at the end of a flame-colored carpet, down which he walked for dozens of triumphant yards, he was greeted by a massive figure in red.

John wiped his face with a gray handkerchief and turned to the last entry in his notebook. He was making his daily report to the gentleman known simply as M, who sat behind a battered desk in an office that had seen better centuries. M wore a gray cape as thin as smoke, and a chronic scowl.

"Merchandise check on Judson A. Wick," John read. "Requested Fame and Influence. Field: none. When pressed, subject chose the film industry, a desire inspired by watching a friend's success. Here is the printout on his mental processes: Settled on becoming a producer, a notion which he got from his ex-wife. Decided to produce a certain novel, an idea which came from the same source. Determined that the novel was brilliant, by checking the opinion of a noted film critic. Selected a screenwriter and director, names he also got from the critic. Subject ended the trial period feeling confident and self-assured, a state which he induced by seeking out the reactions of influential persons at a fashionable cultural event."

M glowered. "Do you mean there wasn't even one of his own? Not one opinion or desire?"

"No, all were derived from other people. I believe he even got the idea of selling his soul from the Gounod opera."

"Damnation!" roared M. "There are too many like him! They're ruining my business! I need some kind of consumer protection. It's fraud, that's what it is—people trying to sell me borrowed merchandise. If I didn't check them out first, they'd bankrupt me." He sighed, in a shower of sparks. "Why are the ones without a soul of their own always the most eager to sell?"

John smiled wryly. "I'll have the incident erased from Wick's mind."

"What mind?" snarled M. "Just suppose I took people

like that. Where's my profit? Where's my pleasure? Turn them into servants, procurers of other souls, and they'd feel right at home. No agony at all." His glance darted hotly over John's face. "Not like you, eh, Doctor?"

"No, not like me."

"Well," sighed M, "get back out into the field. And see if you can find me someone like you. Someone with clear title to his property."

Something in the depths of John Faust's eyes glowed in pain for a moment. Then he closed his notebook and left the office wearily and sadly.

The Facsimile Shop

by Bill Pronzini
and Jeffrey Wallman

James Raleigh had just finished stenciling with gilt spray paint the words *The Facsimile Shop* on the narrow front window when the two men came in.

Raleigh, a plump jovial man with silvering hair, wiped his hands on a chamois cloth and approached them, smiling politely. It was almost three o'clock now and they were the first customers of his first day. "Gentlemen," he said, "May I assist you?"

Neither man spoke immediately. Their eyes were making a slow circumspect inventory of the small shop, taking in the copy of Sesshu's Winter Landscape on the wall beside the door, the gold-painted, delicately amber-inlayed replica of Pectoral of Lioness from Kelermes, the fake gold and ivory Cretan Snake Goddess from the Sixteenth Century B.C., the imitation Egyptian Seated Scribe, of red-hued limestone—each of which, among other items, adorned the single row of display shelves in the center of the shop.

The taller of the two men, dressed in a conservative gray sharkskin suit and a pearl-gray snapbrim hat, picked up the Seated Scribe and rotated it in his hands. He had craggy features and a cleft chin, and he studied the synthetic work of art with cool hazel eyes. After a moment he said conversationally, "Nice bit of craftsmanship."

Raleigh nodded, smiling. "Its prototype dates back to 2500 B.C."

The man looked at him quizzically. "Prototype?"

"Why, yes. You see, everything in my shop is a facsimile of the original *objet d'art.* I specialize in genuine imitations—sculptures, paintings, and the like."

"In other words, junk, Harry," the second man said affably. He wore a Glen Plaid suit that was cut too tight across the shoulders and a green felt hat with a small red feather in the band. His nose had been broken at one time and improperly set, and his ears were large and distended.

"Now, Alex," Harry said in a mild voice, "that's no way to talk."

"Sure," Alex said. He looked at Raleigh. "What's your name, pal?"

Raleigh did not care for the man's tone, but he said, "James Raleigh. Really, gentlemen, if there is something I can—"

The man called Harry continued to study the Seated Scribe, frowning thoughtfully. Finally he glanced at the other man. "What do you think?"

Alex shrugged.

"How much is it, Mr. Raleigh?"

"Forty-nine ninety-five."

"Alex?"

"Too damned expensive."

"I believe you're right," Harry said. He turned toward the display shelves, and then seemed to spread his hands, allowing the sculpture to fall at his feet. It shattered with a dull hollow sound on the hardwood floor.

Raleigh stared down at the shards, feeling heat rise in his cheeks. It became quiet in the shop. At length he raised his head and looked at the two men; they returned his gaze steadily, expressionlessly.

"Why did you do that?" Raleigh asked.

"An accident," Harry answered. "It just slipped out of my hands."

"I don't think so," Raleigh told him evenly.

"You don't?"

"No. I think you dropped it deliberately."

"Now why would I do a thing like that?"

"That's what I'm asking *you*."

Harry turned to the second man, Alex, and shook his head sadly. Then he produced a wallet from the inside pocket of his sharkskin suit and took a small white business card from it. He handed the card to Raleigh. On it were the words *Sentinel Protective Association* in black script. Below the words was an embossed drawing of a uniformed soldier with a rifle, standing at attention.

Harry said, "Accidents happen all the time to small businessmen such as yourself, Mr. Raleigh. There's nothing you can do to prevent them. But there *is* something you can do to prevent a lot of other costly business hazards—vandalism, burglary, wanton looting. This is a very bad neighborhood, you know—out of the way, poorly policed. The Sentinel Protective Association eliminates all such hazards here—all except, of course, simple accidents."

Raleigh smiled faintly. "And how much does the Sentinel Protective Association charge for this service?"

"There is a membership fee of one hundred dollars," Harry said. "The weekly dues are twenty-five dollars, payable on Fridays."

"Suppose I choose not to become a member?"

"Well, as I told you, this is a very bad neighborhood."

"Very bad," Alex agreed. "Why, just last week poor Mr. Holtzmeier—he owns the delicatessen on the next block—poor Mr. Holtzmeier had his store all but destroyed by vandals in the middle of the night."

"I suppose Mr. Holtzmeier wasn't one of Sentinel's clients."

"He was," Harry said. "But he had decided to discontinue our services only three days before the incident. An unfortunate decision on his part."

Raleigh moistened his lips. "They call this kind of thing 'juice,' don't they?"

"Beg pardon?"

"These protective association shakedown rackets, like the one you're working here."

"I really don't have any idea what you're talking about, Mr. Raleigh. The Sentinel Protective Association was formed on behalf of the small businessmen in this neighborhood and it operates solely with their interests in mind."

"Of course it does," Raleigh said.

"May we put you down on our membership list?"

Raleigh did not answer at once. He glanced around the little shop; it was a comfortable old place, one that suited him perfectly, and the rent was moderate. The thought of being forced out of it was not an appealing one.

After a time he turned back to the two men. "Yes," he said slowly. "I haven't any choice, have I?"

Harry's expression was guileless. "I knew you were a reasonable man," he said.

"I suppose you'll want the money in cash?"

"Naturally."

"I can have it for you by noon tomorrow."

Harry shook his head. "We're sorry, Mr. Raleigh, but we couldn't possibly offer you any protection until we receive at least a down payment on the membership fee."

Alex reached out to the display shelf and began to tilt to and fro a sculptured replica of the Eleventh Century head of Divinity. "A lot of things can happen before noon tomorrow," he added meaningfully.

Raleigh sighed. "How much do you want now?"

"I think fifty dollars would be an equitable sum," Harry said. "A guarantee of your good faith."

Raleigh worried his lower lip for a long moment. Then he sighed again, in a resigned way, and said, "Perhaps it would be better if I paid one month's dues in advance, along with the membership fee. I wouldn't want anything to happen unexpectedly."

The two men exchanged glances. Harry raised his eyebrows. "Why, that's very wise of you, Mr. Raleigh," he said. "Most prudent."

"Yes," Raleigh said. "I have some money in my safe. If you'll excuse me for a moment?"

"Certainly." The two men smiled.

Raleigh turned and disappeared through a door leading into a storage room at the rear of the shop. After several moments he emerged and stepped to the small check-out counter, where he placed ten twenty-dollar bills on the vinyl top. "Well, there you are," he said. "Two hundred dollars."

Alex came forward and counted the currency. Then he nodded in satisfaction, put the bills into a leather executive wallet, and removed a receipt book and a ballpoint pen from his coat. Laboriously he wrote out a slip and presented it to Raleigh.

"Congratulations on becoming one of Sentinel's clients, Mr. Raleigh," Harry said. "You can rest assured that your cooperation is appreciated, and that you won't have any trouble whatsoever."

Raleigh nodded.

"Goodbye for now, then," Harry said in a pleasant voice, and the two callers walked out leisurely.

As soon as they had vanished from sight, Raleigh hurried to the front door, locked it, and drew down the shade. Then he went quickly into the storage room.

He sighed a third time, wistfully now, as he set to work. It really was a very nice location—but then, he was reasonably certain, he would have little difficulty finding another quiet, side-street spot, perhaps in another state, where he could set up his Facsimile Shop—and the Old Heidelberg printing press that he was now beginning to dismantle.

He smiled only once during the lengthy task, and that was when he thought of the inferior-quality throwaways he had run off for testing purposes that morning; and of what would happen when the Sentinel Protective Association tried passing those particular genuine imitation twenty-dollar bills.

A Corner of the Cellar

by Michael Gilbert

"And don't forget the boiler," said Mrs. Cotton. "I opened it up so that we can have a nice bath. It'll need two scuttles of coke."

Sam Cotton groaned.

When they had moved into the Old Rectory at Marlhammer, he had felt in his bones that he was making his last move. He was only forty-nine. But the time comes in every man's life when he will settle down to enjoy the fruits of his toil.

Starting as an unskilled, untrained, almost unpaid assistant to an assistant in a shaky firm of chartered accountants, he had worked. How he had worked! Twelve, fourteen, sixteen hours a day—in his spare time, at night, during the weekend. Now he was a qualified accountant, a partner, a director of four companies, and a rich man.

Too fat, not healthy, seldom happy, but rich.

The Old Rectory had cost money. It was a plain, Georgian house, of dark red brick and darker red tile, with more solid wood in its window-frames and box shutters than a builder would put into a row of houses these days.

It stood back a little, isolated by beech trees from the road. It had its private path to the little church, but it was nearly a quarter of a mile from its nearest human neighbour.

"It's pretty," agreed Mrs. Cotton, "but it's got too many rooms."

This, like most of Bertha Cotton's deceptively simple remarks, was true. The house had been designed for and occupied by old-fashioned country parsons. It had many bedrooms and vast box-rooms. It had a pantry, which the Cottons used as a kitchen. A kitchen, which they had used as a storeroom. And range upon range of stores and sheds and cellars.

"I wonder how the Grundsells managed?" said Mrs. Cotton. She referred to their immediate predecessors, who had purchased the house from the last incumbent some five years previously.

Mr. Grundsell had been a small, happy, cheerful person, popular in the village. Not nearly as rich as Sam Cotton, but perhaps happier. His wife, older than he by some years, had been something of a mystery at first. A heavy, dark, foreign-looking woman, who seldom spoke.

However, nothing is hidden for long from the legion of charwomen and daily helps, and it became known – whisper it softly—that she drank. Seldom, but my, how deeply!

"A cupboard full of bottles," reported Mrs. Tyzer. "Gin. And another pile—so big—buried in the paddock."

However, Mrs. Grundsell had not lasted. Perhaps she found the house too isolated. She spoke wistfully of Blackpool. Mr. Grundsell, who gave in to her in everything, gave in to her in this. One night of dark and storm when no one was about, he packed her and her belongings into their big, closed car and drove her off. Or so he reported, when he mentioned it later.

Marlhammer saw her no more. Shortly afterwards, Grundsell had decided to sell.

"Not surprised, really," said Mrs. Tyzer. "A great big house, and him all alone in it."

That was how the Cottons had come to buy it. A handsome house, full of large, cheerful rooms, rooms still redolent of the line of sober, god-fearing clerics that had inhabited them with their industrious wives, their contingents of servants, and their quiverfuls of children. Against the edge of one bedroom door Sam Cotton had found their heights recorded, starting with Benjamin, a mere two-foot-nine off the ground and running up, through eight others, to Ruth.

A cheerful house, with one reservation.

He could not get used to the cellar.

Well, it was not really a cellar at all. It lay down two steps only at the end of a series of pantries, dairies, and wash-houses. A sort of sunken cul-de-sac. It had been designed as a game-larder. As you shone your torch upwards—the electric light did not reach so far—you could see the great steel hooks, deep-rusted now, in the beams of the roof. It had a floor of badly cracked concrete.

"Just the place for coke," said Mrs. Cotton.

It was late summer when they moved in, but, warned by her experience of the winter before, she had ordered four tons. And had got them.

Mrs. Cotton usually got what she wanted in the end.

As autumn turned into winter and winter into spring, and Sam Cotton made his nightly, dreaded pilgrimage, sometimes one scuttle, sometimes two, the huge pile diminished. As it diminished, a curious fancy grew in Mr. Cotton's mind.

There was something evil about the cellar. And the evil lay in the far corner where the coke was piled deepest.

He got into the way of calculating how long, at his present nightly rate of progress, it would be before he uncovered this corner. Two months. One month.

He said nothing directly to his wife, who was not an imaginative woman, and inclined to be impatient of her husband's fancies. But he did suggest, casually and tentatively, that they might perhaps take on a resident servant. At the moment they had only Mrs. Tyzer, who worked like a giant by day, but deserted them at six o'clock.

"I could never stand anyone living in," said Mrs. Cotton. "They'd get on my nerves."

"We could afford it," said Sam.

"It isn't a question of money," said Bertha. "And anyway, it's quite unnecessary. Do I ever ask you to do anything except get the coke at night?"

It was true. She was a splendid manager. Twenty years younger than Sam, and five times as healthy.

"I don't even ask you to wash up," she said.

"I wouldn't mind washing up," said Sam. But he had left it at that. It would have been too difficult to explain. And it would soon be summer—and the last of the coke would be gone.

A fortnight. A week.

He had noticed lately that a crack in the floor seemed to lead directly into the corner. It grew larger as he uncovered it.

That there was something in the corner, he was now certain. He had lived a great deal of his life by instinct, and now all his instincts told him so.

As the pile of coke diminished, as he bent, night after night, to fill the two steel hods, nearer and nearer and nearer to that corner, the corner to which the crack pointed, a prickling sweat broke out all over his body. His heart thumped, and he felt curiously light-headed. He had never felt quite that way before, but it reminded him of an occasion when, as a boy, he had fainted from overwork and lack of food.

There *was* something in that corner. Something inevitable, something deadly that would become apparent when the last scuttle of coke was removed.

But how would it be if the last scuttle—the very last scuttle—was removed by someone else? Like everything in life, it was simply a matter of calculation. The daily woman filled four scuttles during the day. He filled two at night. It was like one of those card games when you have to arrange your play so as to avoid holding the last card.

When he had seen the coke the night before there had been, he calculated, about sixteen scuttles of it. Four would have gone. He would take another two—then Mrs. Tyzer would take four more—

"You've been doing sums to yourself for ten minutes," said his wife. "What's wrong? Money?"

"Nothing's wrong," said Sam.

"Then hurry along and get the coke and we can get off to bed. I don't know about you, but I'm dog-tired."

"We shall have to be ordering some more soon," said Sam, cunningly. "I don't suppose we've enough left for three days."

"We haven't that," said his wife, briskly. "I lent a bit to Mrs. Tyzer. She's right out. You ought to be able to scrape up enough for tonight, though. They're delivering a ton in the morning."

With a curious leaden feeling which centered on the top of his stomach and the bottom of his chest, Sam Cotton walked heavily out to the cellar.

It was as his wife had said. A pathetic remnant of coke and coke-dust covered the corner. The crack gaped, so wide now that he could almost put his fist into it. Two blocks of the cement flooring looked almost as if they had been taken up and carelessly laid down again.

Sam picked up the shovel and bent down.

It had come now. It had to be faced. As he had faced and outfaced other things in his hard life.

His heart was pounding so that it nearly choked him. One scuttle. Then the other. The coke which was left would exactly fill it.

He stooped again and scraped the shovel on the floor. A blinding red light. An uprush of dizziness. He was on his knees. Then on his face, his nose an inch from the crack . . .

"Murder," said the young doctor, savagely, to his partner. "Plain murder. Letting him go out, night after night, with his heart in that state, and grovel for coke and lift weights. But not the sort of murder she can be hanged for—more's the pity."

Every Fifth Man

by Edward D. Hoch

You probably wonder why I'm still alive after all that has happened, and I suppose it *is* quite a story. I'd been living and training with the exiles for two years before the attempted coup, knowing—as we all knew—the penalty for failure. There were months of hand-to-hand combat and paratrooper training and even some explosives practice before we were ready for the big day, the day we returned to Costanera.

I'd lived the twenty-five years of my life in the cities and towns and jungle villages of Costanera. It was my country, worth fighting for, every inch of it. We left with the coming of General Diam, but now we were going back. We would drop from the skies by night, join the anti-Diam military, and enter the capital city in triumph.

That was the plan. Somehow it didn't work out that way. The military changed their minds about it, and we jumped from our planes into a withering crossfire from General Diam's forces. More than half of our liberation force of sixty-five were dead before we reached the ground, and the others were overrun quickly. By nightfall we found ourselves prisoners of the army in the great old fortress overlooking Azul Bay.

There were twenty-three of us taken prisoner that day, and of these one man—Tomas—had a bad wound in his side. We were crowded into a single large cell at the fortress and left to await our fate. It was hot in there, with the sweat of bodies and a mustiness of air that caught at my throat and threatened to choke me. I wanted to remove my black beret and shirt and stretch out on the hard stone floor, but I did not. Instead I bore it in silence and waited with the others.

A certain custom has existed in the country, a custom which has been observed in revolutions for hundreds of years. Always faced with the problem of the defeated foe, governments had traditionally sent down the order: *Kill every fifth man and release the others.* It was a system of justice tempered with a large degree of mercy, and acted as a deterrent while still allowing something of an opposition party to exist within the country. Of course, the eighty percent who were released often regrouped to revolt again, but the threat that hung over them was sometimes enough to pacify their activities.

This, then, was the fate that awaited us—twenty-three prisoners in a gloomy fortress by the blue waters of a bay. We had reason to hope, because most of us had the odds on our side, but we had reckoned without the cold-blooded calculation of General Diam. The order came down early the following morning, and it was read to us through the bars of the cell. It was as we had expected: *Every fifth man will be executed immediately. The remaining prisoners will be released in twenty-four hours.*

But then came the jolting surprise. The officer in charge

kept reading, and read the same message four times more. General Diam had sent down five identical executive orders. No one was to survive the executions.

I knew something had to be done, and quickly. As the guards unlocked the cell door I went to the officer in charge. Using my deepest voice I tried to reason with him. "You cannot execute all twenty-three of us. It would be contrary to orders."

He looked down at me with something like scorn. "Be brave, little fellow. Die like a soldier!"

"But the first order says that every fifth man should be executed immediately. It means just that. They should be executed before you read the second order."

The officer sighed. "What difference does it make? The day will be hot. Who wants to die under the noonday sun? At least now there is a bit of breeze out there."

"You must obey the orders," I insisted. "Each order must be executed separately."

You can see, of course, the reason for my insistence. If the five executive orders were lumped together and carried out at once (as General Diam no doubt intended), all twenty-three of us would be shot. But if they were carried out separately, the orders would allow nine of us to live. I'd always been good at mathematics, and this was how I figured it—every fifth man would be taken from the original 23, a total of 4, leaving 19. The process would be repeated a second time, killing 3, leaving 16. On the third round another 3 would die, and 13 would be left. Then 2 shot, 11 left. A final 2 shot, and 9 of us would walk out of the fortress as free as the air.

You say the odds were still against me? Not at all—if the officer agreed to my argument, I was certain to survive. Because consider—how would the fifth man be picked each time? Not by drawing straws, for this was the military. We would line up in a single column and count off. And in what order would we line up—alphabetically? Hardly, when they did not even know our names. We would line up in the old military tradition—by height.

And I had already established during the night in the cell that I was the shortest of the twenty-three prisoners!

If they started the count-off at the short end of the

line—which was unlikely—I would always be safe, for I would always be Number One. More likely, they would start at the tall end, and for the five count-offs I would always be last—numbers 23, 19, 16, 13, 11, and 9. Never a number divisible by 5—never one of the doomed prisoners!

The officer stared down at me for what seemed an eternity. Finally he glanced through the orders in his hand once more and reached a decision. "All right, we will carry out the first order."

We lined up in the courtyard—by height—with two men supporting the wounded Tomas, and started the count-off. Of the 23 of us, 4 were marched over to the sea wall and shot. The rest of us tried not to look.

Again—and 3 of our number died against the sea wall. One of the remaining 16 was starting to cry. He had figured out his position in the line.

The officer formally read the third executive order, and 3 more went to the wall. I was still last in the line.

After the fourth order 2 of the 13 were marched to their death. Even the firing squad was beginning to look hot and bored. The sun was almost above us. Well, only one more count-off and then 9 of us would be free.

"Wait!" the officer shouted, as the first man began to count off again. I turned my neck in horror. Tomas had fallen from the line and the blood was gushing from his side. He was dead, and the 11 was suddenly reduced to 10.

I was the tenth one as the last count began!

The fifth man stepped out of line—then *six, seven, eight, nine, ten.* I didn't move.

"Come, little fellow," the officer said. "It is your turn now."

You ask how I come to be sitting here, when I was so surely doomed, when my careful figuring had gone for nothing. I stood there in that moment, looking death in the face, and did what I had kept from doing all night and morning. I knew the officer would obey General Diam's order to the letter—to execute every fifth man—and that was what saved me.

I took the beret from my head, let my hair fall to my shoulders, and showed them I was a woman.

The Pro

by Robert H. Curtis

Mrs. Henrietta Marshall looked at herself in the faded mirror. The reflection did not please her. In her bathrobe and out of her girdle, she appeared to herself fat and old. Usually an inborn optimism and energy would have prevented any sort of self-pity, but she felt sad now about leaving New York. The depressing hotel room itself played no part in her feelings. Midtown commercial hotels had been familiar to her for over forty years, and she stayed at places like this all over the country. But she always regretted her departures from New York. She saw so many old friends in this city. Mrs. Marshall spent more time on the road than in the small Iowa town where she lived—hardly a place people would visit on vacation.

"Oh well," she mused. "I've got at least ten years before I have to call it quits completely." She scanned the room and sighed as she contemplated her half-packed suitcase lying like an open-faced sandwich on the bed. She looked at her alarm clock—11:15 A.M. Two hours until plane time and, tomorrow morning, back to work in Chicago. She looked into the mirror again and noticed the doorknob turning and the door slowly opening. The reflection revealed a thin, sallow man in his thirties. Mrs. Marshall was about to tell him that he was in the wrong room, but before she could get one word out the man said, "Be quiet!" in a voice chilling in its hatred. "I want money and jewelry. In exchange for your cooperation, you get to keep all your teeth."

"Nothing I have is valuable," she protested. She was standing now, hugging her bathrobe tightly to herself.

The intruder placed his attaché case on the bed and

opened it. "Listen, you!" the man said. "Don't waste my time. Hand me your purse."

Mrs. Marshall did as instructed, and the man held the purse in his left hand as he rapidly went through her suitcase. He was angry at finding nothing of value. Now Mrs. Marshall watched helplessly as he emptied the contents of her purse on the bed. He picked up her wallet and counted the money. "Two hundred and fifty-three dollars. Stupid women like you always carry a lot of cash. That's cause you can't travel with your mattresses." He stuffed her money into his own wallet which he replaced in the inside pocket of his jacket. Then he put Mrs. Marshall's small gold compact into his case.

"You're not even leaving me cab fare," she complained. "I'm going to the airport in half an hour."

"Don't con me. You got travelers checks right there." He pointed. "You're just lucky that forgery's not my bag. Nothing much from you," he muttered, "but sometimes hitting a dump like this pays off. Look!" He touched the case. Mrs. Marshall saw only some burglar tools and a thin jewel box. But then, the man opened the box and Mrs. Marshall gasped. Outlined against the black velvet was the most beautiful necklace she had ever seen. Made from perfectly matched natural pearls, it glistened so hypnotically that she felt an almost palpable need to touch.

The man laughed unpleasantly. "All your dough wouldn't have bought you three pearls from this baby." He closed the jewel box and then the attaché case. Moving to the dresser, he rifled through the drawers but found nothing. "You don't have any jewelry at all? That's hard to believe."

"You've taken everything from me. Isn't that enough?" she asked as her eyes darted to the closet and back again.

Her eye movement did not go undetected, and the man walked to the closet and pushed each dress to one side after a brief inspection. Finally he spotted a cameo brooch. He tried to remove it but had some difficulty with the clasp.

While the man was struggling with the brooch, Mrs. Marshall eased towards the table and silently removed something from it. Just then, and as the man was about to rip the pin from the dress, the clasp released and the man pocketed the brooch. As he came to pick up his attaché case from the bed, he was almost knocked off his feet as Mrs. Marshall tripped on the rug.

"Oh, I'm sorry," she said.

"Idiot! the man snarled. His face was only inches from hers. "I'm leaving now. You make a move for the phone or call out in the next ten minutes and you'll *really* be sorry." Mrs. Marshall believed him.

The burglar ran to the stairwell and raced down two flights, entering the crowded lobby unnoticed. He calmly walked to the revolving door and disappeared into the noon crowd along Lexington Avenue. A half hour later, he entered the elevator of an apartment house on Third Avenue in the mid-90's. He got out at the fourth floor, let himself into his room, and sat down on the sofa. He paused for a moment, anticipating the joy he would feel when he surveyed the spoils of his most successful morning. Now he was ready. He pressed the latch of the case and opened it. At first he couldn't believe what he saw but then he let out a moan. Gone were his tools, gone was the gold compact, and gone was the thin box with the pearl necklace. Only a black book lay in the case. He felt panic for a moment but then realized that he must have placed the necklace in his inside pocket. He reached in his jacket and broke out in a cold sweat. Not only was the necklace not there but his wallet was missing. Hurriedly getting back to the attaché case, he picked up the black book and turned it over. It was a Gideon Bible. He opened it and found, between the cover and the flyleaf, a sheet of heavy writing-paper, half of which was occupied by a slightly gaudy lithographic heading. It showed a number of men in old-fashioned evening clothes cowering before a younger, slimmer, but easily recognizable Mrs. Marshall, who smilingly held aloft a double handful of watches, vests, suspenders, and wallets. The caption read: *Madame Henrietta, The American Sorceress. Conjuress-Illusionist-Prestidigitator. Bookings Available.*

Nobody, That's Who

by William F. Nolan

Look, Danny, you're my lawyer, aren't you? Can't you get me *out* of this? Hell, it's all crazy, it's a frame. Sure, I can go all over it again for you if that'll help. Sure, right from the beginning outside her apartment.

Well, like I said, I didn't really have anything *definite* to go on. I mean, I had this kind of hunch is all. Just a feeling that she was playing house with some other guy while I footed the bill. When I get a strong hunch on something I usually play it out. So that night I decided to stick around after leaving her apartment. Just in case. I kissed her like nothing was wrong and pretended to leave. But I only took the elevator down one floor, then climbed the stairs back to her apartment. I posted myself down at the end of the hall where it was plenty dark, where I figured I wouldn't be seen. And, by God, I didn't have long to wait, either. Maybe ten, fifteen minutes. Then along comes this guy. Like I told you, I never did get a look at his face. Wore a hat pulled down low and the collar of his topcoat was turned up all the way round, so I couldn't make out any features. Just a tall guy in a dark blue outfit.

Anyway, he tapped on the door, quiet like, two shorts and a long, and she opened it while he slipped inside. Now that was two o'clock on the nose. I checked my wrist watch, because I wanted to see just how long he'd stay in there with her. Hell, I felt like rushing in there and catching the pair of them at it, but I'd have the break the damn door down to do it and by that time he'd be long gone down the fire escape outside her window. So I decided to see just how long he'd stay.

Figured I couldn't hang around in the hall. Too suspicious in case the house dick came along, or maybe another hotel guest or somebody. I knew this guy would have to cross the lobby on his way out, so I took the elevator down and planted myself in a leather chair by the doors and waited. Just waited it out for him. I didn't know, right then, just what the hell I'd do when he finally showed. I was boiling, I'll admit. I hate being played for a sucker. That really ate into me. I mean, after the way I'd set her up and all. I just sat there in that chair and boiled.

Finally, two hours later, the elevator door slides back and he steps out. Same guy. Same dark blue outfit, hat and all. And, damn it, I *still* couldn't make out what he looked like. My chair was too far back and the lobby was pretty dark by then. I would have had to catch him and knock off that hat of his to really get a look, but what the hell, *she* was the one I wanted, not him. So I let him go. That was my first big mistake.

Then I got the idea about scaring her. I mean, I wanted to teach her a lesson. Shake her up good. Not hurt her, understand, just scare her. Sure, I had every right in the world to work her over for two-timing me, but I decided not to lay a hand on her. I figured why play it dumb and get myself in hot water with the law.

So I took the stairs up to her apartment. Four flights, just enough to wind me, get me to breathing hard like I was half nuts, you know. Figured that would help.

I tapped on her door, soft, the same way he had. Two shorts and a long. I knew she'd be plenty surprised to see me—and she sure was. She thought her lover boy had come back until she got a look at me. Then she tried to shut the door in my face, but I just pushed hard and forced my way inside.

"Whatta you want?" she says, and starts backing away from me toward the bed.

I didn't say a damn thing, just stood there looking mean, breathing hard and ragged. She let out a gasp, a kind of little choking sound. Then she dropped on the bed and curled up there, watching me like I was some kind of animal.

I locked the door behind me, then went over to the open

window and shut and locked it. Like maybe I was going to do something that I didn't want anyone else to hear.

Oh, she was scared, all right, *plenty* scared. She didn't know what the hell I'd do next. I could see her eyes shining out at me from the bed, wild and wide. She had on a pink and blue shortie nightgown and her legs were all drawn up under it. She looked like a rabbit you catch in the headlights of your car, kind of frozen with fear.

I eased down into a chair by the window, where she could see my face in the reflection of the outside neon. Then I thought of a beautiful touch.

I began to scrape my fingernails. You know, just sitting there quiet in that chair, with the red and yellow neon lighting my face, breathing slow and hard—and scraping each nail with one of those sharp little silver files. Listen, that threw the fear of God into her. She figured I was just waiting till I finished the last nail before I went for her, so she was as still as a cat. Just her eyes moved, watching me.

Well, this went on for maybe ten minutes. Then she began to see I was bluffing, that I wasn't going to try anything. She sat up and dug out her cigarettes. She lit one, with the pillow propped up behind her. Then she tried some bluffing on her own.

"What's the idea?" she said. "Why the big spook routine?"

"I know all about your boy friend," I told her. "I saw him come in and I saw him come out."

"So what?" she snapped. "So a guy spends a couple of hours in my apartment."

The goddam nerve of her! Here I'd set her up in this place of her own, bought her some nice clothes and things and always treated her fine. And this is what she gives me. I'm telling you, it knocked me out. Then I asked her if she denied sleeping with this guy.

"He made a few passes and we wrestled around some, that's all," she told me.

Oh, sure. I believed that was all like I believed there wasn't any moon in the sky.

When she saw I wasn't having any she got sore. Her whole face changed. I mean, she suddenly turned hard, like some two-bit hustler. All the softness went fast and it was like I was seeing her for the first time with the shell off. She knew the game was finished and she didn't give a damn.

Then I got the full treatment. She began to laugh at me like I was a fool.

"You're not very bright," she told me in that new hard voice of hers. "Sure I had some kicks with this guy. Why? Because I'm fed up with playing around with you, that's why."

Then she told me that this other guy was a real *man*—not just a weak excuse for one—and that one like him was worth ten of me.

God, but she had nerve! Wasn't afraid of me at all by then. Not at all.

And I didn't intend to touch her. She wasn't worth it. Maybe I *was* the dumb cluck she made me out to be. Maybe I deserved what I was getting. I was as sore as hell at myself for playing along with her.

"I'm finished," I said. "This is the end of the line for us."

She just kept on laughing. Told me the sooner I got out the happier she'd be.

And here's where the crazy part starts. I was on my way to the door when it opened—and there, outlined against the light from the hall, was this guy of hers in the blue coat. And right away I saw something glint in his hand and I knew he had a gun.

It was all real freaky. He'd done the same thing I'd done. Come back, I mean. He'd probably seen my car parked in the hotel lot and recognized it. Had come back up and heard our voices outside the door. Figured she was playing *him* for the chump. Hell, it was all mixed up ten ways from Sunday.

Well, this guy didn't give either of us a chance to say a damn thing. Just stood there for a split second, long enough to make out the girl good and clear. Then he just pumped two slugs into her, one, two. Just that quick. Slammed the door and he was gone. Only first he tossed in his gun and it landed right at my feet on the rug.

That's when I *really* played it dumb. I actually picked the damn thing up and looked at it. Now, I've seen guys do that in the movies maybe fifty times and I always figured it was phony. No innocent party, I told myself, would ever pick up a murder weapon and get his fingerprints all over it. But I swear that's just what I did. Who knows why? Shock, I guess. The shock was terrible, the kind you get after a real bad auto accident. I was trembling, I remember, and weak all over.

I knew she was dead without even walking over to her. Nobody could miss at that kind of range. So I just stood there holding on to that damn gun and looking down at it while the outside hall filled up with people.

Next thing I know, somebody is pounding like hell on the door and yelling for me to open up. Oh, I dropped the gun quick enough then, all right. I knew I was a goner if they found me in here with her body, so I unlocked the window and took off down the fire escape.

What else is there to tell? The cops were waiting for me when I dropped into the alley—and I guess I sure looked guilty enough. I told them about the other guy in the blue get-up, but they just grinned and treated me like I was already on my way to the chair.

Hell, Danny, can't you find this guy? *He* killed her, not me. I never even touched her that morning. I don't know what this guy looks like, but he's *got* to be found. What chance have I got without him? Who's going to believe my story?

I'll tell you. Nobody, that's who.

Start looking for this guy, will you? He could be almost anybody. A mutual friend maybe. Hell, Danny, *you* knew her—and I've seen *you* wearing a dark blue topcoat. And . . . the guy's about your height, too.

Just do one thing for me, will you? Quit grinning like that. That's the way the damn cops grinned at me.

Will you *quit* it?

Pigeon

by William F. Nolan

When Vince Thompson entered his apartment, he saw the small white square of paper under the door.

Well, he thought, it's about time. Been a month since the last one.

He locked the door behind him and unfolded the paper. It was like all the others: a phone number and the letter R typed at the bottom. Nothing else. Vince ignited the edge of the paper with his lighter and watched the number blacken and curl into ash. Then he dusted his fingers and reached for the phone.

"Vince?" R's voice was cold and metallic over the wire.

"Yeah. I just got the message."

"Ready to go to work?"

"Just fill me in."

"It's tonight. Top of Bel Air Road off Sunset. You follow it all the way up. To the left, at the summit, you'll see a stretch of open ground. About a hundred feet in is a small white stucco house set into the hill with a two-car garage in front. You station yourself inside the garage. Door's unlocked, so you'll have no problem getting in. Your pigeon should arrive by eleven. You be there by 10:45 just in case."

"Fine. What's my boy look like?"

"Tall. Fairly slim build. Around forty or so."

"This one for the usual?"

"Maybe more if the job's real clean. We'll see."

"Anything else I need to know?"

"That's it, Vince." The voice clicked off.

Thompson replaced the receiver and leaned heavily back

on the couch. He grinned to himself, thinking of a quick two grand for one night's work. Wilma would be real pleased to get that coat he'd been promising her. Tomorrow night they'd celebrate, go dancing, drink some good champagne . . .

Vince lit a cigarette, drawing the smoke deep into his lungs. R was sure some operator. Like a ghost. Nobody sees him, nobody knows who he is. As he'd told Mitch, Vince didn't like the feeling you get working for a guy with no face. A square of white paper, a phone number, some orders, a dead man—and a couple of thousand bucks. No problems. No loose ends. But sometimes it made Vince jumpy. He'd been asking around, among some of the wise boys, but no one seemed to know anything. R was just a voice. Well, for the kind of dough Vince was getting he could keep his curiosity curbed. Actually, with R figuring all the angles, it was a perfect set-up.

Vince checked his watch: 9:30. He estimated a half hour to reach Bel Air, another ten minutes to the top. Which meant he still had time to stop downstairs for a couple of quick ones.

The place was packed. Full house for a Friday night. Vince managed to push his way to the bar. He ordered a scotch and water, and looked over the crowd.

Here I am, he thought, ready to kill a man tonight and it might even turn out to be one of you guys. He sipped his drink slowly.

How many jobs had he done for R? Ten? A dozen? It didn't matter, really. To Vince Thompson, killing was a business and it was up to R to keep the books. A year ago, when he hit L.A. from Frisco, his old pal Mitch had put in the good word on him to R, and he was in.

His gaze swept the room once more. Jerks! Poor dumb jerks pushing trucks for a living or delivering milk or sweating over a desk in some seedy office. Hell, he'd make more tonight with one shot than these dummies would make in three months!

He finished his drink, had another.

When he left the bar, he felt just right: not high, but brought to a fine cutting edge. He knew he could handle the job without any trouble and be back at his apartment by midnight. He might even give Wilma a late buzz and tell her the news.

Just at the entrance to Bel Air Road, under the tall, wrought-iron gate off Sunset, Vince pulled his car to a stop. Nobody around, no other cars. Quickly he reached under the dash and unstrapped the slim Italian Beretta he always carried there. He flipped out the magazine, checked it, and eased the gun into his coat. He sighed, feeling whole once more.

One of the toughest rules Vince had to accept, when he started working for R, concerned the Beretta. None of R's boys packed a gun before a job. That way, according to R, they were always clean if the cops picked them up between jobs. For Vince, the rule seemed all wrong. Without his Beretta he felt half-naked; he'd carried it since he was sixteen; he was never fully at ease without it.

Bel Air Road twisted up sharply past the rich hillside homes, and Vince felt the Merc slide a bit on the turns. He backed off. It was no use pushing it because the road was dark and narrow and he didn't want to get tangled up with another car on the way down.

The climb was a steep one. At the top, he pulled the Merc far over on the dirt shoulder under some trees and cut the engine. His car would be out of sight here. Below him, stretching for miles, Vince could see the glittering lights of Beverly Hills and Hollywood.

He got out of the Merc and stretched. Chilly as hell up here, Vince thought, feeling the cold wind against his face. He looked around.

As usual, R had arranged a perfect set-up for the job. No other houses nearby, a long stretch of open ground between the garage and the road. If anybody heard the shot, it would sound like a car backfiring on the steep grade. Perfect.

Vince checked his watch again. 10:44. He'd better get moving. When he reached the garage, a low modern structure with a sliding door, he nodded. No lock, just as R had said. The door slid up quietly under his hand.

Inside, near the far corner, he saw several stacked

cartons. Vince allowed the door to slide down behind him as he moved toward the boxes.

He eased down on the cool concrete, his back against the wall. When the door opened, his pigeon would make a perfect target against the lights of the car.

Minutes ticked by. A cigarette would be too risky, he knew, so he quit thinking about a smoke. He slipped the thin Beretta into his right hand, letting one finger curl slowly around the trigger. One shot. That's all he needed to do the job. He'd earned a marksmanship medal in the service, and he'd had plenty of practice since. *Plenty.*

Vince Thompson stiffened at the sound of a car on the road below him. The high whine of the straining engine increased in volume. He eased forward, transferring his weight to the balls of his feet; the Beretta was up and ready.

He heard the car pull off the road and bump over the open stretch of ground.

His pigeon all right.

Vince pressed close against the stacked cartons, waiting. Outside, he heard a car door open, the dry scuff of shoes against the ground.

Any second now . . .

The garage door began to slide upward and Vince sighted along the Beretta's thin barrel, ready to squeeze the trigger.

Vince swore, drawing in his breath sharply.

No one was there.

Just the bright cones of two powerful headlights in the open doorway.

Vince felt his mouth go dry and his heart begin to pound inside his chest. He squinted into the glare. Nothing.

Only the lights, the smooth sound of the car's idling engine, and the wind.

Suddenly he was remembering the metallic voice of R: *"Tall. Fairly slim build. Around forty or so."*

Which, Vince realized, was a thumbnail description of *himself.*

Sure, it all figured. His bitching about working for a faceless man, quizzing Mitch, nosing around the boys for information he didn't really need . . .

He was becoming a risk—and R didn't believe in risks.

Okay, then, Vince told himself, get the hell out of here. If you can reach the Merc you've got a chance. But first, fix those lights.

Two shots and the twin beams winked out in a soft shower of glass. In the thick darkness, he was up and running.

Ahead of him, the way seemed clear. He twisted past the car in front of the garage and struck out across ground, crouched low, the Beretta poised for action.

Then Vince Thompson went blind.

A dozen bright flashlight beams dipped up from the dark ground, slicing into his eyes.

God! They were all around him!

If anyone heard the sudden roar, it must have sounded like a car backfiring on the steep grade.

The Prisoner

by Edward Wellen

He absently brushed a few specks of dust from the desk but did not really feel in the mood to get down to work. He looked around the cluttered office. There was so much to do. And, God knew, he desperately wanted nothing to go wrong.

But on impulse he quietly—any sudden loud noise would bring a guard running—opened the bottom right drawer and took out his binoculars. The binoculars were a way of escape. He kept to one side of the window, out of sight of the guard he heard coughing and shifting below the window, and peered out beyond the gate.

It was just past dawn, and traffic was light in the streets outside his prison. He focused the binoculars. At the nearest intersection came the young paper boy riding his bike no-handedly. He could not hear, of course, but from the cant of the head he knew the boy was whistling or singing.

Suddenly a car shot into sight, taking the turn too swiftly, too sharply. It struck the bike, toppling the boy and his basket of papers. The car slammed to a shivering stop.

Instinctively he burned the license-plate number into his mind.

The driver's door opened. The driver got out and with the exaggerated sobriety of the truly drunken walked back to the still form, looked down at it, then with a shock into true sobriety looked wildly around, hurried back into his seat, and drove off.

Watching it all, he himself felt a shock into something beyond sobriety. He should have recognized the car on sight, for he had seen it before, had more than once from this same window seen Pardee breeze by with the top down. And each time he had smiled a twisted smile knowing the thought that must have gone through Pardee's mind as he passed by: by God, *he* was inside these walls of gray sandstone painted white and Pardee was *outside*.

He started guiltily from his trance, hearing the siren of an ambulance, nearing, nearing, then on the spot and moaning into silence. He had known instantly, by the terrible fling and the ragdoll fall, and by the mangled bike, that the boy was past saving. Still he felt thankful someone had quickly sent for help. It was now out of his hands.

Grimly he put back the binoculars and started to work. Someone else must have seen Pardee, just as someone else had seen the still form in the street and summoned the ambulance.

But no. As the day wore on, he managed to listen to the local news broadcasts and learned the police had no leads to the hit-and-run driver.

His mouth tightened. He could not remain silent. But it would be impossible for him to speak out. He thought wryly how much easier it would've been for him to identify Pardee. The man was someone he didn't know.

He could not go into court and permit a clever defense lawyer to cross-examine him and make capital of the dislike he and Pardee had for each other.

"Isn't it a fact that you and Mr. Pardee have been known to be enemies for years?"

He would have to say yes. It was the truth.

But even if he got off with merely giving a deposition, the shadow of suspicion would linger—more than a shadow, a stain—the suspicion that private spite had lurked behind public spirit.

He looked around in frustration at the walls that closed him in.

Then voices broke in on him, voices from the yard outside. He had forgotten. It was a Visitors Day.

The people passing in through the gate were usually a distraction, but now their hushed intensity was a convicing reminder of where he was.

He eyed the phones on the desk ruefully. One disguised call to the local police would suffice; but he could hardly make an anonymous call from here.

Then he had it. The least he could do—and the most—was to write an anonymous note. The time was now, while he thought of it and had this rare chance.

He stepped back to the desk, drew a piece of stationery toward him, stood leaning over it, and picked up a pen to begin. No. First things first. He took up a ruler, covered the letterhead, then lifted the bottom of the sheet to tear it off below the letterhead. But as he did so, light passed through the paper, outlining the watermark. He let the sheet fall flat. All the stationery on the desk bore that revealing letterhead and watermark.

The scratch pad. He took up the ballpoint pen again and printed his message painstakingly in characterless block letters. No one would ever find out he had written it or that it had come from within these walls.

But what now? Even if he found a plain envelope he would never be able to smuggle the letter out. He might manage to pass through the mail room, but how could he slip the envelope into the outgoing mail without someone noticing? He was always being watched.

Cross that bridge when he came to it. He was wasting time. He whirled his glance around the room and saw a book on a shelf in a plain dust wrapper. He grabbed the book and pulled. It was tightly wedged in and pulling it out caused a book alongside to fall to the floor.

The thump of the book on the carpet had an echoing thump in his heart. He waited frozen for a guard to rush in.

No one came. He let out his breath slowly. The carpet had a deep pile and the thump had seemed louder to him than it really was.

He took off the dust wrapper and spread it out on the desk. He found a used envelope stuffed with some news clippings, dumped the clippings into the wastebasket, and pulled the side and bottom flaps of the envelope unstuck. Using the spreadeagled envelope as a pattern, he cut the dust wrapper to its shape and matched the folds. Now he had a plain envelope. He shoved the letter inside, sealed all the flaps with dabs from a small stick of glue, then printed an address on the envelope.

All that had taken only a few minutes. The group of visitors was off to one side still admiring the garden. Now to distract the guard under the window.

He tossed a pen—there were lots of pens—into a bush off to the right. The alert guard whipped around, reaching for his gun in the same motion, and headed for the bush.

Quickly now, while the guard's back was turned. He sailed the envelope out to the left. He agonized over its flight—rather, its fall; watched it tilt and plummet like a broken-winged bird until a swirl of wind carried it out into the open near the path.

The guard came back to his post, shaking his head.

Time passed. The sky darkened. It was clouding up to rain, and rain would beat the address on the envelope into soggy illegibility. The guard had still not noticed it.

Then the man coming on to relieve the guard saw it and picked it up.

"What's this?"

"Dunno. Let's have a look."

They frowned over the address.

"Guess one of the visitors left it there. I better take it right in."

Listening to them he smiled. Then a thought struck him and he stepped quickly away from the window and went to the desk.

He could barely make out the shadow-edged imprint of his message on the top sheet of the scratch pad.

I WITNESSED THIS MORNING'S HIT-AND-RUN ACCIDENT BUT I CAN'T GET INVOLVED.

The message ended with the car's license-plate number.

Hurriedly he tore off the top half-dozen sheets, made a spill of them, lit a match, and burned the sheets to char in the ashtray.

Just in time. There was a buzz. He pressed a switch.

"Yes?" he said, his voice calm.

"Sorry to break in on you, Mr. President, but something politically touchy has just come up—"

Politically touchy, yes. They had done a quick check on the license number. But no one—not even Senator Pardee—could reproach him for forwarding an anonymous letter to the Chief of Police for the District of Columbia.

The Sooey Pill

by Elaine Slater

It was the pill society. There was the morning-after pill, of course, which the government had made obligatory after the first child. Yet even so, the population growth was alarming, and overcrowding was becoming desperate. Then there were the multitudes of tranquilizer pills in almost every color, size, and shape that helped one to cope with the tensions caused by the almost total lack of privacy, by the constant noise, polluted air, continual abrasive physical contact with crowds, and by the harsh and ugly sights of a superindustrialization devoid of trees or greenery of any kind.

Then there were the food pills. One took them three times a day. The endless wheatfields, pastures, grazing lands, and vegetable farms of former days had become ancient history. Even the Grand Canyon was now filled to overflowing with sweating humanity, jostling endlessly for living space. The food pills were processed in huge floating factories, and consisted of compressed algae and seaweed, and plankton. They had a sort of unpleasant fishy taste, but could be swallowed whole with a glass of desalinated water, and they provided all the nutriments necessary to go on living.

But the most important pill of all was affectionately called the Sooey pill. It was the only one that came in a lavender color with a stamp on it resembling a clenched fist. Every person was issued one of these on his or her twenty-first birthday. If one lost the Sooey, another would be issued—but only after much red tape; and, of course, one's name was permanently placed on a "Suspects List," to be consulted every time someone was murdered by misuse of the Sooey. These suspects automatically came under police surveillance and were questioned at great length, and one knew oneself to be at best a possible unwitting accessory to murder. For this reason, and others, people took great care not to lose their Sooeys.

Basically the entire society was built around the Sooey pill. It was not only the individual's escape hatch, but society depended on it as a regulator in a world where nature's own regulators seemed to have fused out, or gone haywire. There had been much talk—and the Radical Demopubs had actually tried to force through a bill to issue the Sooey pill at age thirteen or younger—of issuing the pill before childbearing age. It was a desperate measure, attempting to deal with a desperate situation. But the Demopubs were overruled by the conservative wing of their own party, who joined with the opposition in saying that it was an inhuman solution, and that the situation was not yet *that* desperate—an indication, some people muttered, in itself, of things to come.

But perhaps it would not become necessary ever to pass that bill, as living conditions were indeed fast becoming so intolerable that the Sooey, or suicide pill, was being used with ever-increasing frequency. People rarely reached forty before using it, and then desisted only because of an excessive love for their child and a desire, more sentimental than reasoned, to help the child reach adulthood. Parents who felt less responsible or loving were using the Sooey in greater and greater numbers—in their thirties, when the child was likely to be a teen-ager, or even younger. This was a great help to the government despite the large number of orphans.

But the government did not of course sanction murder as a solution, as this would have opened the gates to total chaos and anarchy. Therefore, when thirteen-year-old Billy Overton was found dead of Sooey poisoning, the police went to work as they always did—to seek the perpetrator of this heinous deed. The boy had been a happy, healthy, loving child, and his parents were beside themselves with grief.

The "Suspects List" was immediately consulted and the computer was put to work. It came up with only three names—all people who had lost their Sooey, of course, and who, in addition, had somehow been near the scene of the crime or had known the murdered boy. All three seemed most unlikely suspects, but the police were determined to track down every clue.

One was a taxi driver, who had lost his Sooey some eight weeks ago, and whose only connection with Billy was that he had dropped off a passenger three blocks from the Overtons' apartment an hour or so before the crime was committed. As it would have taken him about that long to drive to the Overtons', he became a prime suspect. But the fact remained that he insisted he had never laid eyes on Billy Overton, and all objective evidence seemed to bear out his contention. And what possible motive could he have?

The second suspect turned up by the computer was a woman who lived within walking distance of the Overtons, had lost her Sooey pill three months before, and was just about to have a new one reissued. She knew the Overtons vaguely, but never remembered having met Billy, although she may have passed him many times on the busy, frantically crowded street; and surely, she said, she had no wish to kill the young boy. She was married but as yet had no child of her own. And what possible motive could she have? She was known to be a quiet almost apathetic type.

The third suspect seemed even more remote than the other two. The computer turned up the name of Bobby's first grade teacher who had lost her Sooey three days previous to the murder; but she now lived three hundred miles away, and since any type of transport had to be reserved months in advance, she couldn't possibly have been at the scene of the murder even in the highly unlikely situation that she had somehow conceived a hatred for Billy in first grade and, harboring this dislike, had resolved seven years later to kill him! It was utter nonsense and the police knew it. But Billy was dead and someone had killed him.

Inspector Fenner was nearing forty-two and only his deep attachment ot his sixteen-year-old daughter kept him from using his own Sooey. His wife had used hers the year before, after writing him a heartbreaking farewell note begging forgiveness for leaving him to bring up their Hannah; but she could bear the stifling tension no longer. Inspector Fenner had held her in his arms as she gratefully breathed her last, so he knew the suffering of the bereaved.

He now regarded the Overtons with great compassion. Billy's father, while obviously grief-stricken, was trying to console his wife, but she was beyond consolation. Her eyes were red-rimmed, swollen, with dark black circles underneath. She sobbed continually in great gasping tearless sobs.

"Billy is better off, my darling," her husband told her. "You know that. How often have we spoken of the horrors of this world, of the horrors that awaited him, that more and more were enveloping our Billy as he grew older and came to realize what the world is like. You, who never wanted him to stop smiling. You, who protected him and built an imaginary world around him—you must know and be grateful that he is released now from the ghastly, gray, grim unrelieved life that we live."

Inspector Fenner could bear no more. He left. But the call to duty was too strong, too deeply ingrained in him. He returned the next day and in the gentlest of voices asked the Overtons to show him their Sooey pills.

"What!" said Billy's father, in anger. He was afraid the police officer wanted to take them away. Reassured, he brought forth his precious little lavender pill with the clenched fist stamped on it. Mrs. Overton just stood staring at the Inspector.

Three months later, after the trial of Mrs. Overton, the Inspector leaned over his sleeping Hannah, sleeping among hundreds of others in the unmarried-women's dormitory of their apartment complex, and kissed her good-bye. That night he gratefully used his own Sooey pill, unable to bear the reverberating screams that kept resounding in his ears—screams that he had heard that afternoon—screams of Mrs. Overton after the sentencing.

Until his last breath he heard her shrieking dementedly to the Court, "Have mercy! Have mercy! I did it to save him. I loved him so dearly! Don't make me live! For God's sake, don't make me live!"

But the Court refused to reissue her Sooey.

Backing Up

by Barry N. Malzberg

So I show him the gun. This is the great leveler, the great persuader. "I must tell you," I say in my mellow voice, "that we have been dissatisfied with the collections for a very long time." The gun is a point forty-five caliber precision job, not that this really matters since it is not the make of the guns but their function that interests most laymen. "You are five thousand dollars behind," I add. "Not even allowing for the matter of interest."

He looks at me with calm sad eyes. His name is Brown. I believe that I've got that right, and there's no need to look on the card to check as I'm definitely in the right office. He says, "I told you, I need more time. I'm doing the best I can. Furs is a seasonal business, an erratic business, and this is not our season." It is February, I should point out, although a very mild and springlike February. My forehead in this small room is veritably jeweled with sweat. "Next month," he says, "next month I will have something for you."

"Next month is not sufficient," I say. "My instructions are

not to leave without a down payment now. Two thousand dollars is suggested."

"I don't have two thousand dollars," he says. He looks down at the floor, then up at me with curious brightness. "Anyway," he says, "I don't think you have the nerve."

"What?"

"I said I don't think you have the nerve. The guts." He puts his palms flat on the desk, raises himself to military posture. "I don't think you have the guts to blow my head off at high noon on the seventh floor of this building with at least forty people on the same floor right now. The walls are like paper here. Corners are cut in the construction business something awful. The whole place may hear the shot, up to the fortieth story. You wouldn't think of it."

"Don't toy with me, Brown," I say. I focus my mouth into a snarl. "I don't like being toyed with and I have a vile temper, to say nothing of a job to do."

Brown shakes his head. "We all have a job to do," he says, "but I don't think you have the nerve to do yours." He stares at me from his rigid posture. "Go on," he says, "blow my head off. I don't have five thousand dollars. I don't have two thousand dollars. I have nothing to give you so you're just going to have to carry through your threat." His eyes glint disturbingly. He is exactly right about the construction business. Roadways, churches, automobiles—nothing is built the way that it used to be. Corruption and the cutting of corners prevail. Even the silencer on the pistol is flimsy; I don't trust it.

"Come on," he challenges. The position he has taken seems to have given him a sense of release. "Come on, do it. I have nothing to give you."

He is quite right. My orders don't provide for the contingency of defiance. Whether I have the nerve is another issue, but I don't have to consider that now. Reluctantly I lower the pistol. "I'll be back," I say. "Soon. Maybe today. Certainly tomorrow. You can't run. I know where you live—your wife, your children."

Brown's face leers with sudden power. "You won't do it to them either," he says. "You won't do it to anyone. You've lost the fire. You've acquired scruple. You're like all the construction people now, all the contractors. You just want an edge without risk."

"I don't have to take this kind of abuse," I say. I put away the pistol and leave his office quickly. My footsteps clatter in the hallway; the whisk of elevators is audible at fifty paces.

What is the raw material of these modern office buildings? Chewing gum?

Considering the issue of scruple, I make my way crosstown and find in his accustomed place the bartender whose gambling losses are now in excess of fifteen thousand. He is alone behind the counter at this difficult hour of a February afternoon, but his face does not light with pleasure when he sees me. Quite the opposite. "I told you yesterday," he says, "and I told you the day before that too. I don't have it. I need time to get it together. At least a month."

"They don't want to wait a month."

"That's their problem," he says. He dries his hands noisily on a towel. "I have to ask you to leave," he says. "You hanging around here creates the wrong kind of atmosphere. Customers might be disturbed."

"I'll have a rye and soda."

"No," he says, "I don't want to serve you."

I reach my hand into my pocket in a menacing gesture. "Come on," he says, "this business with guns no longer fascinates. I tell you, I don't have it. I have personal problems, medical bills. Maybe by June I can work something out. Right now I can't do a thing."

"You're in no position to make that statement."

He flings the towel down the length of the bar. "Come on," he says, "eighty-six it. I've had enough of this."

Striations and laughter float from the television set—an afternoon celebrity quiz or something. The level of television has deteriorated as much as everything else, I think as I back away from the bar. Nothing works quite as it used to. Nothing can quite be trusted. Quality levels go down. Strapped gamblers and bankrupt fur manufacturers take a dictatorial position and there seems no way to deal with them. None of this would have gone on five years ago. It is part of urban rot, I think.

"And stay out of here," the bartender says as I go through the door.

Who do these people think they are?

I phone in to tell them that collections have not gone well. They grumble if the message comes direct, but for the fourth day in a row it is the answering service and the answering service, of course, assumes a neutral posture. Sometimes I wonder if the messages are even passed on. Sometimes I wonder if they are out of the office permanently. Sometimes I wonder if I need this job, but then common sense prevails; at my age and stage of life there are few new careers open to me. It is one of the hazards of an overly liberal education; I should have learned a trade.

I take the train north and come in at the usual time. Lydia's face is clamped with tension but at least the children are out for the evening—having dinner with their friends, I am told. "Pour your own drink," Lydia says, "I'm not any servant. I've had a bad day myself." I can see from her expression that it is going to be a difficult evening. We will be up until at least midnight and it will be necessary for me once again to explain to her the meaningfulness of life in the suburbs. Since I no longer believe in that, I will find it tedious and agonizing. "If you want dinner you take me out," Lydia says. "I didn't feel like cooking."

"Restaurant food isn't home cooking."

"We can go to the Major."

The Major is the local chain motel. "Franchises are no good," I say. "Franchising has destroyed the nation. Everything is the same and nothing is very good."

Her eyes, infinitely weary, look up at me. "I don't want to hear that now," she says. "Please don't start up on that with me now."

Who does the woman think she is, anyway? What has happened to the institution of marriage?

Wide O—

by Elsin Ann Graffam

Maybe I'll put my head under the pillow—no, that's no good. I can imagine him, whoever he is, sneaking up on me. Okay, that does it! I'm going to get up and stay up, put the lights on in the living room, turn on the television.

Oh, I hate going into the dark... there! Overhead light on, floor lamp on, TV on, nice and loud. Now I'll just sit down and relax and watch the—

Hey, what was that?! Oh. Old houses creak, remember? If it creaked when Bill was here, it'll creak when he's away, and it's just—just something in the house. It's only your imagination, old girl, that's what it is. And the more sleepy you get, the more vivid your imagination will get.

All the doors are locked, right? And all the windows, ditto. Okay, then. So I feel like an idiot, trying to stay up all night. Well, sitting here in the living room is a lot better than doing what I did the *last* time Bill was away overnight! Locking myself in the bathroom and staying there until dawn, for heaven's sake—

Oh! Oh, the furnace clicked on, that's all *that* was! Calm down, girl, calm down! The trouble with you is, you read the papers. You should read the comics and stop there. No, I have to read MOTHER OF THREE ATTACKED BY INTRUDER and WOMAN FOUND BEATEN TO DEATH IN HOME. But, oh, they were so close to us! That old lady lived—what was it, only three, four blocks away? But she lived alone, and nobody knows I'm alone tonight. I hope.

What *is* the matter with me?! I'm acting like a child. Other women live alone—for years, even—and here I have to stay by myself for just one measly little night and I go all to pieces.

Sure seems cold in here! The furnace was on—still is on, in fact. Must be my nerves. I'll go into the kitchen and make myself a nice hot cup of tea. Good idea! Maybe that'll warm me up!

Now, where *is* that light switch . . . there . . . well, no *wonder* I'm cold, with the back door standing wide o—